APPETITE for MURDER

APPETITE for MURDER

CECILE LAMALLE

WARNER BOOKS

A Time Warner Company

WARNER BOOKS EDITION

Copyright © 1999 by Cecile Lamalle
All rights reserved.
ISBN 978-0-446-60762-9   ISBN 0-446-60762-9

Cover design by Rachel McClain
Cover illustration by Theresa Fasolino
Book design and text illustration by L&G McRee

Warner Books, Inc.
1271 Avenue of the Americas
New York, NY 10020

Visit our Web site at
www.warnerbooks.com

 A Time Warner Company

Printed in the United States of America

First Paperback Printing: August 1999

10 9 8 7 6 5 4 3 2 1

To my daughter Juliet
And to the memory of my father,
Charles F. Lamalle

PROLOGUE

✛✛✛✛✛✛✛

Restaurant Review in the
Albany Star-Register

✛✛✛✛✛✛✛

My friend and I dined royally at La Fermette the other night. The restaurant, located on the outskirts of Klover, New York, in Van Buren County, is a mere thirty miles from Albany. Worth the trip!

It was a memorable experience: the personnel made us feel like most welcome guests in a well-run private home. Decor, ambiance, food are all superb. Monsieur Charles Poisson, a Frenchman, has run La Fermette for many years (before that he was affiliated with a restaurant of the same name in New York City). "Charly," as he is known to one and all, is always on hand to see that your gustatory experience is a happy one. "Every customer is an epicure," says Monsieur Poisson, "and we give him the best."

As soon as you sink into your comfortable, chintz-padded chair a basket of homemade rolls appears accompanied by the best butter imaginable, (which comes from Romback Farms, a local gourmet dairy) and a crock of rich mushroom spread. As handsome menus are presented you look up to admire the huge bouquets of autumn flowers and perhaps pinch a sprig from the herbal bouquets at each table.

French, American, and Continental specialties appeal

to every taste. Lobster prepared in a variety of ways is a Saturday special, and on Sundays there is prime rib with Yorkshire pudding and horseradish sauce.

My friend ordered Sole Véronique, the classic filet of sole flanked with grapes in a buttery white wine sauce, whilst your humble reviewer made do with the Steak Marchand de Vin, a perfectly cooked rib steak with a rich wine sauce. For appetizers, we ordered Salmon Gravlax, the silky pink salmon which is "cooked" for several days in dill, vodka, salt, and sugar, and the Shrimps Charly, a garlicky house special; both were outstanding. Our waiter, a genial chap who seemed to anticipate our special needs (i.e., that we were ravenous), appeared with tiny crocks of steaming, fragrant onion soup, "compliments of the chef." Glasses of house red and house white wine were above par (a full-bodied California Gravenstein Vineyards Zinfandel for me, a Happy Valley Sauvignon Blanc for my friend).

As we finished our main courses the owner/chef, Charly, appeared and offered us pots of fragrant herb tea "on the house" and described the desserts, which are made by a member of the staff. Your reviewer opted for buttery apple tart topped with cinnamon ice cream, while my friend delighted in the old-fashioned pecan pie made with Vermont maple syrup. It arrived festooned with a giant dollop of brandy-flavored whipped cream.

Prices are high. Special "natural" veal from Virginia, farm-raised fowl from nearby Southwind Farm, aged, hormone-free beef from Colorado, organically raised vegetables, do not come cheap. Appetizers fall in the $6–$12 range, main courses are between $20 and $30. Desserts are all $7. It is worth mentioning that a special "bar menu" is available in the adjoining bar, with lower-priced items like meat loaf, spare ribs, pastas, omelettes, and sandwiches. La Fermette is closed Mondays, open for *dinner (6 P.M. to 10 P.M.) Wednesday through Saturday and open for Sunday dinner from noon to 6 P.M. Lunches, prices on a par with other local spots, (hamburgers, omelettes, sandwiches, homemade soups) are available Tuesday through Saturday. Dinner reservations are definitely recommended. The address is La Fermette, Route 65, Klover, New York, and the telephone number is (518) 528-6347.*

CHAPTER ONE

Sunday dinner
at La Fermette

Charly Poisson, chef and co-owner of La Fermette, grinned as he stood behind the swinging doors between his kitchen and his dining room and peered out at his Sunday afternoon crowd.

The dining room was filled again, on this cold, rainy October Sunday at nearly four o'clock. Every seat had turned twice, today. *Formidable*. It was Charly's life's dream come true.

Charly, a French *charcutier's* son, had grown up in the Jura Mountains in France: not a bad beginning, all things considered. Then he'd spent time as a waiter, both in Paris and New York. And now, as chef/owner of a fine French restaurant, Charly had reached the summit of his ambitions.

It is dangerous to reach the summit of your ambitions, but luckily Charly was unaware of that fact. He adjusted his beret and chewed on the dandelion root he'd snatched from his kitchen garden (capital for purifying the blood), smoothed his little pencil mustache, and stood proud; five-foot-six if he stretched on his toes, the noble height of Napoleon Bonaparte.

He turned back to his kitchen. Benny Perkins, Charly's

short, muscular, nineteen-year-old sous-chef, was sautée-ing herb-stuffed pork chops and, Charly knew, dreaming of the day when he'd be a black belt in Tae Quon Do and a world-famous chef: his two current ambitions. Julius Prendergast, the rangy, fortyish Albany stockbroker who drove thirty miles down to Van Buren County on Saturdays and Sundays to cook in Charly's kitchen, in training for the country inn he was planning on opening in a few years, was slicing prime rib and eating a few of the little fatty bits. Patty Perkins, Benny's mother, who made all of La Fermette's desserts and substituted for co-owner Maurice Baleine as hostess when Maurice was indisposed, was plating desserts along with Linda Okun, Charly's carpenter's wife and his new Sunday helper. Linda had just started today, and Patty was showing her how to garnish the oozing chocolate cakes, the ice-cream parfaits, the crepes bursting with fruit compotes and whipped cream, the pastries rich with real butter cream and liqueurs. Old Mick Hitchens, the dishwasher, was scrubbing pots and scraping the leftover meats from the customers' plates into a plastic container for his dog Bruno and Charly's four cats.

In other words, it was a Sunday no different from other Sundays except for one thing: All the seats were filled, and all the seats had turned twice. "Bizzy, bizzy," Charly smiled at his crew, calculating: seventy-five seats times two at $30 per seat—minimum—minus 38 percent food cost, payroll, utilities, depreciation, and what Charly called The Relations Public, which meant cases of wine and blocks of his famous Country Pâté to restaurant reviewers, and complimentary meals to friends and useful allies.

Charly returned to the mound of parsley he was chopping. *Hokay. Done.* "Any more mushrooms, Charly?" Benny called. The pork filet with Sauce Bordelaise was served on a bed of sautéed mushrooms. It was a popular item this chilly afternoon.

"More in the cold room, I get and chop," Charly said, and congratulated himself on ordering extra mushrooms.

"Unfucking believable," Tommy Glade, the barman, cried. He'd left his bar and dashed into the kitchen for a piece of sourdough bread soaked in roast-beef blood. "I've never seen 'em drink like this." He ran out again, wiping his mouth with his hand. It would be his six-year anniversary at AA soon: no booze for six years. *He is an excellent barman,* Charly thought, *and a very nice man. One of us. Très sympathique.*

Charly, mushrooms chopped, added madeira to his Chicken Hash Charly which was heating on the big Vulcan burner. It was for Walter Maxwell (his best customer) and his guests, and it must be perfect.

"Maxwell's table's ready for their entrée," said Elton Briggs, hurrying in.

"Yes, yes, Elton, I am heating up. Is last entrée, no?"

"Last entrée," Benny said. He'd just plated the pork atop mushrooms, and was ladling over the Sauce Bordelaise. He topped the tenderloin slices with leaves of fresh sage sautéed in olive oil.

"Hey, Julius," Elton called. "How's the roast beef?"

"Delish," Julius said chewing. "There's plenty, Charly cooked extra." Cooking extra roast beef for his staff was not pure altruism. For a few extra dollars, Charly gained an enthusiastic staff ready to sell their customers appetizers, desserts, beverages, all the profitable extras, and his turnover was practically nil, in an industry where staff turnover of 200 percent a year was par. These people might be Charly's staff, but they were also his family. His human family. His animal family was four robust cats. And if you can't be good to your family, then what else is left?

"Hey, Benny?" Julius reached over Benny's shoulder, plucked a black hair from the plate of pork chops.

"Gee, Julius, thanks. I didn't see that."

"Neither did Charly," Julius whispered. "Not to worry."
Charly dipped his index finger in the creamy hash,
tasted—perfect. Everything had to be perfect for Walter
Maxwell. Walter would taste, and say, "Damn, Charly, it's
better than the '21' Club," and Charly would beam. He
plated three orders of Chicken Hash Charly on triangles of
sourdough toast, wiped the edges with a towel stuck in his
apron, laid on a sprig of lemon thyme, and signaled for
Elton to take them away. He glanced at the big clock on the
wall. Four o'clock, time to go out into the dining room and
greet his customers for the second time today. Such a
crowd. He chuckled with delight.

Charly hurried to his office beyond the kitchen, sailed
his beret onto the desk, removed his soiled white jacket,
shrugged into a clean, starched one from Dupont & Malgat
in Paris, where all the best chefs got their whites, and
plopped an impressive white toque on his head. On with
the show.

CHAPTER TWO

━━━━━━━

Charly Conducts
Les Relations Publiques

━━━━━━━

Charly pushed open the swinging door and entered his dining room: So handsome, he always thought. Barbara Baleine, his partner Maurice's wife, a professional interior designer, had done a beautiful job. She knew all the tricks: the pale apricot walls, so flattering to the ladies' complexions; the overstuffed chintz-covered chairs, so comfortable for ample backsides; the chintz swags at the windows, which framed views of meadows; masses of autumn flowers, which, combined with the bowls of apples and the smells of cooking wine, gave the room an aroma of prosperity; lots of well-polished old pine sideboards and serving tables; and the thick wall-to-wall flowered carpet that masked stains and muffled noise, cocooning the dining room in an air of *luxe*. Charly thought it the most beautiful dining room in the world.

Because of his many years in the restaurant business, Charly knew the importance of a well-appointed dining room. How many people could truly appreciate fine food? The answer was, not many. But if the surroundings were luxurious, customers perceived that the food was luxurious, too.

"It's what we call the Delta Philosophy," a Mississippi

bon vivant stockbroker had explained to Charly, once, when he was head waiter. "Ya see, down in Mis'sippi, those rich delta farmers had lots of money but no real taste. White trash, I guess you'd call 'em. But rich, ya know? So the delta shopkeepers, they'd put in chandeliers and fancy carpeting, and the farmers bought, because they figured that if the store was fancy, the merchandise was, too. Same's with these folks. They've probably never had range-run chickens, prime aged beef, truffles, but they can tell you've spent lots of money decoratin' the room, so they figure the food's gotta be good, too. Makes 'em feel they're gettin' their money's worth."

Charly noted that while the flowers were beautiful, the carpet had a stain over near the corner of the bar, and the armoire where they kept the linens needed waxing again. Trust Maurice not to notice. He glanced over to where his partner was sitting at the pine table in the entrance, pretending to read the reservation book and concealing a glass in his plump hand. Maurice Baleine, Junior, was the son of Charly's original partner, Maurice Senior. Charly and Maurice had been partners in the New York restaurant, the original La Fermette; then Maurice had died of a heart attack and willed his half of the operation to his Princeton-schooled snob of a son. Thus Charly had inherited Maurice. What an inheritance.

Charly stood at the bar, raised an eyebrow and half turned toward Maurice, then turned back to Tommy. "How many?" he mouthed, miming tossing back a shot.

"Two doubles," Tommy muttered. "I think he's shit-faced. He was sort of ossified when he got here, couple hours ago." Tommy, understandably, had no use for drunks, now.

"Ah." Maurice, always a jolly tippler, had, in the past year, become worse, bracing his morning coffee with Glenfiddich, and his noontime sandwich with several

Bloody Marys. By dinnertime, he was often so wobbly that Charly would say, "Maurice, go home, Patty will greet the guests." Maurice would have to go, Charly thought for the hundredth time. Charly walked over to Maurice, who looked up.

"Pretty big people here today," said Maurice, the snob. Charly, preoccupied, heard the word "big" and looked around. "Yes," he told his partner, "that man over there, he look like a *pastèque,* a big watermelon."

Maurice, confused, said, "Millions in this dining room."

Charly walked away. He fished some Sen-Sen out of his pocket and flipped some of the tiny lozenges into his mouth. You couldn't breathe raw garlic on customers, and eating raw garlic—good for the circulation—was a habit of Charly's. Charly's frown turned to a benign smile as he noticed a customer glancing his way. He was onstage. It was Police Chief John Stark and his family, whom Charly always invited, twice a year, as his guests. The Relations Public.

"Ah, Chief Stark. And Mrs. Betty. And Rebecca. And Elizabeth. You enjoy? Everything, it is hokay? You want more rosbif? I can arrange . . ."

"Oh, boy, Charly, you're gonna kill us, all this food." Stark smiled. Six-foot-four, 275 pounds. Betty and the girls were hefty, too.

"No, no seconds," Stark said. "I want to save room for Patty's lemon meringue pie. That really hit the spot, Charly. I needed the fuel, been up so late these past nights. I'm going nuts with these barn burnings, they're driving me up the wall. We had another one last night, did you hear?"

"No!" Charly said, shocked, his hand on his heart.

"Yep, the Bradleys. Their hay barn. No animals perished, but their hay barn's pretty close to the main barn, so we had to get all the cows out. Mrs. Bradley was crying, Mr. B, I thought he was going to have a heart attack, he collapsed, but then he kept going. I never got to bed last night, so this meal saved my day."

An arsonist had been setting fire to hay barns since June. Barns belonging to local farmers, not the barns of rich weekenders, like the fires across the river a couple of years ago, which had been set by a bitter volunteer fireman. Now that was understandable: The rich New Yorkers drove up in their big cars, turned the old farmhouses into decorator-magazine showplaces, and the locals were too poor to appreciate the gentrification of their county. When a sleek Mercedes pulled up at a convenience store next to a battered old pickup, and both drivers had had a few, well, it didn't take much. But this wasn't the case, here. This time, the burned barns all belonged to locals.

"Oh John, this is terrible. The same method? The gasoline? The rag?"

"Yep. The same. And we haven't a clue, not a clue."

"It must be—crazy person," Charly offered.

"Yep. That's what I figure. But who?"

Charly remembered his role of host. "And the young ladies? A big Brownie Surprise, perhaps? Brownie with cinnamon ice cream, hot caramel sauce on top of that, toasted walnut and cherry on top of that?"

The girls giggled at his accent. Tomorrow, at school, they'd brag in a casual way about dining at The Firm, which was what the locals called the restaurant. Everyone knew that The Firm wasn't cheap.

"I will get you the dessert menu," Charly said, and turned so that they wouldn't see his eyes tearing up. Five years ago, young Johnnie Stark would have been here, too. But he'd been killed the night of his senior prom, barreling down Route 24 at 2 A.M. He'd swerved, overcorrected, smashed into a tree, died instantly with a broken neck. The Stark family still wore a mask of pain. Charly's own wife and son had died many years ago, his beloved Claudine dying in childbirth, the baby, a day later. To hear of a child's death tore at his heart. Charly wiped his eyes with his snowy handkerchief.

Charly stopped at table three, where his investment adviser, Jimmy Houghton and Jimmy's office manager, old Evelyn Holmes, sat finishing up their desserts. Jimmy managed Charly's money very profitably, so Charly endured Jimmy's pedantries with as much good grace as he could manage. He was, however, a pest. Charly bowed. "Ah, Jeemy. Madame Evelyn. You enjoy?"

Jimmy, a forty-year-old bachelor, was as skinny as a boning knife, with a petulant look on his face: a real old maid. Now, about to give Charly the benefit of his good advice: "Yes, Charly. Very nice. Very nice. Of course that pork chop was much too rich, much too rich. And that whipped cream on the pecan pie—terrible for the gastric juices. Terrible."

If he has stomach problems, Charly wondered (again), *why order the richest things on the menu?* But aloud, he soothed, "Ah, I will bring you a nice infusion, some peppermint tea—or perhaps sage? *La Sauge* is marvelous for the problems of the *estomac* . . ." Jimmy ordered the sage.

Evelyn, catching Charly's eye, winked. "My chicken was heaven, Charly dear. And I'd like a peppermint infusion."

Charly bowed and moved on, his lips twitching. Poor Jimmy, besieged by ill health. But a real money man. Knew what to do with the dollars, but always complaining about his digestion, his sciatica, his headaches, like an old man. He must have had a terrible childhood, Charly mused. But a rich one. He wore beautiful clothes. Like that blue blazer . . . custom-made, without a doubt. Actually, Charly knew nothing about Jimmy's home life. Several businessmen had recommended him highly. Jimmy helped his clients make a lot of money.

People loved to criticize: part of the fun of dining out, it seemed. So Charly heard about the strange, bitter herb in the salad ("lovage; tastes like celery and is good for the digestion"); the small portion of prime rib ("we will bring you more"); the fact that the waiter had said there were no more Shrimps Charly yet the customer had seen two orders going past ("Ah, the Morrisons, they always order the shrimp by telephone, since they know we run out"); the butter wasn't salty enough; the bread was too salty; the string beans weren't cooked enough; the potatoes were overdone. "That sauce has WINE it it?"

There is nothing that deflates a chef's ego more than discussions of a culinary nature with the general public. And the customer was always right. It didn't matter. Charly's rather large ego was only temporarily incommoded.

Ah—the Vanns, and Honoria Wells. Charly glided up to their table, smiling. He was catering Dinah and Peter Vann's wedding anniversary dinner party on Tuesday. "Everything hokay, mesdames, monsieur?"

"Divine, Charly," Honoria boomed. Honoria was local aristocracy, and looked it: a well-bred, horsy face devoid of wrinkles, thin lips, a trim figure in a cashmere jumpsuit, wrist sporting a heavy gold chain bracelet. Her sleek helmet of jonquil hair was secured behind her ears with gold bobby pins.

Charly knew all about sixty-year-old Honoria's penchant for young men, since she was Julius Prendergast's eccentric aunt. It was Honoria, in fact, who had asked Charly to take Julius on. But Honoria was a kind woman, ready with her checkbook when disaster struck a local family, so people just said, "There goes Honoria, wonder who she's screwing now?" when Honoria's big white Buick whizzed past.

"Everything was fine, Charly," Dinah Vann said. A

petite woman who worried about appearances, she was overdressed, as usual, in silk and sapphires. For the last few weeks, she had been driving Charly crazy over her dinner-party menu: It had to be chic, stylish, totally contemporary, the best. Another good customer of the cosmetic surgeon, Charly noted, admiring Dinah's lack of wrinkles.

Peter, Dinah's husband, a retired Seventh Avenue manufacturer of bathrobes (Luxury Lounge Wear) appeared drunk, as usual. He lolled in his chair, eyes glazed. Now, he'd try to get another drink, free, his usual trick. Sure enough. Peter pointed to his glass, leaned toward Charly, and whispered loudly, "Not Tanqueray in my martini."

"Not what you ask for?" Charly, affronted.

"Nope." Peter shook his head with the vehemence of the inebriated.

"Is Madame driving? If so, another drink will be brought immediately."

Dinah laughed cynically. "I'm always the Sunday driver," she said.

Charly carried the glass to the bar. "Mr. Vann is up to his old trick . . ."

Tommy rolled his eyes. "Is the old sot driving?"

"No, no, the missus, she drive."

The ladies accepted a chamomile infusion, so good for the skin.

Charly finished his dining-room tour with Walter Maxwell and the Warburtons, the horse breeders from Highdale. He hurried to their table and bowed, smiling at his favorite customer and his guests.

"Wonderful chicken hash, Charly," Walter said, right on cue. "Wasn't it superb, Billy, Midge? Much better than the '21' Club's. Just the right amount of madeira, too. Charly, you're a genius. Isn't he a genius, Billy, Midge? Isn't this the best restaurant on the East Coast?"

Charly breathed a sigh of relief. Walter was in a good

mood, today. You never knew with Walter, though he looked like the millionaire he was in his tailored jeans, creamy cashmere sweater, well-laundered custom made bush jacket and hand-sewn Italian moccasins, no socks.

Charly beamed. "My most aristo-cratique customer. I am honored. A small digestif, may I offer you? Or an herbal infusion?"

Walter tossed back his silver head, smiled graciously: royalty, condescending to his subject. "Very good of you, Charly. Billy? Midge?"

As Charly bustled off to give Walter's waiter the order—two peppermint teas and a Benedictine for Mr. Warburton—he reflected, *Ah, if all of my customers were like Walter, what a pleasure life would be.*

Six o'clock. The restaurant was empty. Old Mick was unloading the last of the dishes from the dishwasher, the staff were finishing up their snacks. The telephone rang in the kitchen. "Linda, it's for you," Benny called. Linda picked up, smiling, probably expecting Bob to say he'd be picking her up, shortly. But her face went from smiles to tears, and she said, "Oh, God, Bob, not again, well don't worry, maybe I can get a ride, here." Charly, who had been chatting with Patty about the desserts—everyone said the rum cake with marzipan was too sweet—said, "What?" to Linda.

"It's our youngest, Robby. Fourteen years old. Always in trouble. We can't do anything with him, he comes and goes all hours of the day and night. Now he's down at the police station, cops caught him spray painting a school bus. Bob's down there with him, doesn't know when he'll get home."

"I'll take you home, Linda," Patty said, kindly.

Charly said, "Ah, la la, is always something," and shook his head, wondering what he could do to cheer Linda up. "Take home this half apple pie, Bob will enjoy when he get

CHICKEN HASH CHARLY
Yield: 4 servings

2 Tablespoons olive oil
½ cup onions, chopped
2 cloves garlic, chopped
1 cup mushrooms, sliced
2 cups chicken, cooked and cubed
2 egg yolks, beaten
⅓ cup heavy cream
3 Tablespoons madeira
Sea salt and white pepper, freshly
    ground, to taste
Sourdough toast, as needed
Chives, snipped, as needed for garnish

Heat oil in skillet and sauté onions, garlic and mushrooms until onions start to brown, Stir in chicken. Beat together egg yolks and cream and pour over chicken. Stir in madeira. Heat gently, do not boil. Add salt and pepper to taste. Serve piping hot on sourdough toast and garnish with snipped chives.

home," he was urging, when Tommy, who had been tidying the bar, stuck his head through the kitchen door and gestured to Charly. "Charly, come out here. I want to show you something."

Charly hurried into the dining room. "What? Where? I do not see . . . Ahhh." Underneath the reception desk Charly could see two feet sticking out, then two legs, then the rest of Maurice. Unconscious under the table.

"Ai, Ai, Ai," Charly wailed. "He will ruin us."

"Fuckin' disaster," pronounced Tommy.

By seven o'clock Maurice had been carried to his car and driven home, and Charly had been assured by the restaurant staff—especially the waiters—that Maurice must have passed out after the last customer had left the restaurant, since neither they nor the customers had noticed anything.

By half past seven, Charly, exhausted, trudged back to his little farmhouse, about two hundred yards behind the restaurant. He carried two small bags—one of roast meats, another of fish fillets—for his four cats.

Usually, in the evening, Charly would go home, feed his cats, have a cup of chamomile tea, perhaps a bowl of soup, then take a book up to bed and read. But tonight he felt too tired to do anything except feed the cats and fall into bed.

Maurice was wearing him out. Maurice would ruin the restaurant. He must talk to Jimmy about his investments, what should he sell, in order to buy Maurice out. "Take good care of my son," old Maurice had whispered in the hospital. "Oh, I will, I will, I promise," Charly had replied. He hated to break a deathbed promise, but enough was enough.

As he stumped along the path, Charly looked up and noticed a full moon. Of course. What could you expect? As any bartender or cop could tell you, the full moon always brings disasters.

CHAPTER THREE

Sunday Night with Walter Maxwell, Epicure

Walter Maxwell said good-bye to Billy and Midge War-burton in the parking lot of La Fermette, then got in his Land Rover and drove home to Black Bull Farm. He wanted to catch a quick nap before going down to the Amtrak station. Wanted to be in top form for his ex-wife's visit.

Oh, God, what a stupid thing to do, invite her to spend the night. Why did he do it? Was this the onset of Alzheimer's? Walter was seriously concerned about his state of health, both mental and physical. He'd been so for-getful, recently. Was this old age? Forgetting appoint-ments, like that buyer the other day, and sometimes when he woke up he didn't even know what day it was. And his heart kept racing, he had dizzy spells, numb hands, numb feet. Sometimes he forgot to eat. But seventy wasn't old, he was in the prime of life. The prime—he could go another twenty years, maybe more.

The cunt, Candy Moran, the second Mrs. Walter Maxwell, had called early one morning last week.

"Good morning, Black Bull Farm, Walter Maxwell speaking."

That goddamn breathy little-girl voice: "Oh, Walter,

Walter darling, is that really you? The great Walter
Maxwell?"

Walter hadn't heard that voice in thirty years. His
stomach dropped. His knees turned watery. "How'd you
get my phone number, Candy?"

"Oh, really, Walter, you're so famous. You have an in-
ternational reputation, with your Black Angus bulls. So
many articles about you."

His name had never been in print, never. One of his
phobias. Once a reporter wanted a Black Angus story, said
he was going to write it anyway with or without Walter's
consent, but a visit from Little Ricky had changed the reporter's mind. So, where had the woman gotten his name?
He decided to ignore it.

Now's when he should have said, "Fuck off, bitch" but
instead he said, "What can I do for you, Candy?"

It seemed that Candy had to take the Amtrak on Sunday
to Albany, an art symposium, and she wondered if he could
meet her train at Hogton Sunday night, on her way back,
and they could have, quote unquote, a nice little visit. She
could spend the night at his house and catch an early train
into New York the next morning.

"I've thought about you so much, Walter darling. You
were the most brilliant man I've ever known, really distinguished, a trendsetter, I'm really dying to see you." Etc.
etc. Walter held the phone away from his ear.

Walter said he'd meet the 7:04 from Albany Sunday
night and put her on the 9:06 Monday morning bound for
New York.

Now they were sitting in Walter's living room, with its
oriental rugs, big Steuben glass pieces, metal sculptures,
leather chairs and sofa, and the ten-foot pine library table
Walter was so proud of. Candy was on her second martini;
Walter was drinking San Pellegrino. Now—too late—it all
came back: what a lush she was; the time she "borrowed"

a hundred grand to set up her own business which instantly failed; the money for "home improvements" which all went up her nose—she was into cocaine in a big way then. Now, he remembered. And she still had that mole under her left eye, too. Her trademark when she'd been Candy, just Candy, the fashion model.

"Get you another drink?" She'd reeked of booze getting off the train, still handsome at sixty, looked about forty, face pulled tight from the face-lifts and eye jobs and God knew what else, dressed in a stylish tweed suit with a colorful Hermès scarf of red-and-orange autumn leaves. Bergdorf's idea of country casual. *Cry poor,* Walter counseled himself. *She's out for money.*

"Just the tiniest droppie, darling. That's a beautiful cashmere sweater. You still order them by the dozen from Harrods?"

Walter gave a short bark. "Ha. Those days are gone forever, Candy. Times have changed. I'm barely making it."

"All that Steuben? Those leather chairs? The oriental rugs? That's a Shirvan over there, those are Kashans, not cheap, Walter."

Since when had she been into rugs? "The rugs came from an auction; the Steuben, the leather stuff, that's twenty years old." He hated explaining, making excuses, crying poor. He could feel the rage building up. His hands were shaking, and he steeled his muscles to keep his head from nodding. That no-account user. That filthy, grasping harridan. He brought over Candy's martini. He wanted to kill her. Rub her out, like a horsefly. Like all the others. They used to call him Walt The Stone Killer, when he was doing business with Big Ricky Zampone. You'd better believe it.

Her glass was empty. "You want another one?"

"Jusht the tiniest . . ." Slurring her words, now. *She'd better get to the point,* Walter thought, *she's ready to pass out.*

"I sh—sold over a million dollars' worth of art last year, Walter. Walter, Walterrr, you listening to me? The Hapworth Gallery. I've been there, oh, nearly five years. Forrest Hapworth wants me to become a partner. A hundred thousand, darling, that's all. I know you'll let me have it, for old times' sake. Actually, I can probably pay you back in a couple of years."

Funny, how Candy's slurring stopped when she talked about money. She'd gotten her second wind.

Walter's long face dropped. He looked astounded. "A hundred thousand? Today? Christ, you're raving, Candy. I couldn't raise a hundred gees, or fifty, if my life depended on it. I'd have to sell the farm."

"What about your Swiss bank account? Your Bahamas stashes?"

"All gone, Candy," Walter lied.

"Oh, Walter. I'm so sorry to hear it. Because I'd hate to get that killing reopened. The one where you shot Billy Talbott in Boston. No one knew Billy had lent you half a million dollars and you shot him so you wouldn't have to repay it. I've been talking to an old retired judge about the case, one of your customers. We could start a civil suit, like they did with that football player, what'shisname, Simpson."

"Candy, you're raving."

"You didn't know I listened in on that phone conversation you had with that fat thug, the Mob guy. You said, I took notes, 'I'll do him when the time's right, make it look like an accident.' He lent you the money, as I recall, for the Boston mob—some business thing. It was all arranged. The killing, I mean."

Walter shook his head, smiled at his outstretched hands, as if they could tell him something. "You're in la-la land, Candy. You know what it takes to get a case reopened, after thirty years? Most of the players are dead."

"The judge told me . . . well, it doesn't matter." Candy shook her head, such a pity, she'd have to do it, looking at Walter like he was a naughty boy who'd just sent a baseball through the window. "That poor woman."

"What poor woman, Candy?"

"Babs Talbott. Billy's wife. No one in Boston wanted to have anything to do with her after that. I heard she had to change her name, get out of town. With those two little kids, too. You ruined four lives, not just one." She looked around the room and frowned. "Still have that fake Giacometti, I see. You always did have gangster taste, Walter. Like that Godfather you used to admire, God, I hated that guy. Ralph something or other."

"Ralph D'Annunzio, Candy. And believe me, the feeling was mutual. Ralph died of cancer oh, about fifteen years ago."

"Oh, I'm sorry to hear that." Candy looked at her glass. Empty again.

"Tell you what. For old times' sake, maybe I can did up thirty grand."

"Well, it's a start, Walter. But not good enough."

Walter took Candy's glass. "Let's go out to the kitchen, have a sandwich." He was shaking badly, now, and he knew it had to be done. But not in the living room where the rugs could get messed up. Do her on the tiles, just like Bobby Fingers, they got Bobby into the kitchen so they wouldn't mess up the rug.

"I've got some wonderful country pâté, guy named Charly Poisson makes it for me. You ever go to his La Fermette in New York? He moved it up here. He makes me soups, meat dishes, casseroles, fabulous chef."

"You always were such a gourmet, Walter darling." Candy giggled.

"I prefer the word *epicure*."

Candy giggled again. "Remember Babs Talbott, that

awful onion soup dip thing she made? You always said Wasps ate shit, and they did. Babs and I used to make up these awful messes in the kitchen, Chicken Divan with canned soup and frozen broccoli, remember that?"

That was it. Candy had somehow gotten in touch with Billy Talbott's wife, how else could she remember her name? And the two kids, they'd be in their late thirties, forties by now. They'd all get together and cook up some sort of lawsuit against him. Couldn't let that happen. He was shaking badly, now, head quivering, little white lights dancing before his eyes, flashbulbs in his skull. And now the voices had started, those voices that chanted, "Do it," he'd always heard those voices before doing it. The voices telling him it was okay, the only thing to do, a job, nothing more.

Clack, clack, Candy's smart little suede boots on the tiles. Walter, following, grabbed up his fake Giacometti, and following Candy into the kitchen, swung his good tennis arm. His arm was hard, like steel.

He bashed in the back of Candy's head, aiming carefully so he wouldn't hit that big main artery that spurted blood like a fountain, the carotid artery in the neck, he'd memorized his *Gray's Anatomy*, carotid arteries, subclavian arteries, strangling people was better, no blood, but his hands were shaking too badly, and he didn't know if he still had the strength to strangle.

Candy froze, rigid, and Walter felt that old, remembered surge of intense, almost painful pleasure, better than any orgasm, a surge of power and pride and triumph. No drug could come near this sublime feeling.

Blood seeped from the gash, didn't spurt. Then Candy, making little mewing sounds, was falling, falling, banged her face on a corner of the big steel Traulsen refrigerator, grunt, grunt, and then lay still.

Walter turned her over, felt the pulse at her neck. It was still there, but faint. Walter pressed down on the two carotid arteries on either side of her throat, just below her ear, he'd done it so many times, knew exactly where, cutting off her oxygen, pressed and pressed, counted sixty, seventy, eighty, then a hundred, twenty, thirty, forty . . . then let go. Candy was gone.

Walter straightened up. God, his back was killing him. His nostrils flared. She'd loosed her bowels. He'd forgotten. They always did that.

Now, what? He had to get her out of the house, now, tonight. Marian Arnold, his housekeeper, would be in at 8 A.M. tomorrow. He'd go out to the garage, back the Land Rover up to the back door, get the big painter's tarp, wrap her up, she'd look like a rug. Let's see. What else would he need? His leather gloves, his shovel, take her over to the field just off Route 65 where Charly Poisson let the gardener dig humus. The earth was soft as butter there, or so Charly said. Dig a trench, just a shallow one, dump her in, then come home and call Little Ricky to come and get her tomorrow, take her somewhere, the cement plant in Jersey, probably. Little Ricky would know. Luckily the train station had been deserted, no witnesses, and since she'd lived in New York City, who'd think of looking for her up here?

Walter backed up the four-wheel drive so it was right by the kitchen door. Got out of the car. Jumped. *Christ, what was that?* A rustle in the bushes. Walter stood still, listened. Just an animal, probably. Then he shook himself. *Hey, loosen up, Walter.* He chuckled. Walt the Stone Killer. He'd thought those days were gone.

At 10:42 by his digital watch, Walter was back home, car put away, bloody rags in a garbage bag with crumpled newspapers on top, waiting to go to the dump. He found Candy's raincape, handbag, and overnight bag and stuffed them into the bottom drawer of his desk. Locked it. Then pulled the telephone over, dialed 2-0-1 for New Jersey, and punched in Little Ricky's number, which he knew by heart.

Late to call, but Walter knew Ricky's routine: He'd be down in his den having a final scotch and soda and waiting for the late news at eleven. Bernice, Ricky's wife, would be upstairs in their big bedroom reading a romance novel. Walter was grateful that he'd kept up with Little Ricky after Big Ricky's death. Little Ricky was helpful. And he idolized Walter Maxwell (Big Walt the Stone Killer), as his father had.

"Hello, Rick," Walter said.

"Hey, Big Walt, Big Walt, jeez, how ya been? How ya been? How're they hangin'? Good to hear, good to hear."

In Walter's books, Richard Zampone was listed as "Consultant." Close enough. Walter kept him on retainer, like a lawyer. For times like now, though this, of course, would cost extra.

"Everything's fine, Rick. I have a job for you if you can come up tomorrow night. Probably with someone. Marty, maybe? That possible?"

"For you, Big Walt? Of course. Of course. What sort of job?"

"Some merchandise to dispose of. Female."

"You want I should bring the truck? Maybe a rug or two?"

"Sounds good, Rick. You know the way?"

"No problem. Like last time. You haven't moved. How's the cows?"

Little Ricky couldn't imagine why an important man

like Big Walt Mastrinski wanted to live up there in the boonies, away from all the old gang, raising a bunch of cows. But, hey, it takes all kinds to make a world, huh? Big Walt, today, was as old as his father had been when he died, may his soul rest in peace. Old guys get funny.

"The cows are fine, Rick. Can you be here around half past eight? Be back on the road in an hour? And how's Bernice?"

"Half past eight it is, Big Walt. And Bernice? Co-pacetic. Boy, we missed you at Marcie's engagement party. Bernice went crazy, shrimp, polpo, calamari, mussels, lobster Fra Diavolo, you wouldn't believe. Everyone was here—Marty, Harold, even Frankie Slats. Everyone asked about you. I know you never got on with that side of the Family, but you were missed, Big Walt, believe me. Everyone talkin' about the good old days. Dad woulda loved it."

Walter said he was sorry he'd missed the big reunion, to give his love to Bernice, double pay, of course, like last time, and said good-bye.

"Anything for you, Big Walt," Ricky said. And meant it. His pop had loved Big Walt. "He's such a fuckin' gent," Big Ricky would chuckle, huge belly wobbling with mirth. "Learned to talk like a university professor, goes to England to buy his fuckin' *shoes.*"

Little Ricky had grown up on stories about Walter, the clothes he wore, the women he had ("a regular Casanova") and especially, the guys he hit. Walt The Stone Killer. "For him, it's nothing, like takin' a piss." This was one very cool guy. Even now that he was old.

Walter got up, turned off the downstairs lights, locked the doors, climbed the stairs. He'd deal with Candy's purse, cape, and overnight bag tomorrow. Now, he was exhausted.

He sloughed off his clothes, threw them in the tub of cold water, in case there were bloodstains, and took a fast shower, sluicing down his tired, old body with the warm water. Then he dried himself, put on his silk pajamas, climbed into bed, and immediately fell asleep.

CHAPTER FOUR

✛✛✛✛✛✛✛

Charly Finds Far More Than Fungi

✛✛✛✛✛✛✛

Charly Poisson opened one eye and looked at the red 5 on his electric clock. Uh-oh, too early. He inched down, pulled the down comforter up to his ears, closed the eye. At his head, a cat was poised, waiting for movement; at his knees, another cat crouched; in the wicker basket by the window, another cat; starting to claw at the comforter near his feet, a fourth cat.

Non, Charly thought, *Non et non et non.* He wouldn't get up. Monday, his free day. The restaurant was closed. He made his mind a blank.

Against all odds—a full bladder, four eager cats— Charly drifted back to sleep. And dreamed of mushrooms. Clusters of brown, fleshy fungi, stewed in olive oil, garlic, and parsley; mushroom soup; mushrooms on toast. He saw his father, gaunt, drooping mustache stained with yellow nicotine, holding a basket of *cèpes—Boletus edulis—* picked in the little woods just off the Route de Villeneuve, about a kilometer from the villa. *"Ça, mon p'tit, c'est du bon manger"*—That's good eating, little one, in the *patois* or slang, of the Franche-Comté region in France where he'd grown up. Charly and his father had often hunted wild mushrooms, and it was always an adventure. Of course he wouldn't hunt *cèpes* in America—a toxic variety looked too similar, and Charly was no mycologist. But the less subtle oyster mushroom was good, too.

At 5:59, Charly's eyes flew open. This was it. He raised himself up, toed into his sheepskin slippers, found his indoor beret on the headboard and clapped it on, a guard against the deadly air currents, or *courants d'air*, that every French person knows are fatal to good health. He grasped his little dropper bottle of Bach flower remedies and plopped four drops onto his tongue, to keep his mind clear and to calm his soul. Ah, Dr. Bach, such a pity he was English, for as every Frenchman knows the English were a terrible people who'd burned Joan of Arc at the stake. He tottered up and shrugged into a woolen bathrobe covered in cat hairs. Made his way to the toilet. The day had begun.

Downstairs, the rituals continued: Charly let the cats out; filled a saucepan with water; looked out the window above the sink—ah, a lovely day, grey and misty. Charly thought about his dream. Yes, *tiens,* this would be a pleasant morning to hunt for mushrooms. He went to the back door and opened it: Four cats rushed in. Charly sniffed the air. It was quite warm, unlike yesterday, and the air smelled wet and leafy, faintly salty. Charly stepped out onto his back porch. Breathed the warm, moist air into his lungs, held his breath, then breathed out again ("poooh") to the count of eight.

By now the water was boiling, so Charly spooned a large amount of Puerto Rican coffee into his Melita filter, set it on his pitcher, poured over the boiling water. He poured half a cup, added an ice cube from the freezer, gingerly felt the liquid with his tongue, then gulped it down. Repeat performance. Charly shuddered. Delicious.

He got the plastic bowl marked *chats* from the refrigerator and spooned meat into four bowls, which he set down on the kitchen floor. He stroked four sleek backs: "Ah, Frère, Marcelle, Tin-Tin, Suzanne," he addressed each cat by name: "You are good, good." Charly loved his cats; people, he merely tolerated.

As he lay in his bath, Charly planned his mushroom hunt: He'd found a nice grouping of oyster mushrooms last fall in the little copse beyond his two fields at the end of Hubbard Road, and though it was far from certain that mushrooms would be there, (mushroom hunting was like fishing, the exercise was often more rewarding than the findings), it would make a nice little *promenade* on a warm and misty morning. How many mornings like this were left in the year? And if he did find mushrooms—a bonus.

Charly dressed carefully: silk undershirt; long johns; corduroy trousers; a cotton turtleneck with a wool pullover on top; woolen socks; leather boots.

Downstairs, he added a nylon windbreaker and a cashmere scarf, then stuffed leather gloves in his pocket. A heavy woolen beret covered coal black hair, courtesy of Monsieur Clairol, that grew on a head shaped like a Roman senator's. Charly wasn't at all sure what a Roman senator's head looked like, but an old customer had once paid him this compliment. A Roman senator, eh? Not bad. He patted his pockets: a handkerchief, his folding knife. In addition, he took a cloth shopping bag from the kitchen, with a small paring knife and, as an afterthought, stuffed in two plastic supermarket bags: ever hopeful. He checked his watch: just seven o'clock.

Charly walked to the end of his driveway and turned left on Hubbard Road. He walked for half a mile, then the road forked: turn left and the road soon ended in the midst of Charly's fields. Turn right, and the small road led up to another dead end and Maurice and Barbara's big, modern, white-stucco monstrosity. Ah, Maurice. Maurice would have to go; Charly would have to buy him out. It had to be done, and soon, for Maurice would ruin the restaurant's reputation. Yes, he'd deal with it this week.

At the end of the road Charly began tramping through

his fields. Fields bought parcel by parcel as the restaurant prospered. The most beautiful fields in the world, Charly thought, filled with mice and voles, raccoons and woodchucks, rabbits and opossums. Deer foraged there, and wild turkeys. In the sky above, a hawk drifted lazily on the air currents, and a big V of wild ducks honked as they flew. He could be in the Jura, in France, Charly thought. But no, on his last visit to his hometown, Charly had been shocked to find no more fields, all houses. Suburbia had arrived in the French countryside.

Charly heard the chirping of a thousand birds as he pushed through the goldenrod and the St. John's Wort, the Michaelmas daisies and the dried milkweed pods. There was even an out-of-season dried dandelion flower, all furry and white. Charly bent down and picked it, and blew the tiny seeds over his fields, as he recited the logo of the excellent Larousse dictionary, *"Je Sème A Tout Vent,"* I sow in all winds. Ah, it was beautiful.

Now Charly came to a small wooded area. It had once been an apple orchard, then the trees had died and fallen, and saplings had sprung from the rotten wood. This was Charly's secret mushroom spot. Once, some years ago, he had found fifty-one morels here, but that had never been repeated.

Charly looked into the dark little copse. Blinked. Looked again. Shook his head, closed his eyes, opened his eyes. Was this possible? The decayed logs were blanketed with masses of oyster mushrooms. He'd never seen such a sight in his life. It was magic, with the sunlight breaking through the mist, the fog lifting, and, at his feet, mushrooms and more mushrooms.

Charly recognized that this was a sublime moment. Ten years from now, twenty, he would remember the magic of this October morning, with the shafts of sunlight piercing the fog, and the logs at his feet carpeted in mushrooms. *Oh, Papa,* he thought, *if you could see this.*

Ten, twenty, then fifty, sixty, seventy . . . Charly stopped counting. The three bags were bursting. He was glad, now, that he'd delayed his bowl of hot cereal. Instead there would be mushrooms on toast.

Charly picked up his bags, turned to leave. But wait . . . what was that flash of yellow, over there by the trees? A ray of sunlight picked out something that shone like gold. Not a mushroom, certainly not an edible one. Charly strolled over, his bags bumping against his legs. Ah, yes, something had been buried . . . see the upturned dirt? An animal had been burrowing, Charly could see tiny footprints, a fox, perhaps. He bent down, peered. It was a piece of fabric. It looked like part of a scarf. Charly put down his bags and touched the cloth. It felt like heavy silk. He grasped the corner, gave a little tug. More of the fabric appeared. A scarf? Yes, it looked like the corner of a beautiful yellow scarf printed with autumn leaves, an expensive Hermès, perhaps, an old Hermès, see how the edges had been hemmed outward, a trademark of that famous Parisian saddlemaker? Now, who would bury such a scarf? And on his land? Charly shook his head.

He grasped the scarf and pulled. Stuck. He grabbed the fabric with both hands and gave a mighty tug . . . and fell backwards, as the scarf came out of the ground, attached to a human head and neck, and the neck was attached to a body, the body of a woman, a quite-dead woman, dressed in a tweed garment.

"Ai, Ai, Ai!" Charly screamed. He let go the scarf and fell backwards, bumping the back of his head against a tree trunk. He felt hot and then cold, paralyzed, dizzy, and nauseated. He turned his head and vomited his coffee, tasting the acid, metallic liquid.

He didn't want to look, but he looked: The grey face was set in a grimace, the back of the head appeared bloody and pulpy. One eye was closed, with a small brown birthmark just below the corner of the left eye. At the back of the head, big bluebottle flies had already started buzzing, attracted by the blood. "A hunting accident," was Charly's first, irrational thought. But no, this was no accident. The body had been buried, a deliberate act. Charly crept up and looked into the face. It was a curious face, with a look of age, but no wrinkles. Charly had seen similar faces on some of his wealthier customers—like Madame Wells, for instance, and Madame Vann. Le face-lift, without a doubt. Behind the ears would be found little surgical marks—not that Charly was about to look. In addition, the face was puffy and looked bruised. Charly sniffed: no smell of decay, only of wet earth, a faint scent of perfume and, yes, a smell of alcohol. Charly thought of Maurice, yesterday, thought of his customers downing drink after drink. *My partner is alcoholic, my customers are alcoholic, even the corpses I find are alcoholic,* he thought bitterly.

Charly staggered to his feet, grabbed his mushroom bags, backed away from the corpse, then turned and hurried out of the little woods, which looked sinister now. Clouds had covered the sun, and a chill breeze blew. Charly breathed deep, gasping breaths, panting with shock.

He thought he'd never make it home—each step seemed to take hours—but finally his little house came in sight, and Charly set down his bags and threw open the back door. He stumbled into the warm kitchen, reached up, and grasped the cooking brandy, which stood on a shelf to the right of the stove. He took a swig. What was the homeopathic remedy for shock? Arsenic. He rummaged in his kitchen medicine basket, shook four tiny tablets out. And Dr. Bach? Might as well cover all bases. Rescue Remedy, of course. He found the little bottle, plopped four drops onto his tongue. Then he looked up Police Chief John Stark's number in his address book. Since the emergency number 9-1-1 had been established a few months ago, people were urged to call there, but Charly felt more comfortable dealing with someone he knew. "Stark! Chief Stark!" Charly gasped, as the telephone was answered. "I must speak to Chief John Stark!"

CHAPTER FIVE

❖❖❖❖❖❖❖

Walter Is
Indisposed

❖❖❖❖❖❖❖

Walter Maxwell groaned in his king-size bed. Pain behind his eyes, stiff neck, sore back. He felt awful. Damn woman had been heavy. He should have sent her back to New York with the promise of a hundred gees and called Little Ricky to deal with her at her apartment. He was too old for all this stupidity. He turned over, pulled the covers higher, and went back to sleep.

It was eight o'clock Monday morning. Marian Arnold, Walter's daily cleaner and the wife of Tom, Walter's farm manager, drove her battered white Toyota Corolla into Walter Maxwell's back parking area. She grabbed her big plastic purse and slouched to the house, a hulking woman dressed in shapeless jeans, a baggy sweatshirt, and a polyester-filled nylon windbreaker.

She turned the knob. Still locked. Well now. Mr. Walter got up early, and the first thing he did was to unlock the back door. He'd told her so. Now, where was her key, oh, here. Maxwell's had a red ribbon.

She unlocked the door, entered the small back hall, wiped her feet carefully, walked into the mudroom and prepared to wipe her feet again on the rag rug at the entrance to the kitchen, but it was missing.

Marian Okun Arnold was forty years old but looked older—greying brown hair pulled back in a ponytail with a rubber band, scrubbed face a network of tiny wrinkles. Five-foot-ten and sturdy, she had a bulging, prominent forehead, (mildly hydrocephalic, which was not uncommon to children born of alcoholic mothers) and small, deepset dark brown eyes, like buttons. Her mouth was a thin line.

Marian had quit school in the eighth grade, to the relief of most of her teachers, who found her slow and dull. Only her home economics teacher gave a positive report. "Marian Okun," Mrs. Babcock wrote, "is a tidy worker. She is slow but painstaking, and in cleaning up afterward, she is the best in class. Below average in intelligence, Marian would make an excellent houseworker. She is clean in her person and, I believe, honest." The general attitude toward Marian was, "for an Okun, she's one of the better ones." The vast Okun clan, part Native American, part God knew what, were small farmers, carpenters, basket weavers, with more than their share of drunks and trouble-makers. Down at Stark's headquarters, the Okuns were well-known, if not well liked.

Marian's customers were pleased with her. She always had plenty of work. She might be slow, but she was a thorough cleaner, she charged the minimum rate, and she never tried to cheat you on time. Also, she rarely spoke. Most cleaning ladies wanted to tell you all their troubles, waste your time, be on an equal footing with you, but not Marian. "She knows her place," her customers said.

Marian entered Walter Maxwell's kitchen. Something was wrong, and she felt the hairs on her neck go up, just like a dog's. But what? There were a few dishes piled in the sink—Mr. Walter usually rinsed them off, put them in the dishwasher. She checked the wastebasket under the sink. Empty. It was usually full. The refrigerator was pushed sideways, all catty-corner. The big table where Mr. Walter usually ate his meals—pushed way over to the side. Marian checked the big wicker rag bag in the mudroom—some rags were missing. Marian shook her head. Nothing, really. Nothing important. Then why did she feel all creepy? Was Mr. Walter dead? She could smell death, feel death close by. She was part Passamaquoddy, from Maine; she felt the closeness of the spirit world.

Marian stood still and listened to the silence wrapped around the big house. Usually she could hear bathwater running, a toilet flushing, noises in the study, or Mr. Walter talking on the telephone. She walked to the bottom of the stairs. "Mr. Walter?" she called.

A noise. Walter opened his bedroom door and called, "Who is it?" His voice was all gurgly, like he had a cold.

"It's me, Marian."

"What are you doing here?"

"Like always. Cleaning. It's Monday morning, eight o'clock."

"Oh. I overslept. Begin your day."

Marian usually tidied up the entire house, putting things back where they belonged. Then she'd clean the rest of the house, saving the kitchen for last. But today, she didn't know why, she felt she should begin by washing the kitchen floor. It was all streaked, and something in the room smelled funny. *Gives me the willies*, Marian thought, and remembered a phrase of her grandma's: "A goose has done walked over my grave." She put the dirty dishes in the dishwasher, filled the sink with warm water, poured in some pine disinfectant, got her mop and her rags, and set to work. Marian found a piece of broken glass, a crust of bread wedged in a corner, and a crumb of the meat loaf that the restaurant man made for Mr. Walter over near the sink. *All topsy-*

turvy, Marian thought, as she finished up the floor. *Maybe Mr. Walter got himself liquored up last night.*

"Oh, hello, Mr. Walter." He stood at the entrance to the kitchen, a gaunt old man in light blue pajamas and a navy blue bathrobe, stood there and shivered, as if he was cold. Looked grey, sick, shaky. Not like himself, a mean man, always had been. No smiles for the help. Treated you like you were a machine, a piece of dirt, not a person with a soul.

"I've left some clothes soaking in the upstairs bathtub," Walter said. "I cut my finger, there may be stains. Put them in the washer, will you? Except for my white sweater. Wash that by hand, like all my sweaters."

"Bloodstains? Hope it's cold water. Hot water makes blood set."

"Well," Mr. Walter said, not friendly-like, "do your best."

Marian loved to clean people's houses. She'd feel all dirty inside, and then she'd clean someone's house and it made her feel clean, to leave the rooms all sparkly and smelling nice from lemon oil. "You're a good girl, Marian," Mrs. Babcock had told her. "The Lord takes care of folks like you."

Now she had another person in her life who made her feel all clean inside: Pastor Pflugg, who ran the New Awakenings Church. "Everything that happens to you, it's God's will," Pastor had told her. "You must never fear the fires of hell, God's love will protect you." Listening to Pastor Pflugg, Marian felt the cleansing fires of God's love. She accepted her husband Tom, who liked to get all liquored up and talk big, about how he was going to do this and that to folks; she could bear her brother Bob and his family and not feel sad because God had chosen to give him and Linda children, but not her. Pastor Pflugg told her:

"Marian, you're good." And Marian knew it was so. She was always ready to do the bidding of the Lord.

Marian cleaned Walter Maxwell's house for two hours, not doing guest rooms this morning since the extra washing and cleaning of the kitchen floor had taken a half hour longer. One more cleaning job before lunch, and then she'd go home and make a sandwich. Then she'd spend an hour doing God's work for Pastor Pflugg: going around, knocking on folks' doors, giving them the good news about the Bible.

Marian finished the downstairs, finished the upstairs. Cleaning always calmed her. She'd washed Mr. Walter's white sweater, filthy, it was, with spots that could have been blood. She got them out—it was a job—with yellow soap. There were spots on the back of Mr. Walter's pants, too, what had he done, wiped his fanny with his bloody finger? Well, now. Everything came out, all those spots. Mr. Walter was rich, so many clothes, she wondered if he knew how many pants he had? How many fine, soft sweaters?

Marian never felt envy toward these rich folks she cleaned for. They were too far beyond her ken. There were people who made her feel like crying—the girls who'd snubbed her in school, who'd called her "dummy," grown women now with children. They had children, but she didn't. They were wicked, yet the Lord had given them babies to hold and cuddle.

But the Lord had promised her that they would be punished. "Vengeance is mine, saith the Lord." Pastor had spoken of this just yesterday, in his sermon on the wicked. "There comes a time," he'd said, "when we must mete out punishment with our own hands. When we must take it upon ourselves to punish the wicked." She and the Lord, Marian thought, together, they could do so much.

Driving away from Black Bull Farm, Marian thought about something that Mr. Walter had said. He'd said he had cut his finger. She'd glanced at his fingers, but hadn't seen any cuts. She'd have a good look at his hands, tomorrow.

CHAPTER SIX

Monday Morning with the Klover Police

John Stark, Chief of Police for Klover Township, felt good after ten hours' sleep. More than ten, really. He'd fallen asleep on the living-room couch as soon as they'd come home from The Firm, yesterday, and slept until nine, when Betty nudged his shoulder, asking him if he wanted a sandwich before going to bed. He'd said no. Then he'd gone up to his bed and slept until five in the morning. By seven, he was at the Klover Police Station.

Now, Stark sat at his desk with a mug of coffee, talking to two of his men, Clem Hughes and Vince Matucci, about the arsonist. Those barn burnings were tearing the town apart. Clem, due for retirement next year, knew all the old-timers and was expert at passing the time of day with them, finding things out; Vince, six years on the force, whose uncle Rex Cingale owned a local steakhouse and bar, could pick up more news in a night than Stark could accumulate in a month.

Just last week, for instance, the police had picked up the guy who'd robbed Monte's service station; he'd bragged to a pal, right at the Steak Heaven bar. Bobby Matucci the barman overheard him, and passed the news on to his brother Vince, who was Officer Matucci. In an hour the guy, sitting at the police station, was confessing to four robberies.

"Talked to Jim Halloran yesterday," Clem said. "Says the farmers are going to start a vigilante group, take turns watchin' each other's places at night. Now you know what that means? They catch the guy, have a little accident with a firearm, guy'll never live to stand trial. We gotta catch him."

"They can't stay up all night and work all day," Stark said. "And how can one man be in six, seven places at once? They're desperate. Five months this guy's been burning barns—and we haven't a clue."

They reviewed what they'd done so far: made lists of past barn burners, since 1950; contacted neighboring counties to get their lists; made more lists of known local felons, now out of jail; and alerted the high-school principal, who was to keep his ears open. (And if anyone had big ears when it came to hearing schoolyard bragging, it was Matthew Murdock.) They'd contacted all gas stations, hardware stores, and other purveyors of receptacles for holding gasoline. Who bought gas in jerricans? (Practically everybody, since there were so many gas-powered lawn mowers.) They contacted local psychiatrists and doctors, hospitals and private sanatoriums to ask them to report any potential arsonists among their patients. They'd pursued every avenue they could think of, except hiring a psychic, and Stark was considering this. That old lady down in Hogton had a good reputation for finding things and people. Found the Broderick child—he'd crawled into an old outbuilding and couldn't get out. The old psychic told them where to look.

"I got Bobby listening, my Uncle Rex, too, down at the restaurant," Vince Matucci said. "They all say it's a volunteer fireman. They're the ones usually start fires."

"Practically every man in Rex's bar's a volunteer fireman," Stark pointed out.

"Yeah," Vince went on, "and Fire Chief Tibbetts, he's so mad, the idea one of his men could be the one, he's watchin' 'em like a hawk. And they're all spyin' on each other. This thing's rippin' 'em apart."

Stark sighed, waved a sheaf of telephone message slips. "I know. They've all called. I also got a call from Pastor Pflugg, he runs the New Awakenings Church. Says he's going to pray for us, but maybe the farmers are getting a message from God to mend their ways. You know the man? A weirdo. It's not a church, it's a cult. I want to check them out."

Hughes and Matucci nodded. Stark's telephone rang. "I told Sheila to hold all the calls, except for life-or-death matters. Hello? Klover Police Station, Chief Stark speaking."

Stark held up his hand, signaling his two men to stay where they were. "Charly? Calm down. I can't understand you."

"The body, she is in the woods, all bash up, shallow grave, animals dig, a scarf of Hermès, good cloth, rich lady, perhaps old, the smell of alcohol, I go to find mushroom. *Mon Dieu, elle est morte.* She is dead."

Hughes and Matucci sat up in their seats. Impossible not to hear, Charly was shouting. "She is dead," came through loud and clear.

"Hold on, Charly," Stark said. "You've found a body. Correct?"

"Yes, that is correct."

"It's a woman's body and she's been bashed on the head, buried in a shallow grave and animals dug her up. Correct?"

"Pre-cisely."

"You found her this morning, you went out hunting mushrooms."

("Hunt mushrooms?" Hughes whispered. "What's the guy, crazy?" And Matucci whispered back, "Nope, my granny goes all the time.")

"Exactement."

"Where did you find the body?"

"On my land."

"Well, Charly, you've got lots of land." Charly had over a hundred acres.

"It is . . ." Charly took a deep breath. Directions were a difficulty. "It is, you know, beyond my house. Go to the end of the road, at the fork you turn left, at the end of the road there is a field but you go through the other field, the one with a little woods at the end, on the left . . ."

"Why don't I come, pick you up, we'll go over together, huh? Then when I see the body, I'll call the station, we'll get the coroner, the photographer, you know, the forensic team from the state police. So, Charly, give me about fifteen minutes, okay?"

Stark hung up, told Hughes to alert Hy Bingham, who acted as coroner, to call Sam Higgins the photographer. He told Vince to round up the rest from the state police. Klover didn't have a forensic team—few small towns did. Why should they? Last year Van Buren County had had one homicide, eight attempted suicides, five actual suicides, one drowning, one death by fire and fourteen unattended deaths of old people. No drug deaths, but seven cases of drug overdoses. It wasn't exactly New York City or Detroit.

Clem was skeptical. "You think there really is a body?"

Stark nodded. "Well, yeah. But it might be something buried years ago. Remember those bones Charly found, turned out to be part of an old graveyard on his land, bones were a hundred years old."

Clem snorted. "Guy's dyin' to be a detective."

"Still," Stark said, "he said she was wearing a scarf, he thought she was a rich lady, and he said something about smelling alcohol. I'd say she was recent. He didn't say she was rotting."

"A local?" Clem Hughes asked. "Or city folks?"

Stark shrugged. "Sounds like a city woman." In other words, a stranger, not one of them. He stood up and twisted his mouth into a sarcastic smile. "Hey, it's like we've got nothing better to do, right? We're just sitting here twiddling our thumbs. We've gotta find the arsonist, and now, this. Vince, after you've made those calls, get Abe, all these phone calls from the volunteer firemen have to be returned. I leave it to the two of you to judge if there's anything worth pursuing. But listen: Whatever Charly found is dead. It can't burn down a barn. The arsonist can, and will, burn down more barns. He has top priority. We have to find that guy. Soon."

"Maybe it's a woman, you know?" Vince said. "Maybe this old dead broad, she's got a grudge, or she's crazy, a farmer catches her tryin' to burn down his barn, bashes her on the head, buries her in a trench, he's gonna come by later, haul her up, put her by some old outbuilding, set it afire. That way, everyone'll know it was her, the arsonist. And no one gets in trouble."

"Yeah, maybe," Stark said. "You know what? I think you've got a great career ahead of you, Officer Matucci—as a TV script writer."

"Aw, Chief."

"Sounds like a good idea to me," Clem said, and glared at Stark. "All these damn strangers, come up to Van Buren County, try to rule the roost . . . you know what they charge at that Firm restaurant?"

"I know," Stark said drily. "I ate there, yesterday." He left his office, shrugging on his jacket, Clem and Vince still sitting, Clem opening and closing his mouth like a fish.

CHAPTER SEVEN

A Well-Dressed Corpse

Dinah Vann, Mrs. Peter Vann, by her own estimate one of the richest women in Van Buren County (though not in the same ballpark as Honoria Wells, their guest at La Fermette yesterday) was, in her own words, "at sixes and sevens." Here it was Monday morning, her big dinner party was tomorrow night, and those artichoke hearts surrounding the veal just weren't right. Too 1960s. Not something you'd see in *W. W* was Dinah's favorite fashion magazine, all those lavish pictures of her former customers, when she'd been saleslady, finally head buyer, at Chez Mimi on Park Avenue, the most exclusive women's dress shop in New York City. She dialed Charly's home. The restaurant was closed Mondays, she remembered that.

"Allo? Allo? Charles Poisson, 'ere."

"Oh, Charly. I'm so glad I caught you. It's Dinah Vann. Listen, we must discuss the menu again, I'm not at all happy about . . ."

Charly was in no mood for frivolities, even from a good customer like Madame Vann. "Madame," he hissed, "something tairrible has happen, and I am waiting for the police."

"The police?"

"Yes, madame. I have found, on my land, a body. Of a woman."

"A woman, dear God. Is it Honoria? You know, she's going with that awful young man, I'm so afraid for her, he's a dreadful man."

"No, no, *chère* madame, do not be alarmed. It is not Madame Wells. But it is a well-dressed woman, she wears a Hermès scarf, and a jacket, perhaps a suit, of fine tweed . . ."

"An Armani? A Giorgio Armani? The suit, I mean?"

Charly had no idea. A tweed garment. But to say this would not be observant. Sherlock Holmes wouldn't have said he didn't know. "I think, hmmm, an Yves St. Laurent. Yes, yes, I am sure of it. But, madame, I call you back. The police are coming now and"—importantly clearing his throat—"I am going to take them to the body. So, I call you back in an hour or so, yes?"

Charly called the house of his partner, Maurice Baleine, knowing that he would still be asleep (drunk or sober, Maurice rarely woke before ten), and that Barbara, his wife, would answer the telephone.

"Oh, Charly. I don't know what to say about last night. Passing out, like some cheap, Bowery bum."

"Say nothing, my dear Barbara. You are as distressed as I am. Is everything, you know, hokay?"

"Everything is not okay. He's been sleeping in the big guest bedroom for months, so we rarely see each other. I can't go on like this, Charly. It's been going on too long. I've had enough. But now, I've got an appointment in Rhinebeck, a big house to decorate, I'm running late."

"Then I tell you quickly." And Charly recounted his find.

Barbara said, "What kind of publicity is this for the restaurant? You don't think people will think she's a customer who's been poisoned by your food? Listen, Charly, don't tell the world. In fact, don't tell a soul." After seeing a surge in Charly's business brought about by two modest magazine articles, Barbara was respectful of the power of the press. And she knew Charly's love of gossip. "Restaurateur Finds Decomposing Woman's Body." No, no, press like that Charly didn't need. "Bad publicity, Charly."

"Ah, I did not think of that." Just as he hung up, Charly heard a car crunch on the gravel of his driveway. He grabbed his jacket (he'd never removed his beret) and hurried out. He got in the passenger seat of the police car and nodded to Stark.

"So, you were hunting mushrooms, eh, Charly? You do that often?"

"Once in the fall and once in the spring, usually. My papa used to take me when I was"—Charly indicated a short height with his hand—"small boy. In Jura Mountain in France. Before the war, of course. During wartime, the Nazi occupation, the Germans, they shoot the people in Jura. Especially the *Maquis,* who are the guerillas. And the friends of the guerillas, the doctors and priests who help the guerillas, so many killed and tortured."

"Maybe that's why I'm a cop," Stark said. "To keep the killing down. We don't want murderers like that here in Van Buren County now, do we?"

"No, we do not. And perhaps that is why I feel anger when I see this woman," Charly explained. "You cannot kill people. You cannot. We cannot take the lives of other human beings. We must have justice."

"Of course," Charly continued, "you can die from mushroom poisoning, too. In this way, I suppose, you could kill yourself. But this lady that I find, she did not die from mushroom poisoning. Me, when I hunt the mushroom, I take great care. This morning I find many oyster mushroom, called *Pleurotte* in France. Very safe, very good."

Stark, who thought eating wild mushrooms purely suicidal, changed the subject. "I haven't been down this road for years. Still a dead end, huh?"

They'd arrived at the fork. Charly pointed left. "To right, is house of my partner Maurice Baleine. Big house. Ugly. A showoff house."

"Showing people how rich he is."

"That is correct. You do not want a house that make people say, *Ooh, la la,* rich people live there. To do that is to invite jealousy. Stop here, please."

Together Stark and Charly walked over to the little woods. Charly pointed to the body with his finger, but did not approach. Stark walked up to the body, crouched down on his haunches. The back of the head was covered in flies. He noted the face: old but not wrinkled, sunken eyes, puffy cheeks, greyish, mottled skin. A birthmark, or something, below the left eye. Lips parted, showing a broken tooth. Hair matted with dried blood. Bloody tarp, yellow scarf. Ugly, as corpses always were. He'd never seen her before.

Stark stood up and motioned for Charly to come along. Silently, they walked back to the police car. Stark spoke: "Whoever dumped the body, they drove down Route 16, then across the little field, not the way we came. You notice that? Easy to do in a four-wheel drive. Woman was killed elsewhere."

"No, John, I did not notice. Finding the body, a big shock."

"Well, there was no blood behind her head, for one thing. And I noticed the broken weeds, branches, tire marks over on the other side. Stopped raining last evening, early, so you can see the tracks real well."

"It was not raining when I left the restaurant to go home," Charly pointed out, "around seven, I think."

Stark nodded. "I'd put money on the fact that she was killed elsewhere, like I said. Brought here after the rain. Animal damage minimal, she hasn't been here that long, maybe twelve hours. She's pretty stiff, in full rigor, or close to it. Bet she was put there last night. Yeah, she was killed elsewhere, wrapped in that tarp, they dug a hole, ground's real soft."

"Ah."

"Doc Bingham can tell us more. Body temp, last meal, if there are any maggots underneath her. I didn't see any."

"You notice the smell of alcohol?" Charly asked.

Stark shook his head. "Dissipated, I guess, when you pulled on the scarf. But she looks like a drinker. See those puffy bags under her eyes? And she's got sunken cheeks, looks like she drinks her meals, and those broken veins on her cheekbones, on her nose, she tried to cover them up with makeup, but they're there, all right. That shallow grave, though, that's a puzzle. Why so shallow? Animals would dig her up in no time, body gases would puff her up, she'd start to smell . . . but this area, guess no one comes here much."

"Except me," Charly said. "I walk here. And even if I had not come for mushrooms, I would have come soon to get humus. I have to plant my garlic. Garlic is always planted in October. And always humus for garlic. Garlic is a heavy feeder, it must have humus. I tell many of my customers, get your humus here. And many do."

"Killer didn't know that. Here, I'll drive you home, call it in, wait here for the men. Someone knew about this place, Charly. Looks deserted, the perfect spot, Route 16 goes nowhere, those three deserted farms . . . yep, the perfect spot."

"Not so perfect," Charly pointed out, "since I found the body."

CHAPTER EIGHT

✚✚✚✚✚✚✚

Soup and Supposition

✚✚✚✚✚✚✚

Jimmy Houghton, Charly's investment adviser and the man Charly had nicknamed "the pest," breakfasted on a tall glass of prune juice. That damn pork at Charly's, he'd tossed all night. Now he was constipated. Tonight, if he still hadn't moved his bowels, he'd take some Ex-Lax. They should do it.

Jimmy, looking natty and trim (not constipated at all) in his tweed jacket, checked his watch. Plenty of time to tend to his houseplants. Monday was watering day. He must remember to take a bottle of Maalox to the office, the office bottle was nearly empty. He'd better take some Tums, as well, and Rolaids, and some Pepcid AC. Oh, and some of those wonderful cashews he'd ordered from Williams-Sonoma. Marian Arnold was coming to clean, today, so he'd better tidy the place up. If he didn't, Marian would put things in odd spots, and it would take weeks to find them.

Jimmy first watered his plants—pencil cactus, rubber tree, Jerusalem cherry, Christmas cactus, three African violets (watered from the bottom), four begonias, and picked off dead leaves. Then he walked through the rooms of his little farmhouse stacking his *National Geographic* magazines, putting away a few pieces he didn't want Marian to break, not that she ever broke anything, but she was such an angry person. ("Angry?" his client Walter Maxwell had said. "I never noticed." But Walter wouldn't. He wasn't empathetic at all.)

A small malachite box, a Kaigyokudo ivory netsuke of mice playing, and two small Sèvres bowls went into a drawer. From his dad's family. Irreplaceable. Jimmy often thought about his father but even now, thirty years later, he couldn't deal with the pain. No wonder he was constipated—his therapist often spoke of the dangers of suppressed emotion. He took four Cadbury's chocolate bars from a drawer. He kept them here, at home, didn't want Evelyn to know he snacked on candy, when he made such a big fuss about his stomach problems.

Charly sat at his kitchen table, exhausted. He'd taken Dr. Bach's Rescue Remedy, Ignatia pills, and was sipping chamomile tea. Finding the mushrooms was anticlimactic, now. And, too, he'd felt sad that Stark hadn't wanted him at the crime scene. But, in truth, he'd only get in the way. *After all,* he reasoned, *I wouldn't want the police in my kitchen while I cook, why should I be with them while they do their work?* He decided on a snack: sourdough bread and beef dripping, nice and rich. Just the ticket.

After three pieces of bread loaded with dripping and sprinkled with coarse sea salt Charly felt so buoyant he decided to make a mushroom soup, after all. He called old Doc Ross and made a date: Doc would enjoy hearing about his morning.

Charly got his big cast-iron Dutch oven, put it on the stove and added a good measure of butter and olive oil. Let it heat. Meanwhile he chopped garlic and shallots and added them to the pot, turning them with a wooden spoon. He sprinkled them with flour, turned them again, then added his cleaned and sliced mushrooms. When the mushrooms reduced, he poured in rich chicken stock, brought the soup to a boil, skimmed the scum, and lowered the heat. He glanced at his watch. Thirty minutes would suffice.

On the way out of his kitchen, Charly stopped to look in

his pantry. His spiders were coming along nicely—a big, fat web at the corner of the ceiling filled with spiders' eggs. The eggs were getting larger. Soon, they would hatch. *"Mes felicitations,"* congratulations, Charly said to what he assumed was the mother spider. Charly loved spiders, such busy creatures, and they spun such beautiful webs. Sometimes the female spiders ate their husbands, but wasn't this just like life? People always devoured other people—at least, metaphorically. While the mushrooms cooked, Charly would do a spot of housecleaning, nothing strenuous, just push the Electrolux around, gathering up cat hairs.

As he pushed the vacuum cleaner, Charly thought about the dead woman. *His* dead woman. To Stark, she was just another body. But Charly felt a proprietary interest in the corpse. He thought of his childhood hero, Sherlock Holmes. Now, what would Holmes do? Holmes would perceive, by the dust on the woman's shoe, that she came from a certain city; he would identify her perfume, only available at such and such a shop, and her alcoholic smell—an esoteric brand of, say, gin, which Holmes would easily trace. *Oof.* What nonsense. No wonder Conan Doyle had become thoroughly sick of his hero, finally killing him off.

But wait a minute, hadn't Charly solved the case of Dinah Vann's stolen car? By Holmesian deduction? (Well, by common sense.) Several years ago Dinah's car, a yellow Cadillac, had disappeared from her driveway. Dinah, as usual, had left the keys in the ignition overnight. Charly's new barman (soon to be fired, as Charly suspected not only that he was not ringing up all of the sales, but also that he was stealing bottles and watering the liquor) had dropped an ornate key ring with the initials DV. Now why should Amos Alkins have such a key ring?

Charly went to the barman's house while Alkins was tending bar at the restaurant and peered into the barn: There was a yellow Cadillac. Charly had called the police, who discovered that Mr. Alkins was wanted in Kentucky for car theft. "You're a regular Sherlock Holmes, Charly," Stark had said at the time, and Charly had swelled with pride.

"You're a regular Sherlock Holmes, Charly," old Doc Ross said now. "You'll find the murderer. You like to get your teeth into things. See justice served. Cops won't like your butting in, but you'll do it anyway."

Charly and Doc were standing in Doc's living room, sipping a thimblefull of Blanton's bourbon. One shot of Blanton's before lunch and dinner, that was Doc's prescription for himself. "Mmmm, coats the tongue like velvet." Doc smacked his lips.

"Delicious," Charly said, quite untruthfully. He didn't like bourbon, even Blanton's, at $45.49 a bottle. A nice Pernod, now that was an aperitif.

Dr. William Ross used to have a thriving practice in Klover until Alma, his wife, died of the radiation treatments used to kill her cancer. It had been a horrible death ("like Hiroshima,") and Doc had never recovered. He'd turned against the medical profession, which killed more people than it cured. Now he stayed home, read, played cards with friends, and dined at Charly's.

Doc was even shorter than Charly—five-foot-five and round, he looked like one of the dwarfs in *Snow White*, with a big round head, a shock of white hair, and a flowing white mustache. "Best doctor in the area," Charly had been told when he'd moved to Klover, and he and Doc and Alma had become friends. Now, Charly went to Doc's house several times a month, always bringing lunch. He loved the old man.

"Ah, ummm," Doc said, rubbing the side of his nose, a faraway look in his deep blue eyes. "No, don't talk, Charly, I am vis—ua—lizing the scene. A foggy morning. Barely, yes, with the fog, barely light. The sun shafts through the trees. The mushrooms. The costly scarf. A woman, no longer young. Murdered. Robbed of her life. Murder's a funny thing, Charly. It's the ultimate expression of someone's terror. Now, who do we know who is fearful enough of someone to kill him? Or in this case, her?" Doc shut his eyes. After a few seconds, Charly wondered if he had gone to sleep. But his eyes flew open. "Too many people come to mind. She didn't look familiar?"

"I have never seen her before," Charly said.

"Ah—ummm," said Doc, and rubbed the side of his nose. "The police will put it on the back burner. Stark won't feel pressured if the woman's a stranger—not like he would if she was a local. Oh, and speaking of locals, I've been thinking about that arsonist—next time you see Stark, remind him that Tom Arnold burned down an old house, once. Don't think it means anything, Arnold was just a teenager. But remind Stark."

"Yes," Charly agreed absently. "I feel, you know, compelled. I must find the killer of that woman."

" 'Course you will, Charly," Doc said loyally. "She may be a friend of some of our rich folks, one of 'em killed her. Unless, of course, it was a drug killing, can't rule that out, not near Hogton. I read in the papers that our little neighboring Hogton, population fifteen thousand, is one of the biggest drug centers of the Northeast."

"Well of course," Charly said, "that is always poss . . ."

"But, I don't think it was drugs," Doc interrupted. "Drug dealers are always in a hurry. Why bother to dig a grave? If she was killed in Hogton, why not simply dump her in the Hudson River? And where would a drug dealer get a spade? Or even know where the ground's soft? Most of the ground around here, it's rock-hard. No, someone knew of that spot. Come, Charly, let's eat your good soup."

"Best soup I've ever eaten," Doc said. He always said this.

"You have a good appetite, Doc. You think a customer of mine is capable of killing this woman? The Vanns, for instance, come from New York City. Walter Maxwell had a farm near Boston, he say."

CHARLY'S MUSHROOM SOUP
Yield: 6 servings

2 Tablespoons butter
1 Tablespoon olive oil
2 cloves of garlic, chopped
2 big shallots, chopped
1½ pounds mushrooms, wild
   or cultivated, sliced
2 Tablespoons flour
1½ quarts rich chicken stock
¼ cup sherry or madeira
Sea salt, freshly ground pepper, parsley,
   chopped, as needed

Heat the butter and olive oil and sauté the
garlic and shallots until soft. Add the mushrooms and stir until mushrooms begin to
soften. Sprinkle with flour, coating mushrooms well, and stir. Pour on chicken stock,
bring to a boil, lower heat to medium, skim
well, cover pot and cook for 30 minutes.
Adjust seasoning with sherry or madeira,
sea salt, freshly ground pepper and at point
of service sprinkle with chopped parsley.
The flat-leaf parsley has the most taste.

"Maxwell's so sharp he'll cut himself one of these days," Doc said, slurping soup. "What about that Houghton feller?"

"Jimmy? He help me with my investments. What about Jimmy?"

"He came from Boston money, and there was some kind of tragedy, I don't recall exactly what, father died, I think. Maybe cancer, like Alma."

"Oh?" Charly said. "I did not know."

"Well, it was 1965 when Mrs. Houghton and her two children moved here," Doc said. "I always remembered, because I won a thousand dollars on a horse in the Kentucky Derby that year called Houghton's Choice. Just coincidence, no relation."

"My good customer Win Crozier, he is heir to that concern, Crozier Plumbing," Charly changed the subject. He couldn't imagine Jimmy as a murderer. Too fastidious to get his hands dirty. "Mr. Crozier and his—ah—" Charly coughed delicately, "friend, they have a painting and decorating shop, where are they from, originally?"

Doc was still at his soup, while buttering Charly's sourdough bread. "I don't know. Two nice men. Fairies, I s'pose, but that doesn't mean anything, nowadays. Win's loaded with cash. I think they both are, always running off to France. They surely don't strike me as killers. But they're capable, I'm sure. If provoked."

"Capable?"

"Of killing someone. We all are. If sufficiently frightened. Fear is one of the deadliest emotions of all, Charly. Right up there with jealousy and greed."

"Yes, yes, is true. And what about the Vanns, Peter and Dinah, and Mrs. Honoria Wells?"

"The Vanns I don't know," Doc said. "Honoria's a bit of a town character. Rolling in dough. Sex-crazed. Loves younger men. I suppose if this woman were an enemy, about to steal her latest kiddie . . . Well, possible but not probable. Honoria's too wrapped up in herself, I'd say."

Charly let it slide. "What you say about the soil, Doc, is true. You can fill a bag with your hands, the ground is so soft. Humus. But everyone know about it. I tell many people, go and dig it up, use on your garden."

"And do they? Dig it up, I mean?"

"Oh, yes. Often in the restaurant, people thank me."

"Then the killer chose a pretty stupid spot, didn't he? Unless, of course, the killer's a gardener, and realized that no other gardeners would be there late at night. Do a lot of gardeners get humus in the fall?"

"Well, yes they do," Charly said. "They use it for their houseplants, too."

Doc said, "Then look for a gardener, Charly. That's my advice."

"Very good advice, Doc. Except that almost everyone in Van Buren County considers himself a gardener. Now, I must run to the restaurant, wait for my food delivery. And then, I work in my garden."

It would be a good afternoon to plant his garlic. Everything was ready—the row dug out, the humus in his shed. Charly went home, put on his old clothes, gathered a few heads of garlic from his kitchen, slipped on his rubber boots, and got his shovel and the humus from the shed.

He laid down a bed of the crumbly humus in the shallow trench. Then he broke the garlic head into cloves and inserted each clove root side down. He covered the cloves with more humus and, finally, a light coating of earth. In a few weeks he'd mulch the row well with hay.

Charly admired his work. He took extra humus back to his shed. He had to get that hay down—shouldn't be left in the shed. It was a fire hazard.

Who else should he talk to? Rex Cingale, of course. Tonight, he'd go to Steak Heaven, eat one of Rex's good steaks. And what about Maurice? Would he ever get up the courage to confront the silly man?

CHAPTER NINE

Charly Discusses a Delicate Matter

Charly removed his boots in the little back porch, slipped on his shoes. Took a deep breath. Enough with the shally-shilly, the putting-off of the Maurice problem. Something must be done immediately. Maurice, who'd never cared about the restaurant, who'd never even bothered to learn about the restaurant business, was ruining La Fermette. How many customers would put up with being greeted by a drunk co-owner, swaying and slurring his words? Purposefully, Charly dialed the Baleine house.

Maurice was curt. "Hello? Baleine speaking. Oh, Charly. I was just going to call. I'm angry. That damn bartender put something in my drink. A Mickey Finn. I blacked out. It's all Tommy's doing." Charly took a deep breath.

"Maurice, you are an alcoholic. We cannot work together any longer." Charly knew, as soon as he said this, that it was the wrong approach.

Maurice yelped. "An alcoholic? Like an old Bowery bum? Oh, Charly. That's the most ridiculous thing I've ever heard." He brayed a hearty, forced laugh. "To talk to me like that. A Princeton man."

Charly tried to make amends. "Ah, well, perhaps I ex-

aggerate. But I know you are a busy man, with your Wall
Street investments. Far too important a man to run a small
country restaurant. So here is what I propose. Jimmy
Houghton will give us a figure, and I will buy out your
half."

"Well, Charly, I don't know . . ." Maurice tried, and
failed, to sound reluctant. He needed money. He'd made
some unwise investments.

"Just think, Maurice. Several hundred thousand dollars.
Enough to buy yourself a small apartment in New York
City. You, a Wall Street man."

Charly sighed. He must rid himself of this albatross
around his neck.

"Well . . . we could certainly think about it . . ."

"Of course, I would like to retain you as a consultant,"
Charly lied. "You with your education from the fine university . . ."

Would Maurice really fall for this? Of course. Charly
smiled slyly.

"That's an interesting idea, Charly. Let me think about
it, okay?"

Maurice, still in pajamas and robe, put down the telephone in a pensive mood. His head was still throbbing
from last night. What he needed was a small pick-me-up.
He walked over to the butler's table in the living room,
poured a small measure of Glenfiddich, just to take the
edge off. He downed it in a gulp. Mmmm, that tasted good.
Perhaps just another small one, while he thought about
Charly's proposition? It would be smart to have a tiny place
in New York, to not be under Barbara's and Charly's
thumbs all the time.

As the liquor glowed in Maurice's stomach and spread
through his limbs, he puffed out his plump chest. *Yes*, he
thought, *I am far too important to be involved in running
a small restaurant. What Charly said made sense.*

• • •

Honoria Wells breezed in the front door of the sprawling 1920's stone-and-shingle house, Wells Farm, that had been in her family for several generations. "I'm home, I'm home," she sang. "Estrella? Estrella?"

"Sí, sí, señora, I am here." Estrella hurried in from the kitchen to take her mistress's cape. Honoria could smell Rigaud's Cypres airspray, which Estrella had been instructed to spray through the downstairs. (Upstairs was Rigaud's Chèvrefeuille.)

"You have a nice afternoon, señora?"

"Yes, lovely. And Estrella, would you run my bath?"

"The pine bath oil, señora? To make you smell like the woods?"

"No, the freesia. I want to smell like flowers. I won't be in for dinner tonight, did you remember? Mr. Clark and I are going out."

"Sí, sí, I remember."

"After my bath, I want to have a nap. Will you wake me at five?"

"Of course." Poor, poor señora. In love with that *ladron,* that thief. And old enough to be his *mamacita.* It was too sad.

. As Honoria lay in her perfumed bath, she thought about her busy day: she'd met with her lawyer Jonathan Murray. She'd intended to leave several million dollars to Harry Clark, but dear Jonathan, so wise, had suggested leaving a mere fifty thousand now, more when she and Harry got to know each other better.

"After all, Honoria," Jonathan had said, "you and Harry are a brand-new item. Best to wait, trust me. Look, we'll rewrite the will in six months, I won't even charge you. How about that?" Honoria, like many rich people, couldn't resist a bargain.

Honoria lay beneath Porthault flowered sheets and

closed her eyes. It was a gift she had—to be able to lie down and sleep, catnap she called it, for an hour, then rise, rejuvenated. President Kennedy, that dear man, had had the same gift. She'd known him at Hyannisport, where her family had a summer cottage, and she would never forget that little gasp he gave, when he . . . oh, well, years ago. He'd be eighty, now. He pursued every female in sight, and she had been terrified of catching some horrible disease. But irresistible? Heavens. Better think about Harry, instead.

But Honoria's dream was not about Harry. She dreamed, instead, of a lover she'd had nearly forty years ago, Ralph D'Annunzio, a beautifully handsome, cultured gangster. A Godfather in the Mob, it was reputed. She and Ralph were sitting at a long Renaissance table (in Florence, perhaps?) eating mounds of white asparagus with bagna cauda. Ralph took up each spear in his long, slim fingers, and dipped it in the hot anchovy sauce. "This is the gentleman's way to eat asparagus," he said to Honoria, "but it's a secret; only gentlemen know it."

"What about hot wings?" Honoria had asked. Ralph had smiled gently, lazily, and asked, "What are hot wings, my love?" Then, before her eyes, he'd started fading away, away, away, and she was left alone at the table. In the background, she could hear the waiters murmuring . . . *"Es la cinque, señora* Vell, you want you nice *té con las hierbas?* Nice, nice . . ."* and Honoria opened her eyes to find Estrella in the room, with her mug of herb tea.

Wasn't hard to figure that one out. Honoria would watch Harry Clark eating, chewing with his mouth open, grasping the greasy chicken wings, the hot wings, they were called at the bar, in his none-too-clean fingers. She'd turn away, not able to bear seeing the half-chewed food in his mouth, thinking, *What am I doing with this man,* one-half of her revolted, the other fascinated. Later, writhing around in the big bed in the guest room, where they always went, never to her room, Harry would whisper in her ear, 'you love my big dick, don't you? Say it, say it.' And Honoria's revulsion would turn to delight, and she'd be sixteen years old again, writhing in the arms of the family gardener. Harry made her feel like a kid again. Poor Ralph, he'd be horrified. But white, phallic asparagus? A springtime dish? Lots of symbolism, there, symbolism Honoria didn't want to pursue.

After drinking her tea, Honoria went into her dressing room and opened the big closet. Harry was taking her to that fancy restaurant tonight. That meant . . . her Issey Miyake trousers and top? No, too sophisticated. Her Yohji Yamamoto blouse, the black one, with the baggy trousers by Comme Des Garçons? She didn't want to intimidate the guy. This wasn't Aspen. Okay. The Geoffrey Beene grey flannel top, very simple, with the plain sand-colored Donna Karan trousers. Her gold bracelet. Nothing else.

It was a pity, the way everyone frowned and changed the subject when she mentioned her Harry. Was there something she didn't know? Remembering her dream about Ralph, Honoria thought, *Walter. Walter Maxwell.* She'd met Walter once, years ago, he'd been a friend of Ralph's, then she totally forgot about him until she met him again at a local cocktail party a few years ago. And though Honoria wasn't crazy about Walter, such a cold man, she had to admit, Walter was savvy about people. And hadn't Harry Clark worked for Walter once? Yes, she must call Walter.

No sooner said than done. Strike while the iron is . . .

"Hello, Walter? Honoria here. You what? Can't talk now because the police are there? Dear God, you're not hurt? No, just questions? No, don't call me tonight, I'll be out. Call me tomorrow."

I wonder, Honoria thought, as she slipped into the pale grey tunic, *what Walter's been up to.* She wouldn't put anything past Walter. A cold man with the flat eyes of a reptile. *Walter,* she thought, admiring herself in the mirror, *gives me the creeps.*

Down at the Black Bull Farm office Walter sat at his desk, Tom Arnold sat at his desk, and Officer Clement Hughes sat between the two. He'd been offered a coffee and a Coke, and turned both down. Officer Hughes had been just driving by, thought he'd stop in instead of telephoning.

See, a woman's body had been found this morning, and cops were calling people in the neighborhood, to find out if they'd heard anything, seen anything, if they'd had guests this weekend who might be the dead woman. About sixty, dressed in a tweed suit, no handbag, no identification.

At that "no id" Walter felt his panic ebb a bit. But it was a good thing he was sitting down. He felt faint, thinking of Candy's stuff up at the house. If the cops decided to search . . . but why would they? Dumb hicks.

"Oh, sorry to hear about that, the poor woman," Walter said. He told Officer Hughes he'd had customers for his bulls this weekend, two men on Saturday, a young couple on Sunday. But did Officer Hughes know the Warburtons? He thought Mrs. W. had mentioned at lunch yesterday that she was expecting her sister, maybe the old woman had gone on a walk, gotten lost, had an accident . . . and let's see, the Vanns, did Officer Hughes know the Vanns (Hughes shook his head), the Vanns were having a dinner party tomorrow night, Tuesday, maybe they were having houseguests and one of them came early and had some kind of accident . . . Walter scratched his head, telling Officer Hughes all he knew . . . helping.

Then Officer Hughes turned to Tom. "That's Mr. Thomas Arnold, isn't it? I knew your dad, sir." Clem frowned at Tom.

Tom didn't know what to say. "My dad," he repeated. Cops were always hauling in his dad, his dad liked to bend his elbow, well, he was a drunk to tell the truth, he and the law rarely saw eye to eye, his dad had been farm manager here, and also at Walter's old place in Massachusetts. . . .

"And do you have anything to add to what Mr. Maxwell said, Mr. Arnold?" Hughes still had his pad out, ballpoint pen poised. "No? You didn't go out Saturday night? Sunday night?"

"Only to Steak Heaven," Tom mumbled. Why did cops always make him feel like shitting his pants? Oh, thank God, the cop was getting up now.

Officer Hughes, sitting in his police car outside of the farm office, had noted that Tom Arnold looked frightened, guilty. And he was a volunteer fireman, too. Hughes nodded to himself, smart fella, proud of the way he'd carried it off. Pretended he was really questioning Maxwell, that rich asshole, about the dead woman, when all the time it was Tom he was watching, trying to figure out if Tom could be the arsonist. And if his boss asked, he had a ready answer for Stark: "Well of course I would have called, John, but I was just driving by anyway so I thought I'd look in, see what the guy's reaction was . . ." Dead woman, hell. She was a drug pusher; Hughes knew that. No, it was Arnold he wanted to check out, and he'd seen what he'd come to see: Arnold was scared, with the law breathing down his neck. He'd always had doubts about young Tommy Arnold, and see? He was right.

Tom Arnold sat alone in the farm office, stomach all upset. God. Why did cops always make him feel so shaky? Thank God Walter was running like a bat out of hell, out of the office, he could sit on the pot in peace, shit his brains out. There were times when a man really needed his privacy.

As he sat on the toilet, Tom thought bitterly about the police. Just because his pop was a drunk, they were always after *him*. And so what if his old man bent his elbow a little? Loyal, he was. Certainly loyal to Walter Maxwell, and loyal to his son Tom, too, making sure that Maxwell hired him.

"I'll tell you stories about Walter Maxwell, someday," his dad used to say, and chuckle. "Now that man, he's a bad boy. Nothing but a rascal."

His dad had admired Maxwell, but Tom didn't. Tom was afraid of Walter. Just a matter of time until Walter discovered that Tom had been altering some of the bills, putting some cash in his pocket. "You fucking little creep!" Walter had screamed once, when Tom had ordered the wrong feed, and the bulls got diarrhea. Well, one of these days, Tom would show *him*.

CHAPTER TEN

The Evolution of Walter Maxwell

We're done for the day; shut the place up; go on home," Walter had said to Tom right after the cop left. "I just remembered I have to be somewhere," and he'd sprinted for the house. Ran into his office. Dialed New Jersey. Oh, thank God, Ricky was still there, hadn't left yet.

"Don't come. Bulls have found the merchandise."

"Aw, gee, Big Walt, that's too bad. We was just leaving, Marty and me. Lookin' forward to seeing you. You okay about, you know, the situation?"

"Yes, of course. Don't worry, Ricky, everything's under control. I'll send a check down, I know you set aside some time for this."

"No problem, Big Walt. And, hey, if there's anything we can do, you want to come down here, I mean, we'd be honored, Bernice and me. Plenty of room, like a little vacation for you."

Walter said thanks, and hung up. His heart was pounding so hard he wondered if he was having a heart attack. What was going on? Back in the old days, things like this had gone like clockwork. Was he losing it? Christ. He couldn't believe it. Not him, not him. He went back over the cop's visit.

Guy named, what? Officer Hughes, he thought. Officer Hughes was *just driving by,* thought he'd stop in instead of calling. Oh, God. Somehow, they knew. Walter picked up the telephone again.

"Evelyn, my dear, good afternoon. Yes splendid, and you? Yes, I would, if he's not too busy. . . ."

"Yes, Jimmy, something's come up, I may be in need of some cash. Thought I'd go south, perhaps, around Thanksgiving. Yes, I know the stock market's really going gangbusters, that's why I want to sell now. That Bernheimer Fund, I think, let's see, that would round out to about a million, wouldn't it? Yes, just have the monies put into my bank account here. The checking account, for now, I'll move it around later."

No, Jimmy, you busy little bee, Walter thought, *I'm not going to tell you any more.* "And Jimmy, I'd appreciate it if you didn't—oh, sorry, of course I know you're like a father confessor, no secrets pass your lips . . ."

Walter felt so shaky he went upstairs and lay down on his bed. Had a pain in his chest. Was this *it,* then? The end? Or maybe this was the onset of Alzheimer's. Mistakes, mistakes, he'd made so many mistakes. Take some deep breaths. In—count to five. Out—count to five. Big Ricky would not be proud of him. Ralph, aghast. Killing Candy in his own house? How stupid could you get? He should have said yes, yes, Candy, the hundred grand's yours, then called Little Ricky, have him deal with her in the city. Walter could see Ralph frowning, hear that brittle, polite voice: "Walter, my friend, I'm not positive you acted wisely . . ." *Oh, Ralph, Ralph, I need you. Help me.*

Walter used to work for Big Ricky. Still in his teens, washing dishes at a dump restaurant, he'd become an enforcer, learning the ropes from Big Richard Zampone, an important man in the Mob. This had been going on for a few years when an incident, brought to the attention of the FBI, made Big Ricky decide that Walter should leave the New York area for a few months. So Walter had been sent down to work for Ralph D'Annunzio.

Ralph D'Annunzio (old-timers still spoke his name with the respect due a saint) was a gentleman, and he had a gentleman's farm in southern Jersey. It had impressed Walter so much that he'd decided that this was what he, too, wanted. He loved the fragrant meadows, the big barns, the smell of the stables, fresh manure, beautiful livestock. This was power over nature, not just over men.

Walter loved the man's vast, wide-board–floored old colonial house, the oriental rugs, the big, modern, comfortable leather chairs, the heavy glass tumblers into which Ralph poured small amounts of malt scotch, neat. The library was filled with books—floor to ceiling—that Ralph actually read. But most of all, Walter admired Ralph's well-ordered life.

Everything was run according to a schedule: the cleaning crew (no live-in help, ever, they pried too much, Ralph counseled young Walter), came every morning from eight to noon. Groceries were delivered Tuesdays and Fridays. Dry cleaning picked up on . . . Walter couldn't remember the exact details, but everything in Ralph's life was slotted into a time frame: breakfast, lunch, dinner, telephone calls, horseback rides. Even Helen D'Annunzio, Ralph's wife, made her appearances at designated times.

Ralph took a liking to young Walter. Ralph, it turned out, had begun his life much as Walter had. What had pushed him forward? "Goals, Walter. Goals and discipline. Aim for something realistic, achieve it, then aim for something higher." Ralph said some unkind things about Big Ricky, until then Walter's hero: that he was an uneducated boor who took pleasure in killing, that he was born to the servant class. "But you're different, Walter, I could tell as soon as I saw you. You want to better yourself, don't you?" Walter nodded sincerely. "Yes, Mr. D'Annunzio." "Ralph, Walter, call me Ralph." "Sure, Ralph." Walter had found a new guru. "Never be greedy," Ralph cautioned. "Never take more than you need, but set your sights high. And keep your priorities straight. A man's number one priority is himself. You understand that? Oh, and lose the Jersey accent."

Walter watched the way Ralph dressed: pressed, well-fitting jeans on the farm; V-necked cashmere sweaters; tailored tweed jackets; custom-made suits; imported shoes and boots. Walter took elocution lessons from a retired actress on Fifty-seventh Street in Manhattan, who told Walter she had many clients like himself, who wanted to better themselves in the business world but knew they couldn't get far with a dese and dems accent, as she put it.

After that memorable summer Walter often visited Ralph. He learned how to lay a proper table, how to eat asparagus and artichokes with your fingers like an English gentleman, how to deal with caterers and servants. "Hey, get da fuck over here," Big Ricky's customary mode of address, was not, Ralph cautioned, on the right side of couth. Kiss scungilli at Vincent's Clam Bar good-bye. Don't drink soft drinks, liquor, or coffee with your meal. Always underdress. Learn to order wine in a restaurant and what to lay down for your cellar. Walter lapped it all up, like a puppy at his food.

So it came to be that Walter led two lives: the life of a New Jersey thug at Big Ricky's beck and call, and life as an aspiring gentleman with Ralph D'Annunzio as his coach. Walter read and studied by day, intimidated and killed by night. He definitely preferred the days. Killing a man was no more bothersome to Walter than swatting a fly;

but, as Ralph said, it was messy and socially degrading. Why be a butcher, Walter reasoned, when you could hire a whole string of butchers?

"Make your money and get out," was Ralph's advice. "Don't spend your money on stupid things; the IRS is watching you, and so are the cops. Get a money manager. I'll introduce you to mine." Walter quietly changed his name from Mastrinsky to Maxwell and started to plan his future.

Walter followed Ralph's advice on nearly everything. He slipped, however, when it came to women. "Marry a quiet one but a rich one," was Ralph's advice. Helen D'Annunzio had been Helen Farquahr, of Farquahr Pharmaceuticals, and she was so quiet, so plain, that Walter didn't even notice her most of the time. Ralph's mistress, Honny Wells, was gorgeous, but Ralph's visits to her were so discreet that few people knew about her. Walter had met her once, by accident, when he'd walked into the Waldorf's Peacock Alley where Ralph and Honny were having tea. (Ralph kept a suite at the Waldorf Astoria). It was then that Ralph counseled, "If you have a mistress, keep it very, very quiet."

Walter's first wife, a Boston blue-blood, had made Walter sign a prenuptial agreement. (Ralph, of course, had been aghast.) Walter's second wife, Candy Moran, a brainless but beautiful model, was the second mistake. ("You don't *marry* a woman like that, you go to bed with her, period," was Ralph's comment there.) After the third mistake—another one who'd tried a spot of blackmail on Walter—had been killed going eighty on a country road, losing control, hitting a tree (wising up at last, Walter had let the brake fluid out of her Cadillac convertible), Walter had finally gotten the picture: Marriage was not for him.

One day, when Walter was in the process of divorcing

Candy, he had driven down from Massachusetts, where he had a farm, and he and Ralph D'Annunzio, an old man by then, had lunched at Ralph's favorite restaurant in New York, La Fermette. Charly Poisson, the maître d', had recommended the Sweetbreads Financière, a rich dish. Walter was enchanted.

"What a superb restaurant," Walter had said to Ralph.

"It is superb," Ralph agreed, "But old Maurice Baleine has made some terrible investments, and he's drinking too much, and I don't know how much longer the restaurant will stay in business."

"Would you ever consider investing in a restaurant?"

Ralph had laughed. "If you want to throw your money down the drain, invest in a restaurant. No, no, Walter, leave that to the doctors and dentists."

A few years later Walter found himself in New York again and dined at La Fermette. Charly remembered him. The restaurant was still hobbling along. Maurice Sr. had died, and Charly was now co-owner; but, he told Walter, he wanted to get out of the city. "I hear Van Buren County property is still reasonable. I think I look there."

"You think they have any big farms going cheap?" Walter had asked. Massachusetts, suddenly, wasn't a good place for Walter to be.

"I do not know," Charly shrugged, "but it is beautiful country, much of it poor country, real-estate prices are down. This is the time to buy."

Both Charly and Walter bought places in Van Buren County, though neither knew of the other's purchase at the time. When La Fermette opened, however, Walter was one of Charly's first customers. Charly was fascinated by Walter, who appeared so polished, so cosmopolitan, who knew so much about food, and was eager to learn more. Walter thought Charly's food superb.

Walter gave Charly advice: "Start a take-out business.

Lots of weekenders up here, you're on a main road, they can stop in on their way up from the city, buy a weekend's supply of food. Lots of skiers, too."

"Not a bad idea," Charly said.

"Another thing," Walter continued. "Don't have an exclusively French menu. That's too sophisticated. Have some plain dishes for the locals. They're the ones who will keep you in business, so cater to them. The weekenders come and go. So go heavy on the prime rib, the pork roasts, the steaks. Your food cost will be higher, but that's what people like to eat, not Sweetbreads Financière or sole with quenelles."

Charly had already noticed this. "You are right again."

Every week Charly delivered food to Walter's kitchen—pâtés, soups, stews, vegetable dishes—and Walter dined at the restaurant twice or thrice a week, besides. Charly catered Walter's cocktail parties, and he had catered Walter's deceased wife's memorial service (Charly barely knew her, she was always dieting). Walter was, indeed, Charly's best customer.

It worked both ways. Walter was charmed by Charly, so exotic, so French (Walter had never been to France), who never tried to step out of his role of restaurateur to socialize, as an American might. Charly never asked personal questions. His behavior, always, was correct. Charly treated Walter like a respected dignitary; Walter treated Charly like a culinary sage. Best, Walter discovered, to stay away from politics: When Charly got going on his theories of justice or the brutality of the Nazis (who sounded exactly like Big Ricky and the Mob) Walter backed off.

Now, late Monday afternoon, Walter lay on his bed and relived his horrible day. The visit by that damn policeman. Why had they suspected him? True, they now had that OCCB, the organized crime control bureau. Could they trace his movements when he'd been a part of Big Ricky's setup? Would it mention Maxwell? He'd been Mastrinsky then. What about the NCIC—National Crime Information Center? He'd never been accused of any criminal action. He'd never gone to jail, he'd never been fingerprinted—or had he? Maybe in the early days? He couldn't remember. Had they found prints? All these sophisticated methods they had now. Christ, he'd heard they could even get prints from fabric. Klover cops would send everything up to the crime labs in Albany. Oh, Jesus. His head was spinning.

The telephone rang. Groaning, Walter reached for the receiver. "Maxwell." He cleared his throat.

"Mr. Mexweyull?" The high, piping voice of a kid.

"Yeah?" His tough Mastrinsky voice.

"I seen you last night, Sunday night."

"Yeah? So what?"

"I seen you a-draggin' a body wrapped in something, a-draggin' it out your back door, puttin' it in your car, drivin' away."

Walter was stunned. He'd been seen? By some child? That funny little voice sounded oddly familiar. He knew that voice.

In a flash, he remembered an incident down at the barns last summer. The stablemen had one of the youngsters hired to stack hay bales tied to a post: He'd stolen a man's wallet. They were going to whip him with a leather belt. Walter recalled the scene vividly—the three grown men, furious, the kid, white-faced and terrified. "Let him go," Walter had commanded. The men had untied the skinny little runt. "I'm a-movin' them bales, not a-stealin' your bucks," the child whined. A strange, hoarse voice with a hillbilly accent.

Now, holding the telephone, it all came back. "Yeah?"

"I'm a-goin' to the cops, 'less you pay me a hundred dollars."

Oh, right. Now I'm the kid's private banker. A hundred now, a hundred next month, and the month after . . .

"You're the kid from last summer, stole that wallet."
The name, miraculously, flashed into Walter's head.
"Okun? Robby Okun?"

There was a gasp, a squawk, then Walter heard a dial
tone.

Walter knew he had to get rid of Candy's things—the
purse, the cape, the overnight bag. He hurried down to the
office, unlocked the desk drawer. If the little creep went to
the cops, if they searched the house . . .

He upended Candy's purse, picked out the objects with
no identification—sunglasses, reading glasses, makeup
case, handkerchief—and swept them into a big manila envelope. The keys he thrust into his desk drawer. The
checkbook he tore into shreds. The driver's license, health-
care card, train ticket, he cut into pieces with scissors and
flushed down the toilet. There were no credit cards since
Candy had been on every credit company's blacklist for
years. He pocketed the two hundred dollars that was in
Candy's wallet. That left the canvas pouch (underwear,
toilet bag, blouse, sweater, flimsy negligee) and the cape.
He carried the toiletries bag and the manila envelope up to
a guest room on the second floor and dropped them into a
bureau drawer. If the cops did search the house—"Well, officer, I do have women friends come to stay, and they do
sometimes forget things." Man to man. A grin, a wink.
There was nothing to tie this stuff to Candy.

The quickest way to get rid of the rest of Candy's be-
longings was to burn them. Now. Walter gathered it all up,
went to the back porch. No wind. Good. He found charcoal
lighter fluid, matches, and carried everything to a clearing
just beyond the little deserted shed.

Walter had a good brisk fire going when one of those
tricky little winds blew up. Sparks flew, blew into the
window openings of the little shed . . . and a explosion rang

out, as the little shed burst into flames. What the hell was in that shed? Explosives? Walter had thought the shed empty.

He ran to the house to dial 9-1-1, terrified of the inferno he had created.

CHAPTER ELEVEN

+-+-+-+-+-+-+

Charly Spots
a Clue

+-+-+-+-+-+-+

Although Charly's staff, snobbish in their workplace, frowned on Steak Heaven and its owner Rex Cingale, (Tommy Glade called it Snake Heaven referring to the clientele), Charly enjoyed a night out at Rex's. Steak Heaven was a big, vulgar, busy steak house and bar; Rex Cingale, Van Buren County-born and-bred, was an absolutely bottomless pit of knowledge about the county's residents, most of it less than salubrious.

Rex knew, for instance, who was spending more than he earned; who could only get an erection if whipped; what bank president's wife had to spend a vacation at a drying-out spot in the Adirondacks; which bank officers were into cocaine. His liaisons with a bank cashier, a lawyer's secretary, a waitress, a nurse, a saleslady, and several other ladies resulted in much pillow talk. In addition to which Rex was an officer in the Sons of Italy, a volunteer fireman, an Elk, and a member of the Citizens for a Cleaner County. But, as Rex said, "My lips are sealed." Usually.

Charly was amused by Rex. They were hardly competitors—they enjoyed a vastly different clientele. But, Charly felt, Rex was the place to go for information. He'd called to reserve a table, and Rex had said, "You kidding? You can have any table in the place—fucking tomb. But come on over, Charly, we'll chew the fat." Rex's newspaper ads boasted that Steak Heaven not only had the finest steaks in the Van Buren County, but also the longest bar. Both statements were probably true. Rex's frozen vegetables and his factory desserts were inedible, but his steaks were superb.

Charly entered the sprawling log cabin and nodded to Maria, the cashier. All of Rex's employees were family or friends of family. Maria, one of Rex's sisters, was aunt to both Bobby (the bartender) and Bobby's brother Vince (the cop), and the three of them could have written a book on the county's scandals. Throw in Rex's knowledge and you'd have an encyclopedia. Charly walked past the crowded bar, TV blaring, jukebox thumping, and stopped at the entrance to the empty dining room, where Rex dozed at a deuce, a glass of club soda in front of him. "Hum, hum," Charly said, clearing his throat.

Rex looked up, sprang to his feet, agile for a corpulent man. "Charly! Good to see ya. Come on, we'll sit farther in, away from the noise." Rex was formally dressed: dark blue sharkskin suit, deep blue shirt, light blue satin tie, diamond pinkie ring. A man of substance. He shook Charly's hand, grinning, radiating herbal aftershave. With his black, curly hair, his Roman nose and heavy, drooping cheeks, Rex could have been a gladiator, albeit one who had tarried at too many orgies.

The two men sat toward the back, as the noise at the bar was deafening. A waiter hovered. Charly ordered a porterhouse, very rare, a salad, and a glass of red wine. Rex ordered his steak medium-rare, with a baked potato, salad, spinach au gratin, and another glass of club soda.

Rex looked around the dining room. "Your place ever

look like this, Charly? Like you could shoot a cannon down the middle, not hit anyone?"

"That is why we close for dinner Mondays and, after Labor Day, Tuesdays. Maybe we start closing Wednesdays as well."

"How about Thursdays?"

Charly made an undulating motion with his hand. "So by so. Not great, believe me. I put on inexpensive item for the patron. You know, meat loaf, pasta. But today, nothing is cheap." Both men sighed.

"The bar keeps me going," Rex admitted. "Then Friday is payday for a lot of the men, they'll bring in their families, have a steak. Hey, I'm not headed for the poorhouse, but . . . it's not easy."

Charly cleared his throat. Time to get down to business. "You have heard about my body that I find this morning?"

"You bet we have, Charly. Vince called Bobby. But of course I'd rather hear it from you."

It took two glasses of the acid red wine for Charly's story to unfold, and his flair for the dramatic did not desert him. "And I will never forget the look on the woman's face," he ended up. "So desolate. So . . . final. A look of great sadness, as if, in her final moment, she has regrets about her life." Charly sighed, and put his hand to his heart. It is always easier to embroider on empty cloth, and as Charly had scarcely glanced at the woman's face, his imagination could supply many details.

"Ah," Rex told Charly enviously, "I never found a stiff."

The waiter hovered. "Watch out, hot plates, very hot," and indeed, the steak was still sizzling. The two men addressed themselves to their food.

"Superb as usual, Rex." Charly's steak was blood-rare under a thick caramelized crust.

"I read somewhere," Rex said, chewing, "that the Mob,

when they rubbed someone out, they never wanted red meat afterward." Rex was an authority on the Mafia. "They'd order spaghet, or fish, never meat."

"Interesting," Charly said. "How you get this crust?"

"Easy, Charly. Angelo and Ricky, my broilermen, they rub the meat with salt and sugar just before broiling. The salt brings out some of the juices, the sugar caramelizes them on top."

"Brilliant. So, Rex, who you think kill my lady?"

"Vince says all the cops, they think it's drug-related. Old broad is dressed pretty fancy. And she's skinny, like a druggie. Me, I dunno. But one thing I wonder about." Rex stopped to take another bite of steak.

"What is that, Rex?"

"Why was she buried? Bodies around here, they generally get thrown in the river. And Vince says the grave was shallow, hardly more than a—what do you call it—a depression in the ground. Something sounds fishy to me. I mean, it was a dumb thing to do. All the forensic stuff the cops have at their fingertips, it's just a matter of time until they find out something."

"The woman was well dressed," Charly mused, "so I think she must have been visiting rich people. I try to make a list of my customers who have money. The Vanns, Walter Maxwell, Jimmy Houghton, Win Crozier and Morty Cohen, the Warburtons, many other. But, you must realize, I do not know these people well. Do you?"

Rex chewed. "Peter Vann's a drunk. He's come in here lit a couple of times, I told Bobby not to serve him. Martinis. I hear he starts off his mornings with a shot of schnapps. Every goddamn morning."

"Is true," Charly said. "He is often drunk."

"Mrs., I don't know, though Maria's cousin's granddaughter was a waitress up at their place when they had a party a few years ago. Said Mrs. was real snotty to the help, and that she propositioned the bartender."

"Hum. I will ask Tommy Glade, my barman."

"Maxwell? I heard he used to be connected. I know he's tough. He fired Harry Clark for dippin' into the till, know what he told Harry?"

"No, what?"

"'You want to end up in my shredding machine? You wouldn't be the first.' Doesn't drink, never comes here, I don't know the guy personally. Harry said some tough guys used to visit in a big black car, Jersey plates."

Charly gulped. "That does not surprise me." Though it did, in fact. Charly had always imagined Walter springing full-blown from the aristocracy, dancing his youth away while sipping champagne and nibbling bouchées of lobster and caviar. Well, well. "And Winthrop Crozier?"

"Ah, he and Morty are nice guys. Faggots, of course. They stop in every now and then. I get my paint from them. Win's loaded. Crozier Plumbing."

"Yes, that I know. And Jimmy Houghton?"

"He never comes in here. Supposed to be from a rich family, big bucks. Some kind of scandal with Houghton's dad, a long time ago. The Houghtons came over on the *Mayflower,* I heard. Real fancy. Sorry, Charly, can't help you there. I think Jimmy moved here from somewhere else."

"Ah, well . . ."

Their waiter hurried up. "Excuse me, Rex? Everyone's clearing out of the bar, big fire over at Maxwell's. All the volunteer firemen are goin' over."

Rex stood up so hurriedly his chair tipped over. "Shit, and me in these clothes. But, hey, it might be the arsonist again. You coming, Charly?"

Charly scrambled to his feet. "Let's go."

They drove over in Rex's big grey Lincoln Continental. Rex was excited. "Think it's Maxwell's barn? Or maybe his house?"

In less than ten minutes they arrived at Black Bull Farm. Seeing the smoke and the cars, they veered left, toward the big house. Rex parked and they got out. Charly's throat constricted from the powerful smoke, and he coughed. In a clearing behind the big garage at the back of the house two hoses played on what looked like the remains of a medium-sized wooden shed that was now a smoking, charred skeleton.

"What happened?" Charly asked a man standing at the rear of the crowd of firemen. Rex had forged ahead to talk to his buddies.

"Nothing much," the man said. "Maxwell says he was takin' a walk out here, saw flames coming out of the shed, he called the fire company. Don't blame him. See how close to the garage it is?"

Charly nodded, then looked around. Ah, there was Walter, at the head of the small crowd, talking to Fire Chief Harold Tibbetts. Then Tibbetts walked away. Walter turned and saw Charly, gave him a wave.

"Nothing to get excited about, Charly." Walter's voice was casual, almost amused. "I panicked when I saw the flames."

"What is in the shed?" Charly asked.

"Well, I thought it was empty. Haven't been in there for years. But Chief Tibbetts says there's traces of rags, jerricans—you know, for gasoline. They'll examine it when the fire cools down, tomorrow. But you know what that means? Maybe this is where the arsonist is storing his supplies. At least, who else would want cans of gasoline and rags?" Walter shrugged. "Is it someone who works for me?

Or who lives nearby? Or who simply knew about this old shed? Quite an end to a busy day, eh?"

Charly lowered his voice. "You hear about my busy day? That I find a body on my land, the body of a woman?"

"Good Lord, I'd heard about the body, but I didn't know you found it." Walter sounded genuinely shocked. He looked at Charly in a strange way.

"Yes," Charly said. "I went out hunting for mushrooms. That is a good mushroom spot. Oh, *Mon Dieu,* you not feeling well?" For Walter had suddenly swayed, and grasped a sapling for support.

"It's the smoke. It's getting to me. Excuse me, Charly, I've got to get away from the smoke. I think I'm allergic." Walter stumbled off.

He is not well, see how white his face is? Charly thought about Walter. *But of course, his shed going up in flames is a shock . . .*

Charly strolled up to Rex, noting that his suit was still immaculate. Rex was talking to Fire Chief Tibbetts. "And a couple of plastic jerricans, half-melted," Chief Tibbetts was saying, "and a mound of ash, that's ash from paper, like newspaper, some cloth ash, too . . ." He broke off when he saw Charly. "But keep it under your hat for now, Rex, huh?"

"My lips are sealed," Rex said. "Charly, you ready?"

In the searchlights from the fire trucks Charly spied a little mound of burnt matter beyond the smoking shed. It had been trampled down, but you could see that it was a separate fire. Charly noticed a button, some shreds of fabric, twisted metal. But he shouldn't look now, with everyone about. "Yes, yes, Rex, I am ready."

"If that's really the arsonist's little hiding place, it might be important," Rex said. "Chief Tibbetts is pretty sure it is, but he doesn't want to spread that around. 'Course, if the arsonist's a volunteer fireman, here tonight, he knows. But the chief doesn't think it is a fireman. Me, I don't know. Anyhow, Charly, don't say anything about it, huh?"

"My lips," Charly told Rex, "are sealed."

CHAPTER TWELVE

Charly Does
Nothing Wrong

Charly's lips might be sealed, but his mind certainly wasn't. He was disappointed in his dinner with Rex—Rex knew a lot of gossip, but not about the right kinds of people. *Snake Heaven*—Charly chuckled at Tommy Glade's unkind remark. He'd question Tommy about Mrs. Vann. Not that the Vanns had anything to do with his dead lady, but, he thought, you never knew what might turn up.

As Charly approached the entrance to Black Bull Farm, he thought, *Why not? No one will see me, firemen gone.* He turned in at the gate, parked near the fork, grabbed his flashlight, and slid out of the van.

As quietly as he could (which wasn't very quietly,) Charly made his way across the back field to Walter's garage and the still-smoky little hut. Now, where was that mound of burnt stuff? Just beyond the hut—ah, there.

Charly played his flashlight around the trampled ashes, bending down to see better. A piece of leather, a buckle, a metal button. He poked with a stick, stirring up the ashes. Something that looked like a pen. Charly picked it up, rubbed off soot. Gold-colored. Couldn't see much. He took out his handkerchief, wrapped up the cylinder, the buckle and the button, put them in his pocket, and trudged back to the car. Some twigs snapped and Charly stopped and listened. Why should he worry? He was doing nothing wrong.

By the time the firemen left it was ten o'clock and Walter lay in a hot tub, soaking his aching back, then got into bed. But he'd no sooner stretched out than he heard a noise, and saw the flash of headlights down by the road. Someone was turning into his gate. Raising his bedroom window, Walter looked out, but couldn't see anything. Then he heard a car door slam.

Walter wasn't taking any chances. His aching back was forgotten. He slipped on jeans and sweater over his pajamas, pulled on his boots. Grabbed his flashlight, crept downstairs to his office and got his Beretta out of his desk. It was a 9mm Parabellum semiautomatic, a solid piece well over two pounds. Fifteen rounds. He checked the slide safety and tucked it into his jeans, at the small of his back. Walter sighed. It was all crashing down on him, he couldn't take it. He retrieved his windbreaker from the hall closet, shining the flashlight at his feet, and crept from the house by the back door.

Walter heard twigs snapping. He strode through the back field, following the sound of crackling brush. It sounded like an elephant thrashing around. He stood still and listened. The crackling was getting closer—someone was down by the garage, near the burnt-out shed. Jesus, and with a flashlight, too. Walter stood behind a clump of privet.

By the light of the moon he could make out a small form, a short man wearing a beret. Charly? What the hell would Charly be doing here? Fire Chief Tibbetts? He was short, too, but Walter didn't think he wore a beret. The figure was poking through the debris where Walter had burned Candy's stuff. Now the figure bent down, picked up

something, peered at it with his flashlight. Now the figure
moved away, stumbling loudly through the underbrush.
Walter followed, down to the farm entrance. He saw a van.
In the moonlight, the van looked maroon, maybe red.
Charly had a red van.

Walter reached around and grasped the Beretta, pulled
it from his waistband. One pop, and Charly was history.
He'd tell the cops he heard a noise, thought it was the barn
burner returning, panicked and shot. Should he or
shouldn't he? In the moment of Walter's indecision, the
figure hopped in the van, slammed the door, revved the
motor, backed away, and drove out the main gate.

Walter still held the Beretta. It was Charly, all right.
Somehow Charly had found evidence to tie him to Candy.
Had he seen them in Boston together? Walter's thoughts
were jumbled. Had he been with Candy when he'd first met
Charly? No, he'd been with Ralph. Memories, dates were
whirling around in Walter's head. Charly knew. Somehow,
Charly knew. Charly would have to disappear. He'd do it
right, though. Give Ricky a call, have Ricky and Marty
drive up and do the job. No mistakes, this time.

Charly, who loved to walk in his fields, would meet
with a tragic accident. It was bird-hunting season. These
things happened. Jimmy was selling some stocks for him.
He'd take the cash and run. Down to the Bahamas, where
the rest of his money was. Get in that friend of the Warburtons to manage the farm, give him a cut of the profits.
Plead illness. It would all blow over. Police up here weren't
too swift, and they were grossly overworked. They couldn't
stay long on Candy's case.

Charly, jubilant, flicked on his kitchen light and retrieved his loot: the pen, the button, the buckle. Something
the arsonist was burning. Carefully, he wiped the pen with
a paper towel, then ran it under hot water, wiped it again.

Peered at it with his magnifying glass. Something was written on it. C-A-N. or C-A-V. Can or Cav. Maybe part of a name? He put the clues in a plastic bag and stashed them in his windbreaker to take to the police.

Grunting with pleasure, Charly climbed upstairs, slipped on his flannel pajamas, and crawled into bed. To the amazement of the police, the farmers, and the entire countryside, he, Charly Poisson, would find the barn burner. Charly chuckled as he imagined Stark's face. "You, Charly. You found the arsonist. Why, you're the greatest detective in Van Buren County."

As he settled into sleep, still smiling, Charly thought of his find and congratulated himself on the stealth with which he'd crept up to Walter's shed. Not a sound had he made. Truly, there was a career as a detective in front of him.

CHAPTER THIRTEEN

Party Planning

Charly heard the telephone ringing as soon as he arrived in the restaurant kitchen Tuesday morning. *Ai,* he'd forgotten to call Madame Vann back.

"Allo, allo, La Fermette, 'ere."

"Charly, it's Dinah Vann. About the dinner, tonight."

Charly tried to put enthusiasm in his voice. Dinah had already called at least fifteen times. The artichoke hearts, that's right. She didn't like them.

"But of course, madame. The dinner will be *splendide.* And instead of the artichoke heart (although, you know, *la Duchesse de Windsor* always used to have artichoke heart) I have a suggestion. One that I find in *W.*"

"Oh, in *W.*" *W.* was Dinah's favorite magazine, as Charly well knew.

"Served at Café Provence in New York, is favorite of a movie star."

"What movie star?"

Charly pondered. He rarely went to the cinema. "He ees small, like me. Very good actor. Everyone love him."

"You mean Dustin Hoffman?"

"Yes, perhaps." Had to be careful, that guy still alive, whoever he was. "The dish is a ragout of artichoke heart with tiny little potato. Very simple. Ragout of vegetable very big now, very styl—ish. Very," (Charly flipped through his mental index cards) "very Beel Blass."

"Yes," Dinah said, "it sounds very nice. Now. Tell me about the body you found. A policeman called yesterday, to see if Peter or I had guests over the weekend. He said she appeared to be a stranger."

"Is true. I have never seen her. She wear a Hermès scarf, costly. I will speak to the chief of police today," (Charly cleared his throat importantly) "and if there is any news, dear madame, I will bring it at half past four."

"Perfect, Charly. Now, let's go over the menu one last time."

"Of course, madame."

And Charly recited: "We begin with blini, filled with Ossetra caviar and sour cream, with the drinks. Then at table, smoked salmon roses; then the roast loin of veal with the sauce of the morel mushroom, vegetable ragout. Then a *salade* of bibb lettuce, radicchio, and Belgian endive with fresh herbs, chervil and Oriental garlic chives and the dressing of *echalote,* virgin olive oil and balsamic vinegar; then yellow raspberries with *crème chantilly* flavored with framboise, and the delicate tuiles with almonds."

"Oof," Charly told Benny, who had come in during the menu recital. "She is big pain, that one. Now, you hokay? We all set for lunch today?" Charly slipped out of his windbreaker, and took it to his office. He put the plastic bag of evidence in his desk drawer.

Benny called, "I'm fine, Charly. I'll just shape the hamburgers, cut the potatoes for french fries, the pea soup's cooking, chicken stock heating for chicken noodle, everything's set. So go ahead with the Vanns' dinner."

Benny set to work, still thinking about the Vann party. Fifteen hundred dollars Charly was charging them, and

RAGOUT OF ARTICHOKE HEARTS

Yield: 4 side-dish servings

- 4 Tablespoons olive oil
- 4 cloves garlic, chopped
- 2 shallots, chopped
- 1 10-ounce package frozen artichoke hearts
- 16 potato balls, made from russet potatoes with melon-ball scoop
- 4 Tablespoons butter (½ stick)
- ½ cup chopped flat leaf parsley

Heat olive oil, sauté garlic and shallots until soft; add artichoke hearts, potato balls and butter, cover, and cook over medium-low heat for 30 minutes, or until potatoes are done. Sprinkle with chopped parsley and serve.

though the raw materials were expensive—those fish eggs, for instance, the smoked salmon, that special natural veal from Virginia—it was still a tremendous amount of money.

"I do not think I charge Mrs. Vann enough; I think we will lose money on the dinner tonight." Charly muttered to himself as he prepared the beautiful loin of veal in the roasting pan, dusting it with salt, white pepper, and herbs. "I will preroast the veal, cut the vegetables, the dried morel are soaking, the veal stock is reducing for the *demi-glace* to make the sauce."

"Mr. Vann must have made a lot of money, before he retired," Benny said to Charly. "They have two fancy cars, and that big house . . ."

"He was in the bathrobe business. Can you imagine? But, why not? I once had a customer, he made *soutien gorge*, brassiere (here, Charly made motions around his chest to indicate breasts) and he was millionaire."

"Oh. Are the Vanns, uh, nice people?" Benny really wanted to ask if Mr. Vann was in touch with his inner self, but that sounded silly. Benny was taking martial-arts lessons, Tae Quon Do, and was into self-realization this season. Actually, Benny decided, Peter Vann probably wasn't in touch with his inner self. He'd had a talk with Tommy Glade about this, Tommy being an ex-drunk and a philosopher of sorts.

"See," Tommy had told Benny, "if a guy's into drinking, he can't be in touch with his inner self, he's too busy coverin' up the pain. That's why drinkin's so bad, because you're always covering up your inner self."

"No," Charly said. "They are not bad people, but they are not good either. They like to impress people with the money they have." Charly was anxious to teach Benny right from wrong. "Now, Benny, I am going into my office to write up the menu, and to make a list of all of the items we must take to the dinner tonight."

"Right." Benny slapped down the last hamburger. Was Charly in touch with his inner self? Once, he'd mentioned the inner-self question to Charly. "My inner self is concerned with the restaurant kitchen," Charly had told Benny. "Find happiness in cleaning the deep fat fryer. Very zen belief. It will bring peace to your soul." Benny had told Charly he doubted that. "Well," Charly had said, "it will bring peace to *my* soul."

"Don't worry about the lunch, Charly, it's all set." Benny set about changing the oil in the deep fat fryer. That was the secret to proper french fries, Charly said. Beautiful, clean oil. And the proper temperature, of course. And the right potatoes (russets). And the proper presentation (a large heap). There was so much to learn. From Charly, master chef.

"The egg pies?"

"No, I forgot them," Benny admitted. "I'll do them soon."

Charly had tried to introduce quiches for lunch, since quiches had a low food cost. But it seemed that real men didn't eat quiche, that was for the ladies. So Charly introduced egg pies. Same ingredients—eggs, sauteed onions and peppers, cubed ham and cheese all baked together in a pie dish, no crust. A hefty frittata. Served with a mound of Charly's french fries, they made a filling and profitable lunch. Real men, it seemed, loved egg pies.

When Benny finished cleaning the deep fat fryer and filling it with new oil, he made the egg pies and Charly mixed the salad dressing, three parts olive oil to one part balsamic vinegar with salt, pepper, and mustard to taste.

After Walter Maxwell had breakfasted on toast, a slice of Charly's pâté and several cups of strong coffee he felt ready to face the day. Firmly, he put yesterday, the worst day of his life, out of his mind, the way Ralph had taught him to do. "Everyone makes mistakes, Walter, but you never dwell on them. That's the secret. You forget them and go about your business."

Now, let's look at today, Tuesday. Men were coming this morning to look at his bulls and he wanted to tell his bank in the Bahamas that he was forwarding some money. Then down to the farm office. Don't worry, Walter told himself. It will all work out. But this time, he wouldn't do it alone. His first telephone call was to Little Ricky Zampone.

"Yes, Rick. Everything's fine with that other business. It'll all blow over, I'm sure. But, in connection with that, I wonder if you and Marty could help with another piece of work. An accident. Rifle. Next week?"

Little Ricky was heartbroken, but next week was out of the question. "NCD, No Can Do, Big Walt." He was taking Bernice to Vegas, a Romance Week, with all the romantic novelists that Bernice loved. Had Walter ever been? Chocolate tastings; heart-shaped beds; gourmet food; romantic videos; fancy drinks—terrific. A great time.

Walter had never had that pleasure. He thought for a bit. The party was arranged, the menu set. If Charly wasn't there, the party would go on anyway. He hated to do it so soon, but . . . the sooner the better, really.

"How about tomorrow, Rick? Could you and Marty come Wednesday? Come in time for dinner, we'll have a wonderful meal at the guy's restaurant, you can spend the night at my house, then the next day, the work could be done. Merchandise left here, like a hunting accident."

"You want to do a *restaurant owner?*"

"What's the difference?" Walter asked.

"Well, jeez, Big Walt, I don't know. I mean, there's so few good restaurants. . . . You've told me about this guy's food. Remember?"

Walter didn't recall. "Triple pay," Walter said. "No, better. Fifty each."

"A hunnert grand? This guy's worth that much?"

Walter said, come up tomorrow evening, we'll discuss it. Hung up, dialed again. He heard Marian Arnold in the kitchen, talking to someone.

"Oh, good morning. Is Mrs. Wells available?" Honoria liked to be called early. *I'll see her tonight at the Vanns'*, Walter thought, *I wonder if she's bringing Harry? Probably not. She doesn't trot him out to her friends' houses.*

"Darling Honoria, how are you? I'll see you tonight at the Vanns', won't I? You going alone? Want me to pick you up? No? Fine. Twenty-five years they've been married, Dinah tells me. Harry? What do I think of Harry?"

So that was the reason for the call. Walter knew better than to bad-mouth Harry to Honoria, but what could he say? That he loved the guy?

"Well, Honoria, Harry and I never did get along. Yes, a year, he worked here. I had to let him go."

Honoria asked Walter if Harry was difficult to work with.

"Oh, well, yes he was. And I didn't like the way he handled the books. I didn't need a bookkeeper. I've got Tom Arnold. Harry wanted to be more creative. Thought up all sorts of ways he could sneak past the IRS. But I stay clear of that stuff. Once those people start nosing around, it's the end. No monkey business with me."

Walter wanted Honoria to know that Harry was a crook without actually saying it. But Honny wasn't biting. The woman was blind. Poor Ralph, he'd turn over in his grave if he could see her now. There was a knock on the study door, and Marian called, "Policeman to see you, Mr. Walter."

"Excuse me, Honoria," and put his hand over the receiver. "I'll be right out," he called. And to Honoria, "I've got to go, sport, someone to see me, but we'll talk tonight, all right?"

In the kitchen stood a short, dark-haired, muscular cop.

Walter was at his most urbane. "Yes, Officer, what can I do for you?" Walter took a deep breath. They're fishing, he told himself, they don't know anything.

"Officer Vince Matucci, sir. I wonder if you'd look at this picture, it's touched up, picture of the woman we found." Officer Matucci brought out a manila envelope, pulled out a photograph. He gave the snapshot to Walter.

Walter looked, felt nothing. "No, Officer, I've never seen her before."

"Oh." Disappointed. "Maybe we'll have better luck elsewhere."

"Looks like she's sleeping." Candy's face had been cleaned up.

"Well, undertaker did a good job. So did the photographer."

"Excuse my manners, Officer. You want some coffee?"

"No, thanks, Mr. Maxwell. I'll be on my way."

A few more days of this, Walter thought, *and they'll forget all about it.*

At twelve-thirty, lunchtime, Charly wandered out into the bar, which was the only room open for lunch. Between twelve and one they served about thirty lunches. After one o'clock, they cleaned up. Lunches were fast: a wedge of egg pie, a hamburger, a sandwich, a bowl of soup, coffee, that was it. Fewer profits than in New York City, but less hassle, too.

Sam Higgins, the photographer, motioned Charly over. He showed him the photograph of the dead woman. "Look, Charly."

Charly looked. "But, she look alive. Looks like she is asleep, only."

"Yep, Brad did a good job. So did I. Here, Charly, why don't you take a couple. You can show it to some of your customers, see if they recognize her."

"Of course," Charly agreed, though he had no intention of showing his customers, intent upon their Shrimps Charly, a photograph of a corpse. It might ruin their appetites. But he could show the photograph to Peter and Dinah Vann. Their dinner was already half-paid for. Charly greeted Win Crozier and Morty Cohen. "Gentlemen. You enjoy your lunch?"

"Yes, Charly, delicious hot roast beef sandwiches." Win said, "Vince Matucci, you know, works with Stark, stopped by the store this morning, showed us a picture of the dead woman. I understand you found her. Any idea who she might be? She didn't look familiar."

"Except for the birthmark," Morty Cohen reminded Win.

"Yes, that's right, the birthmark," Win said. "Morty reminded me, way back in the sixties, there used to be a model, her trademark was a birthmark or a mole, whatever you want to call it, just below her left eye."

"*Tiens,*" Charly was interested. "And she look like this lady?"

Win smiled. "Well, Charly, sort of. I don't look the way I did at twenty"—Win patted his nearly bald head—"and can you imagine Morty with black hair?" Morty's hair was grey as stone. Win continued, "It looks like she's had some face-lifts. Skin's too smooth. That changes your appearance a lot."

"I told Officer Matucci," Win continued, "and he said he'd look into it. But, you know, I get the feeling the police are just making motions. The woman's a stranger, they're not really interested. They're caught up with that arsonist. And who can blame them?"

Charly nodded. He was interested, and passionately so. Justice must be served. Too much injustice in the world. Charly thought of all the people in his town in France, slaughtered by the Nazis. Four of his young schoolmates, shot for helping the Maquis, the guerillas who were fighting for a free France; the young doctor Jean Michel, shot for dressing the wounds of the Maquis; the old priest in Moirans, in the Vosges Mountains, made to sit in a bathtub of water, February, until he froze to death. What had his crime been? Perhaps to hear the confessions of the Maquis? Justice had never been served, there.

Charly's mission in life (so he imagined) was to right that wrong. All wrongs. To pursue justice for people who could not pursue it for themselves. Charly saw himself riding off to battle, like Joan of Arc, with JUSTICE emblazoned on a banner, held high. He might not be the savior of the world, but at least, he'd do what he could in his little corner of Van Buren County. Every bit helped.

CHAPTER FOURTEEN

Charly Makes an Enemy

Because of the Vanns' dinner this evening Charly would not take a nap. After lunch he liked to lie down on the comfortable leather couch in his living room, but private dinners, shopping, and gardening interfered too often for naps to become a habit. Today, he would simply bring in his mail and check on his cats. Two cups of Puerto Rican coffee, so strong they would take varnish off a table, would keep him awake.

Fred Deering and Max Helder, Charly's catering helpers, had arrived at two o'clock and were turning the slices of smoked salmon into rose shapes, making the blini, and ticking off the items on Charly's list. Catering dinner parties and preparing frozen dinners had become a significant part of the restaurant's profits, and Fred and Max, two of Benny's martial-arts classmates who worked mornings preparing lunches at a local private school, were now afternoon and evening regulars on Charly's catering team.

Charly hurried into his house with the mail. No personal letters. He strode through the downstairs, sniffing: a good, homey smell, earthy and damp, from the plants he'd watered that morning. He checked his pantry. The tiny spiders were wriggling in their big web. How many would die, how many would survive? Charly saw very little difference between animals, insects, and people. They all, he believed, had souls. They live, they die. Perhaps their souls live on. Charly's dead lady had been swatted on the head like a fly. Charly, unlike a fellow fly, would seek vengeance. But perhaps flies did avenge human cruelty, in ways that men didn't comprehend, by causing sickness, famines, plagues? Charly pondered this and decided the restaurant kitchen needed his attentions. No time from philosophical musings.

As he prepared to leave the house, there was a knock on the door. Now, who? With the formality of the European, Charly disapproved of casual visitors. If you wanted to see someone, you made an appointment. So it was with a frown that Charly peered from a window that flanked his front door. A woman, holding leaflets in her hand. "Who is it?" he called.

"Word of God," Charly heard. He opened the door.

The woman was tall and sallow-faced, wearing a dark raincoat and a kerchief. No makeup. Charly noted her thrusting forehead, her deep-set, dull eyes. Poor thing, so ugly, he thought.

"Yes, may I help you?" Charly's voice was impatient.

"I come to bring you the Word of God," the woman said hoarsely.

"Thank you, madame, but I am busy now."

The woman thrust out her pamphlets. "From the Bible."

Charly glanced at the leaflets: *The Sacrificial Lamb*; *The Bible Has The Answers*; *Christ Shed His Blood For Us*. He shuddered.

"All the answers are in the Bible," the woman recited in a dull voice.

"Perhaps," Charly said. "Hitler thought he had all the right answers in *Mein Kampf*, too. Now, madame, if you please . . ." He inched the door shut.

"Other people think they have the answers, but we know we have the answers," the woman persisted. "We know. The Bible tells us so."

"Does the Bible tell you it is wrong to force beliefs on others?" Then something clicked: "You are Mrs. Marian, who clean for Mr. Maxwell."

"I am."

"Do you try to convert Mr. Maxwell to your Bible?"

Charly noticed a frightened look cross the woman's face. She thrust the pamphlets at him and, turning, hurried away. She got into an old white car.

Charly felt a stab of pity. Poor woman. Theological fascism was as frightening as Nazism, that's why cults were so terrifying. Because cultists thought they knew the truth. No one could know the ultimate truths. Such arrogance. Charly's pity vanished: "How dare she invade my home?"

Back at the restaurant, calm descended. Charly made his morel sauce, sautéed vegetables, and chopped parsley. He bit into a blini. Perfect. "You have your clothing for serving?" he asked his helpers. They wore black trousers, white shirts, plaid cummerbunds with matching bow ties. *Très chic.*

Max and Fred nodded. "Everything's on target, Charly. Don't worry, we'll do you proud."

"Worry? I never worry," Charly fussed. "Everything will be perfect, I know that. Although I think about the veal. It must be done just so, it must not dry out. And the vegetables—they must have a buttery flavor, but not be swimming in butter. I must remember to tell Patty to drain them if necessary. But of course, I do not worry."

• • •

At precisely half past four Charly, Max, and Fred rolled up the Vanns' white-gravel drive. Charly parked outside the kitchen door. Looking at the house made Charly smile, as always: a white brick faux-château, which would have been quite at home in Beverly Hills or Palm Beach, but looked out of place in upstate, rural New York. Ah, he thought, this is a movie set. But not *cinéma verité*. A movie set showing rich people, as the middle classes thought they should look. Charly knew quite a few rich people who lived like paupers. This, however, was not the case with the Vanns. The kitchen door to the movie set opened.

"Yo, Charly." Peter Vann, lean and weather-beaten, lurched out followed by a blond, ponytailed, slender young man dressed in a dark blue tuxedo. Peter, who did not appear too steady, was grinning.

"We've come to help you unload," Peter said, nodding to Max and Fred.

The blue tuxedo said, "Tiger Cavett at your service."

"No, no, is our job," Charly said after a look at Peter's red cheeks. "But monsieur, you carry the bread. And you, Monsieur Tigre, the tub of butter."

Tiger giggled. "Oh, *Monsieur Tigre*, don't you love it, Peter?"

"We've just hired Tiger to be our driver and general handyman," Peter explained. "And he's the barman tonight. Damn good man."

Patty Perkins, Charly's catering manager, came out to help. "He's pie-eyed already," Patty whispered to Charly.

"Who is that Tigre guy," Charly muttered. "Is he drunk, too?"

Patty shook her head. "No, no, Tiger doesn't drink. That's the whole point. Dinah's hired him to be their driver."

"Yes, but who is he?"

Patty shrugged. "Maybe a chum of Peter's? Peter has lots of chums."

Max, Fred, Charly, and Patty unpacked the van. Charly and Patty ticked off their identical lists: caviar, sour cream, blini; salmon roses on sheet pans to be garnished with cream-cheese rosettes and salmon-roe-caviar "raindrops"; veal roast; ragout of artichoke; herbs for garnish; the famous morel sauce; the salad greens wrapped in a linen towel, then in a plastic bag; the dessert . . .

"Well, that's that, Charly. Everything's here."

"Who are the guests?" Charly asked.

Patty counted: "Mr. Maxwell; Honoria Wells; Mrs. Collins, rarely comes to the restaurant, she's over eighty, drinks straight bourbon; Win Crozier and Morty Cohen; Evelyn and Michael Crisp, you remember them, Charly, he's Crisp Combines; Billy and Midge Warburton, they were at the restaurant Sunday with Mr. Maxwell; Jonathan Murray, the lawyer, and his wife; and Hy Bingham and his wife."

Dinah appeared in the kitchen, dressed in ruffled fuchsia taffeta, rubies and diamonds winking at ears, neck, wrist. *Mon Dieu*, Charly thought.

"Ta-da," Dinah said, twirling around.

"Oh, Mrs. Vee, you look good enough to eat," Patty told her.

"Just like Paris," Charly said faintly. Now, who would dress like that in farm country? The girlfriends of *les gangsters*, Charly decided, recalling certain underworld chieftains who brought their wives to La Fermette in New York City. The women always dressed in black, very correct. But Charly had seen Mafia chieftains with their mistresses, and these ladies dressed like Las Vegas showgirls. Like Dinah Vann, in point of fact.

"Hey, babe," Peter said, entering the kitchen. "You look like a million bucks." Peter still wore his work clothing—jeans and a plaid woolen shirt.

"Get dressed, Peter," Dinah said. "And no more to drink."

"Okay," Peter said without argument. "You know I'd never get boiled."

"I don't want you even the tiniest bit simmered."

It appeared to be a bit late for that. Charly wondered if he was in the house of real, live people, or onstage at a wacky but not very amusing sitcom. Did Dinah not notice that Peter could barely stand up?

"Ah madame," Charly said, digging into his pocket, "I bring news of my body. The photographer Sam Higgins, he give me this photo to show around, to see if anyone recognize the lady."

"Yes, yes," Dinah said shortly, "a policeman dropped by this afternoon, showed us the picture. No one we know. I agree with the police, it's someone dealing in drugs. Not our kind of person."

"Perhaps." Charly put the snapshot away. What was Dinah's kind of person? Now wasn't the time to discuss the dead woman, but Dinah had seemed so curious, before. Now, she wanted to dismiss the matter.

Peter stumbled in, holding a giant snifter half-filled with brandy. "Remy Martin," he told Charly. "Just a sip before you go."

"I drink all that, I wind up in the ditch," Charly said, smiling, but he took the snifter and bowed. Really, you had to enter into the spirit of the thing. He sniffed and sipped, twirling the brandy around holding it to the light. "Excellent." He looked at his watch—5:30—and made a great show of its being so late. "I go, now, so that you can dress, monsieur." Charly gave his nearly full glass to Patty.

Driving away, Charly tried to imagine tonight's scenario at the Vanns' party. Unimaginable. Would Peter make it through the evening?

There was little traffic on the road and through his half-open window Charly could smell burning leaves. A strange American custom, burning leaves. Why not put the leaves on the compost? But Americans loved burning things. This thought, of course, led to speculation about the arsonist. Charly couldn't imagine who it could be, and now, after a day, he decided his "finds" at Walter Maxwell's would amount to nothing. Someone had been burning something, possibly months ago. It probably didn't relate to the arsonist at all.

Dinah Vann confronted Peter as he dressed for the party. "That dead woman the cops asked us about this afternoon, did you recognize her?"

"Yep."

"It's Candy Moran, your old showroom model, isn't it?"

"Yep."

"Did you know she was up here?"

"Nope. Didn't know she knew anyone up here. She didn't know we lived up here, I'm sure. I haven't seen her since we moved out of the city."

"So you didn't kill her."

"Nope. But I don't want to get involved, and I don't like cops, so let's keep our mouths shut, okay? Hey, maybe you killed her, but if you did, I don't want to know."

Dinah ignored this. "Who did she know up here?"

"Beats the hell out of me. You like this yellow tie?"

"Your blue Dunhill looks nicer." Dinah turned around, gave a little jump and said, "Oh, Tiger, I didn't see you."

"Sorry, Mrs. Vee, didn't want to startle you. I knocked

on the open door, but I don't think you heard me. Patty asks, should she top the blini with caviar now? Almost six."

"No, tell her to wait until the first guest arrives. Charly said they get soggy pretty fast." Damn, how long had he been standing there? And what had he heard?

CHAPTER FIFTEEN

An Incident at
the Vanns'

Chief of Police John Stark pulled his grey Plymouth into
his garage next to Betty's maroon Ford Fiesta. Just after six
o'clock, Tuesday evening. *Please God,* he thought, *don't
let me be called out tonight.*

If Johnny were still here, he thought, we'd go down to
Clover Creek, see if the fish are biting. But no, if Johnny
were still here, he'd be twenty-two years old, probably
graduated from college, have a job somewhere. He sighed
at the waste of a young life. Even after five years, he was
still asking, "Why? Why?" He'd be asking till they carried
him to his grave.

"We can eat right this minute," Betty told him. "Eat
now, rest after, never know when you'll be called out. I'll
call the girls."

"Not tonight, I won't go," Stark said. "I'm beat."

When he'd finished his meat loaf, mashed potatoes,
gravy, creamed corn-with-peppers, iceberg-lettuce salad
with plenty of bottled dressing, and two pieces of Betty's
apple pie with vanilla ice cream, Stark leaned back in his
chair. Elizabeth and Rebecca took the dishes into the
kitchen to wash them, and Betty and John talked about the
arsonist.

"I used to think it was kids," Betty said, "but not anymore. Now I think it's a crazy. Some poor, deranged person. Probably just as normal as can be on the outside, no one would ever know."

"I know," John said. "That's what frightens me. I got six calls from volunteer firemen, all telling me they're pretty sure it's another fireman—they're all different people, too: Tom Arnold, Hank Browning, Roland Field, oh, I can't even remember the others. Now we've got to check all those people out. Arnold's a real loser—little sneak. Works for that rich guy, Maxwell, has that Black Bull Farm. Always wondered, if the guy's so successful, why does he hire a loser like Arnold?"

Betty said, "Old man Arnold, Tom's father, worked for Maxwell. So Maxwell probably took on the son out of loyalty to the father. But why would Tom Arnold burn down barns? He's white trash, but he's not unhinged."

"That's the trouble," Stark said. "So often, when people are crazy, you know, paranoid, psychotic, whatever you want to call it, it doesn't show on the outside. Come on, let's go watch the news. I'm sick of thinking about it."

"Why watch the news?" Stark asked after half an hour. "It's always the same. All over the world, people killing other people. Why don't they ever report happy things?"

"You know how many loonies we have here?" Betty asked, after the news had been turned off. "I read in the paper the other day, man in his sixties, troopers up in Sturdevant caught him having sex with his thirty-year-old daughter in the backseat of his car. They called it felony incest."

"He's probably normal in every other way," Stark said. "Probably been doing it for years. Just got lucky, I guess, troopers driving past."

"I told you about the kid, the arsonist, when I was a girl?"

"Remind me," Stark said, stretching out on the couch.

"Well, in addition to burning barns, he tried to set fire to old Bob, Aunt Mattie's handyman."

Stark yawned. "Yeah? Go on. I don't remember hearing this one."

"See, every Saturday night, old Bob would get drunk, then he'd go to the barn, sleep it off. One night Bob woke up, not as drunk as usual, and he heard someone tiptoeing into the barn. This kid came up, sloshed kerosene all over Bob's legs, then started to light a match."

"Nope," Stark said, "you definitely never told me this one."

"Bob jumped up, kicked the can, spilled it all over the kid's legs. The kid dropped the match on himself and went up like a torch."

"Killed him?"

"Yep. And the fires stopped after he died, so they're sure it was him."

"Who was he?"

"Rich farmer's son. Did it to get attention; his father was always picking on him, telling him how stupid he was. Father was a horrible man. He's the one should have been punished."

Stark slid into sleep. Betty took up her knitting: a lovely brown V-necked pullover for John, with the wool from Mrs. Becker's sheep. Now, wasn't that nice of Mrs. Becker. . . . The telephone rang. Please, not for John, Betty thought, though of course it would be, the girls had a separate number, which they paid for out of their baby-sitting money.

A minute later, Stark pulled on his jacket. "It's the Okun kid, Bob Okun's youngest. Vince says he was brought to the emergency room, he stole his uncle's motorcycle, big Harley, and he lost control and smashed into a tree. You know, Sunday night, he was caught spray painting a school bus. That kid, all he does is get into trouble."

"Poor Linda," Betty said. "She works so hard at the luncheonette, now she's working Sundays as well, got herself a job at Charly's place. Oh, speaking of Charly, you find out who that woman is he found?"

"No, but I'll bet she's from New York City. Charly says that scarf she has on costs $250. Can you believe anyone'd pay that for a scarf?"

"City folks are another breed," Betty said. "I'd believe anything of them."

Dinah Vann was as pleased as she could be: Patty Perkins, looking out from the round window in the pantry's swinging door, could see her smiling, laughing, getting up from the table, putting her arms around people. Well, she should be pleased. The party was going very well. They'd gobbled everything up, most had seconds. Peter, God love him, was almost sober, and he got up and toasted Dinah, "The happiest twenty-five years of my life were spent with this gorgeous broad," he'd said, and everyone clapped and whistled. Max and Fred poured more champagne. Yes, it was a lovely party.

Nearly time to wheel the coffee-and-cordials cart out to the living room. She'd better go check, make sure the ashtrays were emptied, no glasses around, placed neatened up after the cocktails. Tiger's job, but Patty just wanted to make sure. She didn't trust anybody a hundred percent.

Patty left the kitchen by the doorway that led out into the back hall, and opened the door that led to the front hall. Uh-oh, two people out here, talking; she'd thought they were all still in the dining room. It was Mr. Maxwell and Mrs. Wells. Patty pulled the door almost shut, and listened.

"So in other words, Walter," Mrs. Wells was saying, "Harry Clark is nothing but a common thief." Patty was shocked. Mrs. Wells was slurring her words, swaying. Drunk? She'd never seen Mrs. Wells drunk.

"I'm sorry, Honny," Mr. Maxwell said. "I didn't want to say anything. But when you told me you'd changed your will to include Harry, well . . . he's a crook, Honny. You ought to know better, at your age."

Suddenly Patty heard the sound of a slap, and peeked out again, to see Honny, her hand raised again against Mr. Maxwell, saying, "You creep. You think I'm nothing but a cheap slut," And Mr. Maxwell, stepping back, saying, "No, no, Honny," and then Mrs. Wells screamed, "Walter!" and there was a very loud crash and Walter fell over backwards.

Patty rushed out into the hall. The wooden column at the base of the stairs had toppled over, and the big terra-cotta urn filled with autumn leaves and chrysanthemums had smashed on the marble floor. Walter lay on the floor, passed out or dead, shards of terra-cotta and flowers over him, his head resting on one of the lower stairs. The guests from the dining room poured out into the hall. "Jesus Christ," said Peter Vann.

Max and Fred materialized and stood over Walter. "Don't let anyone move him," Patty said. "I think that big urn fell on his head, knocked him out. He might have a concussion, might have hurt his back."

Tiger Cavett knelt in front of Walter. He reached into his pocket, brought out a small cotton-covered phial, broke it, and held it under Walter's nose. "Ammoniated spirits," he murmured, "I always carry them."

Walter Maxwell groaned and opened his eyes. He tried to stand up, then yelped, and sat down again. "My ankle," he said. "My head," he said.

"Why don't you all go into the living room?" Patty told the guests. "Here, Max, get some rags, clean up the water so people don't slip, pick up the flowers. Fred, why don't you get the coffee cart in the pantry and bring it round? Mrs. Vee, Tiger and I will stay here with Mr. Maxwell, you go with your guests. I'll clean up the mess. We'll phone the emergency squad to send an ambulance round, he might have internal injuries. Better let the paramedics move him."

"You're quite the general," Tiger told Patty, when the guests left the hall.

"When Charly made me catering manager, he made me take some courses in emergency procedures," Patty said. "Mainly in case there are lawsuits, afterward. Folks love to sue. You'd be surprised how often things like this do happen."

"No," Tiger said, "I'm not surprised at all."

"Yes," Patty said, "with your ammoniated spirits, I can see that."

The paramedics arrived and strapped Walter to a back board to minimize stress. "Had a little too much wine, Walter?" One of them asked.

"I don't drink," Walter told them. "But I think that vase of flowers was drunk; it walked up and belted me." The paramedics, Tiger, and Patty all chuckled. Honoria, swaying badly, now, hurried into the hall.

"Ish all my fault," she said. "I'd better go wi' em. Poor, poor Walter."

The paramedics took one look at Honoria. One of them said, "No, ma'am. I don't think so. Against regulations." And rolled up his eyes.

Walter, strapped to his board, looked up at Honoria. "Ralph's going to haunt you, Honny, you don't dump that guy."

"You' right, Walter darling," Honoria said, and started to cry, smearing her mascara. "I'll dump him ver', ver' soon."

Peter strode into the hall, looking sober and responsible. "Tiger and I will take Honny home," he told Patty, "then we'll swing round to the hospital, make sure Walter's okay."

"Very nice party, sorry I had to leave early," Walter said, and chuckled as they carried him out into the night. It was one way to make a fast exit.

Charly, surrounded by cats, pondered. He'd eaten a bowl of soup, drunk a glass of Beaujolais, and now he sat in his living room, thinking about his contacts in Boston and in New York. Whom could he call? He was sure the root of that woman's killing lay in some episode in the past. At the moment, his interest was pinned on the Vanns. They came from New York, and he was positive Dinah knew something she wasn't telling. She'd been evasive when he'd brought out the picture of the dead woman. He could have sworn she recognized the woman.

Tiens—he just remembered. Once, Peter had said his favorite restaurant in New York had been Le Brouilly, and the owner of Le Brouilly was none other than his old friend and fellow waiter Jean Maille. Perhaps Jean might know something?

And in Boston? Andre Chenier of course; he'd owned Café Ricard for years. Would Andre know anything about a tragedy involving a certain Houghton family thirty years ago? Or would he know Walter Maxwell?

He got out his address book and dialed Jean Maille's restaurant.

"Allo, Allo, Le Brouilly."

"*Monsieur Jean Maille, s'il vous plait. Ah, Jean. C'est Charly Poisson, ici.*" Since the two friends hadn't spoken in several months, there was a certain amount of catching up. Then Charly posed his question. Jean Maille thought for a bit: Monsieur Vann, a customer ten years ago, no, it did not ring a bell. But he had a little black book put away, listing good tippers, bad types, drunks, bad credit risks, perhaps he could find it, call Charly back?

Charly then called Andre Chenier at Café Ricard in

Boston. Again he was in luck: Andre was in, and naturally they reminisced about their lives in New York together, Charly and Andre and Jean Maille, so many years ago. But no, the name Houghton didn't ring a bell. And the man named Walter Maxwell. Well, Andre said, his restaurant wasn't here in 1965, but one of his old waiters had been at Café du Midi, a well-known French restaurant, then. Andre would ask him, and call Charly back. Waiters have notoriously long memories. But it might take a few days; the old man was on vacation.

Now, who else could Charly call? For the moment, he could think of no one. He decided to read about spiders. Murder was nothing in the spider world, the females ate their lovers every day. He would peruse Jean-Henri Fabre, of course, the great French naturalist. His *Life of the Spider* was more exciting than any murder mystery:

The spider has a bad name: to most of us, she represents an odious, noxious animal, which everyone hastens to crush underfoot. Against this summary verdict the observer sets the beast's industry, its talent as a weaver, its wiliness in the chase, its tragic nuptials and other characteristics of great interest . .

Charly smiled. He loved Jean-Henri Fabre, a gentle man who respected all of nature. *And I am like a spider*, he thought, *weaving a web in which to catch the murderer of my poor lady.*

CHAPTER SIXTEEN

The Perfect Day for Scotch Broth

Charly shivered, on Wednesday morning, as he walked the few hundred yards to his restaurant. It was a raw day, with the promise of icy rain.

His spirits lifted, however, when he entered his warm and fragrant kitchen. Today would be the perfect day to make Le Scotch Broth. Charly climbed down to his basement freezer, and retrieved a big bag of lamb bones.

"If you can perfectly roast a chicken and make a good soup, you are on your way to becoming a chef," Charly instructed Benny. It was exactly what an old chef had told Charly many years ago.

Charly had high hopes for Benny, who had, Charly thought, a "feel" for food. And also, when Charly looked at Benny, he always thought of the son he'd lost: Benny looked like a French youth, with his short, squat stature, his pink cheeks, his dark, straight hair. Was Benny Charly's son in another incarnation? Anything, Charly felt, was possible.

Benny placed the lamb bones on a sheet pan and they were now roasting in a hot oven. Next, they peeled and chopped carrots, onions, garlic, celery, leeks. Charly explained that Americans liked big, hearty soups, "one-dish

SCOTCH BROTH
Yield: 8-10 servings

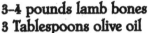

3-4 pounds lamb bones
3 Tablespoons olive oil
1 cup carrots, chopped
1 cup onions, chopped
6 cloves garlic, chopped
1 cup celery, sliced
1 cup leek whites and greens, chopped
2½ quarts rich chicken stock
Bouquet of rosemary sprigs and
   parsley stems
2 cups cooked barley
Sea salt and freshly ground pepper,
   to taste

Roast lamb bones in 350° oven for 1 hour. Heat olive oil in big stockpot and sauté vegetables until they begin to turn brown and sugar in them caramelizes. Add lamb bones to pot, then chicken stock and herb bouquet. Bring to a boil, lower heat, cover and cook 1 hour. Cool. Remove lamb bones, pick off meat and add to soup. Add cooked barley. Add salt and pepper to taste. Serve piping hot.

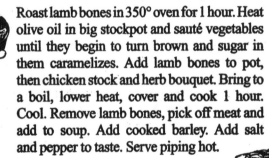

meals" so to speak. "Like the Scotch Broth prepared by a chef named Henry Jones, I have eaten it many times in the Soup Bar in the department store Lord & Taylor," Charly explained. "Long, long ago."

The vegetables sweated in oil; the barley cooked separately. "My Tante Jeanne," Charly reminisced about his old aunt, "she cook the barley along with the soup, makes it nice and thick. But cloudy. For family is hokay, but in a restaurant, customer do not like to pay for soup that look like dirty water. But save the barley water and drink it, very healthful."

After the bones, vegetables, and chicken stock were combined in the big soup pot, and a bouquet of rosemary and parsley stems was dropped on top, Charly left Benny to the lunch preparations. As was usual after a dinner party Charly would drive over to the Vanns', collect his equipment, present the final bill, and hear a report on the dinner. In addition, Charly, the spider weaving his web, was hoping to ensnare Dinah Vann, his latest suspect.

"Everyone loved the food, Charly," Dinah reported. "Lots of compliments. And Patty, Max, and Fred did a terrific job."

"Ah," Charly beamed. "That is what I like to hear. And so, the evening, it was a success." One nice thing about the Vanns, they rarely criticized.

"You heard about Walter Maxwell?"

"No. What happen?"

"Walter slipped and fell in the hall, knocked against a column with a vase of flowers on top, and he sprained his ankle. He hit his head, too, so they carried him off in the ambulance. And Honoria and Walter had been arguing, earlier; they left the dining room together, went out into the hall."

"*Mon Dieu.* Did she hit him?"

"I don't know. It sort of put a damper on what was left of the evening. But apart from that, it was a good party."

"I am pleased, madame. Tell me," Charly continued, "can you think of anyone who might have known my dead lady? The police are anxious to identify her . . ."

"Neither Peter nor I have ever seen her before," Dinah snapped. Charly could see that she was beginning to get annoyed. "As I believe I told you yesterday. I told the police the same thing. So that's that."

"My apologies, madame. And is Mr. Maxwell still in the hospital?"

"They were doing tests this morning, in case he'd had a heart attack, and then he was going home. We called the hospital this morning."

"In that case, madame, I shall leave you." Charly reached into his pocket. "The remainder of my bill."

Dinah took the envelope. "I'll look it over, Charly, and mail you a check. Everything went very well. It was a lovely party."

Back at the restaurant, lunch preparations were under way. Charly put on his apron and was busy with his egg pies when there was a knock on the back door and John Stark put his head in.

"Mind if I come in, Charly?"

"Ah, Chief, we have missed you. You do not stop in as often, now."

"It's the damn arsonist," Stark said, accepting a cup of coffee and a slice of pound cake. "And now there's your dead lady, and the drugs, plus a few other matters. We're understaffed. I need three more officers, at least."

"And the fire at Maxwell—was that the arsonist, too?"

"Fire Chief Tibbetts is handling that one. But they think it was the arsonist. At least, they found rags and jerricans. Oh, and did you hear about Robby Okun?" Stark told

Charly about the accident. "His mother, Linda, works for you, I hear. Poor woman."

"Perhaps Robby Okun is the arsonist?" Charly speculated.

"Only if someone paid him to do it. He's been blackmailing kids at school who smoke pot, threatening to tell their parents unless they pay him. One kid stole money from his mother's purse, she caught him, it all came out. So, yeah, sure, it's possible. Anything's possible." Stark shrugged his shoulders and looked glum. "I'm at the end of my rope."

After Stark left, Charly took up his little bottle of Dr. Bach's remedies, and plopped a dropperful onto his tongue. The story about Robby had upset him. Having no children of his own, Charly had a rather romantic view of youth: good little boys and girls, faces scrubbed clean, attentive for instruction from their elders. And, oh, *merde*, he'd forgotten to give Stark the clues he'd picked up near Walter Maxwell's burnt shed.

Walter Maxwell sat on the side of his bed at the Van Buren County Hospital, room 412. He was in a strange mental state, head muzzy, felt like he was swimming underwater, everything murky. Now, his ankle was taped, and thanks to painkillers he could hardly feel it. He could hardly feel anything. He'd had an electrocardiogram, and there was no heart problem. But his heart was pounding and, looking around, he wondered where he was. It was strange. He couldn't remember. Where was he? Who was he?

Walter swung his legs back on the bed, stretched out and closed his eyes. Of course. He knew where he was and who he was. He was Walt Mastrinsky, fourteen years old, in the old hospital in Newark, New Jersey. He'd slipped on the sidewalk, running from the cops after that

B & E. Walter chuckled. They'd never gotten him for that. But he'd ended up in the hospital. He opened his eyes, stretched out his arm, looking for the ID bracelet the teenaged Walter wore. He was not prepared for the thin, old man's arm he saw. He shut his eyes and tried to make some sense of it all.

Honoria . . . the Vanns . . . that stupid dinner party . . . the ambulance. It had frightened him very much. "You must never be afraid," Ralph said. "Fear can destroy you. There's always a way out, if you keep your head."

He'd lost his head, killed Candy, a bad move, cops had found the body. Correction. Charly had found the body, then come spying around Walter's place Monday night. A pity, but he had to do Charly. Or rather, have it done. And then that kid had telephoned. The Okum kid. Funny how he'd remembered the name. The Okun kid reminded Walter of himself, as a child, always getting into trouble. Both of them were outsiders, outside society. And Candy? What would happen? Nothing. Another month, she'd be forgotten. And Walter would be somewhere in the Caribbean, with enough money to last him the rest of his life. Maybe he'd sell the place up here. He dozed, floating away on the waves of the pain medication.

Walter started up, looked at his watch, it was after one. He was taking Ricky and Marty to dinner at La Fermette at half past six. He got up, tried to put pressure on his taped ankle. Not great. With the hospital cane, though, he could probably manage. Ugly fucker. He had an elegant cane at home.

Walter hobbled out into the hall, walked up to the nurse's station. Deserted. There was no one around, at all. Well, so what? He'd get dressed, get out of here. They'd mail him a bill. They knew where he lived.

Walter retrieved his clothing from the minuscule closet in his room. Sat on the edge of the bed, put on his socks, briefs, Sea Island cotton shirt with the monogram on the cuff and the trousers to his dark blue wool suit. Maybe he should walk up and down the hall for a bit, just to make sure he could navigate without falling. Yes, good idea. Walter reached for the heavy, old-fashioned glass carafe to pour himself a glass of water, but his foot slipped, his arm holding the carafe banged against the metal bed frame, his fingers involuntarily tightened around the neck of the carafe and the receptacle exploded, cascading water down the side of the bed. Damn. Well, at least he hadn't gotten wet, nor, a small miracle, had he cut himself. Bed was still dry if he wanted to lie down again. But he was amazed at the strength in his hands. He'd always prided himself on his powerful hands.

The corridor was still deserted. No doctors, no nurses. Silence, rolling over everything. Strange. More like a morgue than a hospital. He'd read how the old place was understaffed. He peered into the rooms. Many were empty. In others, old people slept, muttered, waited for death.

At the end of the corridor, just as Walter turned to walk back to his room, he saw a young boy in one of the rooms, all alone, sleeping, leg in a cast. For a moment Walter was back in the old hospital in Newark, seeing himself as the kid on the bed, his leg in a cast. It had been just before he met Big Ricky Zampone.

He didn't exactly meet Big Ricky. Big Ricky had been walking—well, waddling—down the street at 2 A.M., amazingly without his bodyguard, and just as Big Ricky passed Walter, walking the other way, a man stepped out of an alley with a gun. The shooter didn't see young Walter at all. Walter, who knew who the fat man was (everybody in the neighborhood knew Big Ricky Zampone) had whirled around, snapped his hands around the neck of Big Ricky's assailant, and squeezed. Big Ricky, aware, by then, of what was going on, had shot to kill, and showed his gratitude to

Walter by hiring him. Soon, Walter became the gangster's star enforcer. A dream come true.

Walter, coming back to the present, stopped outside the kid's room and read the name on the card: OKUN, Robert. *Oh, my God. Is this the kid from the barns, who called me?* Yes, Walter recognized that little pinched, ugly face. The kid who had called and threatened to blackmail him. Wasn't that a coincidence, they both were in the hospital at the same time. Coincidences like this didn't just happen. They meant something.

Walter stepped into Robby's room, closed the door, hobbled to the bed.

The boy's eyes fluttered open. Robby stared at Walter, then he shrank back. He opened his mouth, but nothing came out but a croak.

"You call me the other night, kid?" Walter whispered.

Robby nodded. "Just—joke. Didn't—mean . . ."

Walter laid down his cane, centered himself, put his hands around the boy's neck and pressed his thumbs into the carotid arteries on either side of the neck's base. The boy's hands flew up and beat against Walter's arms, then they lost strength and flapped feebly. Walter pressed harder, and the boy stopped flailing, his body stopped thrashing. The boy's face was a mask of pain, as if he'd been stung by a thousand wasps. Walter kept up the pressure, never removing his thumbs. The blood supply to the boy's brain was being cut off. All systems shutting down. Death was just seconds away.

Walter laid his index finger along the artery. No pulse. He looked around, expecting to see a nurse, a doctor. He heard nothing. He looked down at the boy. His face was contorted. Walter tried to smooth the muscles, make the face look more natural, but he couldn't. The muscles were set. He turned the boy's face to the left, away from the door, and half covered his head with a pillow. All you could see was the tousled hair. It looked like the kid was sleeping.

Sweating, shivering, Walter walked over to the door, opened it, peered up and down the corridor. Still empty. He checked his watch. *My God, it's three o'clock. Better get out of here, go home, grab a snack, wait for Ricky and Marty.* They'd sit in the living room, reminisce, laugh, he'd feed them drinks to loosen them up, talk about Big Ricky and the good old days, then they'd go to La Fermette for dinner. Then they'd do that job, probably wait for the restaurant to close down and Charly to walk back to his little farmhouse.

Walter shed his hospital scuffs, sat down, and pulled on his shoes. Then he got his suit jacket from the closet, and shrugged it on. Felt like a million.

Walter hobbled past the nurse's station—one nurse, dozing, didn't notice him—and caught the elevator going down just as another elevator opened up, disgorging three chattering nurses. The elevator took him down to the ground floor.

He thought he'd have to call for a taxi, but there was one right by the front entrance, letting off a passenger. *This is my lucky day,* Walter thought, as he leaned back into the cab's interior and gave the driver his address. The fog was rolling down in earnest, and it was starting to rain, but Walter thought it looked beautiful out there, grey and misty and mysterious. He shuddered when he thought of the Okun kid. Boy, he'd taken a terrible chance. What would he have done if a doctor walked in? That's how he'd killed Little Augie, fifty years ago. One of his first jobs. What a place, Walter thought about the hospital—no nurses, no doctors, the corridors deserted. You could die in there.

• • •

A nurse's aide pushing her cleaning cart down the corridor stopped at room 412. Looked empty, but it wasn't down on her card. She went in, opened the closet, then stopped, annoyed, as her feet crunched on broken glass. Another one of those dumb glass carafes broken. She got her little broom and her dustpan and swept up the glass, picked up the rest of the carafe, taking care not to cut herself on the jagged edges. Then she continued down the corridor.

CHAPTER SEVENTEEN

✛✛✛✛✛✛✛

Do Not Eat—
Poison

✛✛✛✛✛✛✛

Wednesday lunch was over, thirty people. Charly figured it just about covered the lunch payroll and the food. It was good advertising, though, and a lunch regular was more inclined to bring his family here for a celebratory dinner. Evenings, here, were the money-makers.

"Here, Mick, take the rest of the egg pie home to Bruno," Charly urged.

"See you, Charly," Benny called out—on his way to his martial-arts class, paid for by Charly, though no one knew this but Charly, Benny, and Patty. Certainly not Maurice, who would have made a big fuss. The telephone rang.

"Allo, allo, La Fermette, 'ere. Ah, Elmo, 'ow are you?"

Elmo Richards was the president and CEO (it said this on his card) of Richards Dairy and Produce in Albany. Charly was fond of Elmo, who was a tough, self-made young man. Charly recalled the exquisite, needle-thin string beans, the yellow fingerling potatoes, the big round of cheese that had been delivered. The man had magnificent stuff.

"Mad as hell, Charly. You still have that round of domestic Gorgonzola we delivered Monday? I just got a fax, company's recalling it because of, and I quote, 'a precautionary measure because of the possible presence of *Listeria monocytogenes,* a bacteria that causes listeria with flulike symptoms.' End of quote. They're recalling it in ten states. God, I fucking hate stuff like this, we could get sued, customers complain, ta da–ta da. The whole ball of wax."

"*Ah, la la,* but no, we have not even opened it yet."

"We'll pick it up next time we come by. Credit your account. I'll try to find another domestic Gorgonzola that's edible; most of the stuff's shit. Well, so the cheese producers have troubles too, right? Stuff's probably harmless."

"Is always something," Charly agreed. "The apple with the Alar, the watermelon, the egg with the whatever it was . . . I will put the cheese in a paper bag and mark it DO NOT EAT—POISON."

"There you go, Charly. And, hey, no hard feelings?"

"No, of course not, Elmo. What a thought. You are the best produce company in the entire United States. Beautiful, your stuff."

"That's the ticket, Charly. You're the best, too."

Charly smiled and hung up. Everyone has his troubles. He walked over to his cold room, picked up the offending cheese, put it in a big paper bag and marked it DO NOT EAT—POISON and put it back on the cold-room shelf. He put on his jacket, grabbed his keys, slammed the kitchen door shut, and hurried to his van. No time for a nap, today.

It was half past two and Maurice Baleine, his state of consciousness severely impaired by alcohol, tottered down the stairs to his front hall. A little while ago he'd heard Barbara's car backing out of the garage—going to visit her mother. Now, he felt in need of fresh air. A walk down to the restaurant would be ideal—and no one would be there at this hour. He might even find something to eat, and he was feeling decidedly peckish.

Maurice knew that he was an important cog in the

restaurant's wheels, that it needed him to give it that special
tone. Charly was all right, but he had the mentality of a mere
cook. Whereas he, Maurice, a Princeton man . . . Maurice
smiled. The place needed his superior talents.

Maurice set down his drink. Amazing. It seemed like
he'd just cracked open a new bottle, and now it was half-
finished. Time was playing tricks. He got his wool-lined
Burberry and his deerstalker hat from the hall closet. And
he set off for a bracing stroll down to the restaurant.

Maurice breathed in the moist, chilly air and walked
briskly, without staggering, down the road, which seemed
to undulate in a pleasant way, as though he were on ship-
board. Soon, Maurice fantasized, it would be time for the
deck steward to come round with tea and sweet biscuits.
He was famished.

He was amazed when the front door of the restaurant
loomed up. Why, he hadn't been walking more than a
minute or two, and he knew that it was a good ten or fifteen
minutes' walk. Strange.

Maurice fumbled with the front door and finally inserted his key. The restaurant's barroom was clean and
flowery-scented by the bouquets that dotted the room.
Maurice walked through into the kitchen and opened the
refrigerator. Cold foods covered in plastic wrap. Any of
that good roast beef left? Maurice poked, opened boxes,
nothing. He moved on to the cold room. More food, un-
cooked. Bins of potatoes, onions, carrots, fruit.

He was about to exit the cold room when his eye fell on
a paper bag topped with a note: DO NOT EAT—POISON. *Well
of course*, Maurice thought, reading Poison as Poisson,
Charly's saving something good for himself. He ripped off
the paper and opened the bag. It was a round of Gorgonzola, his favorite cheese.

Maurice maneuvered the cheese into a plastic bag and
left the kitchen. He stopped at the bar and poured himself

a very small Glenlivet, just enough to get him home. He'd been running purely on alcohol since Sunday night, and the tank was beginning to go dry. He poured another short one—merely maintenance—Mmmm. A gentleman's drink.

Maurice locked the front door behind him and started up the road, his parcel under his arm. Again, the walk seemed miraculously short. Could the whiskey have given him wings? Smiling at this amusing and witty thought, Maurice unlocked the front door and headed straight for the kitchen.

There, he found a box of Carr's Water Biscuits and in the refrigerator, a block of butter. He set the cheese on the table and found a knife. "And let the feasting begin," Maurice smiled to himself, as he unwrapped the covering on the cheese and cut himself a manly wedge.

Charly parked in front of a small, grey clapboard house on a quiet street in Hogton. This was a street of lawyers, doctors, and a few investment firms. The renovated century-old houses had a subdued air of prosperity about them. "You can trust us," the handsome old houses seemed to promise.

Jimmy Houghton's office had window boxes at all the front windows, spilling over with red and white geraniums and ivy. It bore a bronze sign, Houghton and Houghton, Investments though old Averill Houghton, Jimmy's uncle, had died long ago. RING BELL AND WALK IN, said a notice. Charly rang the bell and opened the Williamsburg blue front door.

"Charly, how good of you to call," Evelyn Holmes said, making it sound like Charly had been doing them a favor by telephoning. Evelyn sat behind a receptionist's desk, surrounded by a telephone, a fax machine, a computer, and a copier—the only modern fixtures in the room.

"I think Jimmy's free, but let me just make sure," Evelyn said, and picked up the telephone. Charly sat on a Federal-style sofa, not very comfortable, and smiled at Evelyn. "Ah, Madame Evelyn," he said when Evelyn had put the telephone down, "So distinguished-looking, always."

"Now, now, no passes at my office manager," Jimmy said as he came in. "Come on into my office, Charly."

Charly explained that he wanted to buy Maurice's share of the restaurant. What stocks should he sell, and how much should he offer? Jimmy explained that the restaurant was worth around two and a half times annual profits, and that he would work out the exact figures.

"That is all I come for, really," Charly confessed. "I could have asked you on the telephone, but I also wanted to talk to you about the dead body I find in my field. You have heard about her?" (Somewhere, far back in Charly's head, a voice murmured, *this is the job of the police, they won't be happy with you, Charly*, but Charly shook his head impatiently. He, the Great Detective, must solve this affair himself. His self-esteem demanded it.)

"Only what I read in the paper," Jimmy said. "I didn't even know you were the one who found her. The article said anyone with ideas on who she might be should call the Klover Police. Now, tell me your version."

Charly obliged with a dramatic rendition, then reached into his pocket and brought out the photograph. "The police give me this, to show around and ask. Does she look familiar to you?"

Jimmy looked, and caught his breath. "But she looks dead, here."

"But of course," Charly said. "No one know who this lady might be, or where she come from. She was buried in my field. The police are asking people if they recognize her. But how many people can they ask? I think of you, because I know . . . I think you did not grow up here. You came from big city. You came from a family of social prominence, no? And this lady, she is dressed as if she come from a big city, and I would guess she come from Boston or New York . . ."

"Charly, Charly," Jimmy said, laughing. "You're totally confusing me. I don't even know what you're saying. Boston and New York have millions of people. Why should I know this woman, just because she's dressed like a city person? None of this makes sense."

Charly sighed. "No, it does not make sense. But you are a man of affairs, and you know a lot of people not only in Van Buren County. You have wealthy client, like Walter Maxwell, and Mrs. Wells, and Win Crozier. I simply wonder if this lady, the age of your *papa* and *maman*, might look familiar, and if you have ever come across her. In Boston or New York."

"Oh, Charly," Jimmy said, shaking his head. "Where I came from is immaterial, though I did come from Boston, we moved here when I was ten years old, after the death of my father. My mother wanted to be near her people, the Houghtons in Albany, and we took my mother's maiden name."

"Ah. So your father's name was not Houghton?"

"Dad's name was William Talbott. He was killed in a hunting accident. It was a great blow to my mother, so she came back to her folks and changed her name. Very few people, if any, know this down here, and I hope you'll respect this confidence. Down here I am James Houghton. Period."

"Of course, of course," Charly murmured. "I am so sorry."

"And as for your dead lady, well, what can I say? She doesn't look like a very nice person, does she? She looks hard and calculating. Now, instead of concentrating on her, think of people you know up here who would know a woman like that. Does that make sense?"

It made no sense to Charly. How could this dead face look calculating? It looked empty. Death had erased all emotions. Or perhaps Jimmy was not telling the whole truth? Maybe Jimmy was lying to him. Charly didn't argue. "Of course it makes sense, Jimmy. And you are right. That is what I shall do. Think of people who would know a cold and hard woman like this."

"She's had a face-lift," Jimmy pointed out. "And she's wearing an old Hermès scarf, all the ladies of my mother's generation wore them."

Charly said, "Win Crozier tell me that little mark beneath her left eye, you see," and Charly pointed with his finger, "it make him think of someone, perhaps a fashion model, but he cannot think who."

Jimmy stood up. "Well, Charly, I'll think about it, and let you know. In the meantime, I'll try to figure out what you should offer Maurice. Does he want to sell? Did he approach you?"

Charly sighed. "Now, I will tell you something in confidence," and Charly told about Sunday night in the restaurant, finding Maurice passed out.

Jimmy said primly, "He'll ruin the restaurant, you're right. Maurice's a city snob. He's better than us yokels. Whenever I see him, Maurice keeps trying to give me financial advice. The city slicker, telling the country bumpkin the score. And *entre nous*, just between us chickens, Charly, he's invested in some pretty shaky stocks."

"Yes, Jimmy, I know. And that is another reason why we cannot work together any longer. He know everything, I know nothing."

After Charly left, Jimmy Houghton stopped by Evelyn's desk. "Did you know that Charly was the one who found Candy Moran's body?"

"Good God," Evelyn said. "I certainly did not."

"If Candy's past comes out, mine will, too . . . it could affect my business."

"Now don't worry, Jimmy," Evelyn comforted. "It'll all blow over. Just go eat one of those nice Cadbury's chocolate bars you've hidden away."

Jimmy opened his mouth to say something, then closed it.

By the time Charly returned to the restaurant it was four o'clock and time to set up for dinner. Benny had the roasts and the chickens in the oven, and Charly set about grinding more fresh salmon for his famous salmon rillettes. There were twenty reservations. For a Wednesday night, this wasn't bad at all. There would be walk-ins, too, and barroom customers.

Charly found Tommy Glade setting up the bar. Since there was little call for an active barman on Wednesdays and Thursdays, Tommy doubled as a waiter on these nights. Charly remembered his conversation with Rex, about Dinah Vann's propositioning a barman. *Let's see,* Charly thought, *how can I question Tommy in a discreet manner?*

"The dinner party of the Vann went very well," Charly told Tommy. "And now the Vann have a driver, he was the barman last night. A gentleman called Tiger Cavett."

"Oh, Tiger," Tommy said. "He's a nice guy. He helps me sometimes, when I do my painting jobs. He and I were in AA together. Hey, Charly, someone's left a glass in my sink, did you?"

"No, no, not I. But you know Tiger. *Tiens.* Small world."

"Yeah, isn't it? So he's going to work for the Vanns. Good luck to him."

"You think he will not enjoy the work?"

Tommy snorted. "The Vanns aren't very nice people, Charly."

"No, they are not," Charly agreed. "And Rex Cingale, he tell me that Madame Vann, she make the barman a proposition, at one of her parties."

"Fuckin' A, Charly. Remember that time, a few months ago, she came in with a sprained ankle, wanted me to help her to her car?"

"Yeees, I think so."

"Well," Tommy continued, "we'd almost gotten to her car when she pretended to slip, and she grabbed me in a, uh, sensitive spot."

"You mean she grabbed your . . . your . . ." Charly couldn't say it.

"Yep. Un-fucking believable. Right there in the parking lot. And she's not the only one. Old Mrs. Wells, she's another one. Asked me if I'd like to work as her butler, 'and other things' she said—and she winked. Now, I ask you, is that the way an old broad should behave? I don't know what it is with the old dames, but I meet 'em, do a job for 'em, they're practically wavin' their bush at me. I'm a marked man. Gotta watch my step."

"You do not encourage their—ah—attentions?"

Tommy rolled his eyes and grinned. "My sexual horizons are very narrow. I've been with the same guy for fifteen years. 'Course, Charly, I don't talk about that, as I told you. People up here don't mind drunks 'cause there's so many of us. But a lot of doors are still closed to gays in these small towns."

Charly nodded solemnly. "I am like the priest in the confessional. My lips, they are seal. But tell me, Tommy, do you think Mrs. Vann, or Mr. Vann, for that matter, they could kill that lady that I find?"

"Charly, remember what that writer F. Scott Fitzgerald said, 'the rich are different from you and me'? The Vanns are only interested in themselves. If someone were to threaten their wealth, their way of life . . . of course they'd kill. They don't care about anything, outside of their little world. And, hey, Charly, I'll make you a bet: that Tiger Cavett doesn't last two weeks working for the Vanns."

"Ah, a bet," Charly chuckled. "I like the bet. I bet you . . . fifty cents."

"Nah," Tommy said, "let's go for broke. Make it a dollar."

Charly disappeared into the kitchen and Tommy poured himself a glass of good well water. Best drink in the world.

Of course, it hadn't always been like that. "Man, the suds were rippin' me apart," he'd tell the folks at AA. But now, he'd turned his back on the suds, loved that twelve-step program. Just like a religion, placing himself in the hands of a higher power. Just where he belonged, after having lost a zillion jobs on account of his drinking.

"Booze never turned me on," he'd tell the folks, "neither did wine. Just beer. I'd start suckin' 'em down, and I couldn't stop." Then Charly's barman had gotten arrested for car theft, and Tommy went to talk to Charly.

"I won't kid you," Tommy told Charly. "I'm in Alcoholics Anonymous, haven't touched a drop in two years, my painting business is going fine but it's not something I want to do every hour of the day. I need another interest. Always liked mixing drinks."

"Well," Charly had said, doubt in his voice, "why don't we try it?" He was impressed by Tommy's appearance, clean, with a handlebar mustache and a shiny-haired ponytail. Looked the part.

"And I'll tell you something else," Tommy confided.

SALMON RILLETTES
Yield: 4-6 appetizer servings

1 pound skinned salmon fillets,
  ground or finely chopped
1 Tablespoon vodka
1 Tablespoon Dill, chopped (or more,
  depending on intensity of flavor)
Pinch sugar
½ teaspoon sea salt, or to taste
1 large shallot, finely chopped
Dash or two Tabasco—or to taste

Combine all ingredients, tossing gently
with two forks. Let the flavors marry in the
refrigerator for 5–6 hours.

"I've always been attracted to drunks. I don't know why. You have a lot of drinkers among your clientele. Now that I'm not drinking, I see a part of myself in them. They're on the downward slope. Self-destructive. Some kind of death wish. I watch them and I say to myself, 'Unh-unh, Thomas, my boy, that could be your destiny.' Every day, they remind me. Remind me to stay sober."

CHAPTER EIGHTEEN

✚✚✚✚✚✚✚

Walter Dines at La Fermette

✚✚✚✚✚✚✚

Stark couldn't believe it: five o'clock and no disasters today. No real disasters, that is. One missing person, old Mr. Crowley, his daughter phoned it in, but they knew where he'd be and he was: He'd thumbed a ride to the bar at Steak Heaven. Two collisions, cars totaled, but no real injuries, a broken leg and rib on one, broken arm and concussion on another. Two other collisions, just fender benders. Alice Finn beat up her husband, again. Four farm injuries, no deaths. One DWI, though they usually happened at night.

Stark was just thinking. *A day like today is too good to be true,* when the telephone rang. Robert Okun, the kid who'd crashed his uncle's motorcycle and broken his leg, was found dead in the hospital.

"Dead, you mean, he died as a result of treatment?"

The nurse didn't know, and the doctor—there was only one in the emergency room, afternoons—was attending to the victims of another multiple-car crash. These folks were still alive. Since Robby Okun was undeniably dead, he could wait.

"I'll be right over," Stark told the nurse. "Has anyone told the parents?" No one had told the parents, yet. Stark figured it was the doctor's job, but he'd bet you anything it would become his job. All he could think was *Poor Linda. Poor Bob.* Didn't matter how much of a disaster the kid was, he was theirs. Their baby. And he was dead. Stark's throat tightened as he thought of his own dead son.

The lovely dining room of La Fermette, pale apricot walls aglow, masses of flowers filling the air with the scent of meadows, was half-filled with people on Wednesday evening, as Charly, peeking into the dining room, watched for the entrance of Walter Maxwell and two friends. Walter, Charly's best customer, must be greeted personally by the owner.

There was a nice atmosphere of luxury: aromas of cooking meat and wine, the hushed footfalls of the wait-staff on the thick carpeting, the hum of conversation, the chink of glasses. Patty Perkins, in a long black dress, was acting as hostess in Maurice's absence, and Tommy Glade, the barman, was doubling as extra waiter. Lights were dimmed, candles lit; Charly, as always, swelled with pride. This was his. This is what he'd worked all of his life to achieve. A beautiful place. "If only my customers were as beautiful as my dining room," he mused. For some reason, Charly had become convinced that the murderer of his dead lady was a customer of his.

Charly hurried out. "Welcome, welcome," he cried to Walter Maxwell and his two guests, plump men with small, cold eyes. They did not look . . . chic. Not the beautiful people. They looked like garbagemen.

Charly hid his surprise. Walter made introductions: Richard Zampone, Martin Scungilli. Charly bowed and said it was a pleasure, it was his honor, friends of his best customer, and so on. What a beautiful restaurant, the pleasure was all theirs, everyone had a good appetite . . . niceties and compliments were exchanged. Charly led the three men to an alcove. Walter was leaning on a silver-topped cane, very distinguished-looking, his white hair brushed back from his forehead. Tommy Glade hovered, ready to take an order for drinks. "Enjoy your meal," Charly said, and returned to the kitchen. He would personally deliver a complimentary order of Shrimps Charly, Walter's favorite, to go with their drinks. That would be the proper thing to do for such a valued customer.

"Compliments of the house," Charly murmured a bit later, setting down the platter of shrimp. "And, I tell you a little special, not on the menu. This afternoon I have delivered the most beautiful lobsters from Maine that you have ever seen. If you like, we can make special lobster dish."

Walter glared at Charly. His voice was cold, formal. "Very nice, Charly. But I'd told Richard and Martin about your famous steak with the wine sauce. That's what we have our hearts set on."

"We do?" the plump man called Richard asked. "I love lobster. I told you, Big Wa—I mean, Walter, about the lobster Fra Diavolo that Bernice made . . ." and the other man, Martin, added, "Maine lobster? Oh, boy."

What was the matter? Charly could detect an air of tension, almost of hostility. Had he angered Walter in some way? Perhaps the men had had a disagreement earlier. Or perhaps he imagined it.

"Well, then order the lobster, what do I care?" Walter said petulantly. "It doesn't matter at all, I don't give a damn," he added, childishly.

The man called Richard looked pensive. "I tell you what, Walter. We'll order both. We'll have an appetizer, then we'll have the lobster, then we'll have the steak. My parents used to eat like that all the time. First the antipasto, then the pasta, then, little fish, then, little meat. Oh, these shrimp are terrific." The two plump men filled their mouths with shrimp.

"Lobster à l'Armoricaine," Charly said happily. "Is very much like the Italian dish, Lobster Fra Diavolo, but there are differences, flambéed with brandy, for instance, you shall see. Then the Entrecôte Marchand de Vin. A splendid meal, you shall have." And he hurried off to the kitchen.

Charly immersed himself in the cooking. First he killed the lobsters by plunging a knife into their spinal cords. Then he dismembered them and flung the pieces in hot olive oil. Garlic and shallots were added, and when they browned, Charly threw on cooking brandy and ignited it. "Ah, they will love it," he congratulated himself.

"Hey, we're fallin' behind," Hubert the waiter chided a bit later. "And Mr. Maxwell, he says to hurry it up in here."

Charly was surprised. It wasn't like Walter at all, to want to rush through dinner. In fact, Walter was behaving very oddly indeed, brusque, almost rude, to both Charly and his own guests. Charly, adept at reading the body language of his customers, felt waves of hostility flowing from Walter's stiff, unbending form. Tonight he was rigid, muscles clenched. Very strange.

The lobsters had been served, devoured, and empty plates piled with shells were returned to old Mick's station. Now, Charly took the marrow sauce off the fire and poured it in a puddle on three plates. Benny set the steaks on the plates, and Charly poured over the remainder of the sauce. Hubert, tray on shoulder, hurried out of the kitchen.

By nine the pace in the kitchen had slowed down to a trickle. All of the entrées were out in the dining room, and now desserts were beginning to be plated. Charly changed into his clean white jacket, his high white toque, and went out to greet his guests.

Charly, looking into the little alcove, noticed that Walter and his guests had finished their steaks. He caught Walter's eye, and Walter nodded. "You enjoy your meal, messieurs?"

"This," the man called Richard said, "was the best meal I've ever had in my life. This was—*fantastico*. I'm only sorry my wife couldn't be here. You been up here long, Mr. uh, Charly?"

Charly explained about the restaurant in New York, about his move up to Van Buren County a number of years ago.

The man called Marty said, "Best fuckin', excuse me, best damn restaurant I've ever eaten in. You ever think a movin' down to Jersey?"

Charly said it hadn't occurred to him, but it was an idea.

"You move to Jersey, you'll be packed from day one," Richard assured him. "We'll see to that, me 'n' Marty, here."

Walter was frowning. "Perhaps a salad, Charly? To clear our palates before dessert?"

Charly bowed his way out of the alcove. "It's this guy? *This guy?*" Charly could hear the man called Richard whispering. Charly smiled. Once again, he'd delivered a superior meal to his favorite customer. Walter had evidently been bragging about him.

It was after ten when Charly locked the kitchen door. He smiled as he recalled Walter's guests and their big appetites. They certainly hadn't stinted themselves, and the two men, Martin and Richard, had drunk three bottles of wine, besides. Walter, whose ankle must have been paining him, appeared to be in a sour mood. He drank nothing but San Pellegrino water, as usual, and hadn't ordered the lobster. Ah, well, he'd had a painful fall, and he was not young . . .

The telephone was ringing as Charly let himself into his house.

"Ah, Jean, *comment ça va?*" It was Jean Maille, from Le Brouilly in New York. Charly could hear a lot of noise in the background. Jean had found his black book. He had taken notes on Mr. Peter Vann: always tipped well, paid in cash, wanted blank receipts (well, nothing new, there), sometimes came in with an older woman, presumably his wife, sometimes came in with another elderly woman, a model from his showroom Jean had understood, sometimes came in with young men. Possibly *un pédé*.

Charly wasn't interested in *pédés*. "Do you know the model?"

Jean had one name written down, Candy. All of the models back in the old days, they used to have silly names like that. One name, to make themselves sound unique. And Jean remembered her, this famous Candy. She had a beauty mark just below her left eye. She had been on a few magazine covers, and then . . . no more Candy. It was like that in the world of fashion. Hot one day, dead the next. He'd heard this Candy had gotten married, moved out of town. Then, one day, she was back, a model in the showroom of Peter Vann. Showroom models were nobodies. And Candy had been drunk most of the time . . . Then Monsieur Vann closed his factory, Jean had heard the IRS was after him, and Candy disappeared, too.

"You have a fax machine? No? Then I will mail a photograph of the woman," Charly promised. "You must tell me if it is the same Candy."

But it would be the same, Charly felt sure. And this woman—he felt sure of this, too—had been murdered by Peter Vann.

CHAPTER NINETEEN

✛✛✛✛✛✛✛

High Drama with
Honoria and Harry

✛✛✛✛✛✛✛

Honoria Wells couldn't get that damn dream about Ralph out of her mind. It haunted her. She knew that she was acting the fool with Harry Clark, but there were two sides to her: the side that lusted for Harry and the side that stepped back and viewed (and condemned) her behavior.

Furthermore . . . she overheard Estrella and Juanito giggling in the kitchen, heard the word *abuela*—grandmother. She was old enough to be Harry's grandmother, that's what they were saying. And then Walter Maxwell had practically accused her of being a slut. And even last Sunday, lunching with those nouveau riche Vanns, Dinah had said, "Do bring your—ah—*friend*—Tuesday night, if you wish"—making it clear that Honoria shouldn't bring Harry, pretending she couldn't even recall the man's name. Lots of little things. Honoria imagined people sniggering about her. She'd walked into the feed store, and a conversation had stopped abruptly.

Right. This was it. Tonight was the last time. She was sorry, now, that she'd mentioned to Harry that she'd met with her lawyer. Harry's eyes had lit up and he'd become even more amorous, though he'd murmured, "I only love you, Honny, not your money, you know that." Oh, right.

Harry was a crook, Walter said so. Walter wouldn't lie about that.

They were driving up to Old Chatham, to dine in a stylish new place. After dinner, Honoria decided, they'd come back to her place, have a nightcap, and then she'd tell Harry . . . tell Harry what? After all, he was her farm manager. That he was fired? That she didn't want to see him anymore? That she'd heard he was a crook? That she'd had a dream about an old boyfriend and the dream had told her she must dump Harry? What the hell could she tell Harry?

Honoria listlessly scanned the clothes in her closet. Oh, hell, she'd wear that old Missoni knit, it was so baggy it always made her feel ancient. She'd tell Harry that she didn't want to continue the relationship. Period. And that she was going away for the winter, yes, yes, that was it, she was going to spend the winter in her condo in St. Croix. Oh, and hint that she and Walter Maxwell had something on. Harry Clark feared Walter. Walter was an old fart, but he'd go along with it. If you confront your current lover with another lover, your current lover will be happy to fade away . . . wouldn't he?

"Darling Honny," Harry said, "you're looking tired, baby, not your usual self." They were in Honoria's living room, six o'clock.

"I feel tired, Harry. I'm sixty, too old to be kicking up my heels. I'm—ah—thinking of going away for the winter. Maybe down to St. Croix."

"Great idea. You already said we'd go in January together."

Honoria took a deep breath. "Not you, Harry. You'll have to stay here and manage the farm. I want to go alone. Do some thinking."

"Oh."

Harry Clark, tall, thickset, muscular, his handsome, vacant face framed by a mass of glistening brown hair caught up in a ponytail, toyed with the remainder of his drink, fingered his crotch, and smiled at Honoria.

"Well, Hon, that's fine. Just fine. Now, let me make you a nice drink, a Manhattan, I'll bet that's what you feel like. A couple of my Manhattans, and you'll feel like new. And then we'll go off to that place, have some food."

Not the time to ask for more clothes, Harry thought, as he mixed a double Manhattan. The guys down at the bar had told him, "She'll drop you quicker 'n a live coal, that's her way, so live the good life while you can." He wondered how much she'd left him in her will. Several million, at least. But once she went down to the Islands, got to thinking about it . . . she could change the will, cut him right out.

"Harry, did you remember to make a reservation?"

"Nah, it's a weeknight, there'll be plenty of room."

By the time Honoria and Harry left, Honoria had downed two of Harry's killer double Manhattans and was feeling no pain. She didn't notice that he'd switched to club soda. In fact, slumped in Harry's car, she didn't notice anything since she'd fallen asleep.

Harry drove along Route 42, then turned onto a dirt road that led to the creek. It was a chilly, misty autumn night, drizzling a bit, and Harry had his windshield wipers on. Recent rains had turned the lazy little Trout Creek into a rushing torrent. Harry knew this part of the creek well, since he often fished here. Just up ahead was a little waterfall, and beneath the falls was a deep pool lined with jutting rocks.

Harry had often thought of this moment. How he would do it. He knew his affair with Honoria was a sometime thing, a brief fling, and that she'd dump him just like she had dumped all the other studs. A quick blow to the head knocking her out in the car since she wouldn't want to get out and walk, get her shoes wet. Then he'd carry her to the falls and just dump her over. Drive away. Any head injuries would be consistent with her head bumping on the rocks. See, he really knew how to plan. It was—Harry smiled at his own wit, a honey of a plan—for Honny.

Harry pulled the car over to the side of the dirt track. Honoria still dozed, mouth open, snoring. Old douche bag. Harry took the rock out of his pocket, wrapped it in his handkerchief, positioned himself, grasped the rock in his right hand, and smashed it into the side of Honoria's head.

Honoria gave a start, opened her eyes. "What? What?" Harry hit her two more times, dull thuds which did not break the skin: he didn't want to deal with blood, too messy. Now Honoria slumped, apparently lifeless.

Harry got out of the car, unwrapped the rock, and threw it in the bushes, stuffed the handkerchief into his raincoat pocket—the stylish Armani she'd bought him—and walked around to the passenger side of the car. He opened the door, grasped Honoria under the armpits, and dragged her out. She didn't weigh much.

Harry carried Honoria to the edge of the falls, where the embankment was steep. He heaved her in and heard the splash below. "So long, Hon."

Now, back to the car. The hardest part was still ahead of him: back to Honoria's house, express surprise that she still wasn't there, call the cops, then sit back and wait for them to find her body . . . and then, eventually, the lawyer would call. "You probably don't know this, Mr. Clark, but Honoria Wells has mentioned you in her will . . ." Oh, really? No kidding. Big surprise.

"Sí?"

"Mrs. Wells, is she here?"

Juanito and Estrella looked amazed. "Here, señor? But, you leave with her not an hour since."

"We had an argument. A fight. She got out of the car, walked into the woods. I went to look for her, but she was gone. I think she went back to the road, thumbed a ride. Came home."

Juanito and Estrella looked at each other, eyebrows raised. They hadn't really understood what Harry had been saying, except for the fact that Honoria was missing. Estrella looked at handsome Harry and saw the face of evil. "She is no here," she said, and firmly shut the door.

Estrella's English was better than her husband's, so she looked up the telephone number for the *policía* and dialed. She told the policeman that Honoria Wells, her mistress, had gone for a ride with Harry Clark, and had disappeared. Though her English was poor, she made herself understood.

Officer Matucci's first question was, "Where?"

"*Yo no se.* Not know."

"Then let me speak to Harry Clark."

Estrella gave the policeman the telephone number of Harry Clark. He lived in an apartment over the stables.

Estrella and Juanito went to their room, and Estrella knelt down before a statue of the Virgin of Guadalupe. Harry Clark had done something terrible to her mistress, just as she'd feared. Estrella had what her Tia Luzon called "a sense of evil." She knew when bad things were about to happen. But the bad man wouldn't get away with it. She could sense that, too. God protects the innocents and the fools, and her mistress Honoria was both.

CHAPTER TWENTY

✛✛✛✛✛✛✛

Charly Thinks
a Bit

✛✛✛✛✛✛✛

Honoria woke up in icy water, something was banging in her head, she had to get out, had to get out . . . she felt that she was in the middle of a nightmare, but the cold and the wet were real. Semiconscious, her head thudding so loudly she couldn't think, Honoria tried to stand up and felt her feet touch bottom. Where was she? Wherever it was, she had to get out.

The moon was out, so it was night. She waded to the edge of wherever she was and felt herself climbing out of the water. Mud. Her feet—where were her shoes?—were stuck in mud. Branches. Could she pull herself up? She pulled, the branches held, and Honoria was out of the water. She could feel weeds and leaves under her feet. She was cold. Her head hurt. She tried to stand up, and she did stand up, by holding on to the trunk of a tree. She didn't know where she was, but she started walking. Walking, stumbling, staggering, crawling . . . and then she felt macadam underfoot: This was a road. But where did it lead to? Should she just start walking down the road? What else was there to do? Honoria started walking.

It felt like Honoria had been walking forever, and she was relieved to see lights in the distance. As she came closer, the lights became brighter and Honoria saw that the

152 CECILE LAMALLE

lights were in a house, a small house by the side of the
road. She could hear talking; it sounded like a television
set. She leaned against the door and banged with her fist.
An elderly man opened the door. He peered at Honoria
and she peered back. *Harmless,* she decided. The man said,
"Why, it's a lady. All dressed up. What are you doing here?
You're soaking wet. It's not raining, is it?"
Honoria told him she thought she had been walking in
the woods and something had hit her on the head, and she'd
fallen in some water. Could she come in and rest for a bit?
Get dry?
"Yep. Trout Creek's high, now. Bet that's where you fell
in. Just across the road and down a piece. A branch probably
hit you, the trees are thick. You think I should take you to the
hospital? You don't look too good. Kinda late at night to go
walking, ain't it? All dressed up like that?"
Honoria said she just wanted to sleep for a bit. Could
she do that? She didn't want to go to a hospital until she
could figure out what had happened to her, her head was
still spinning. This man seemed like a simpleton, but
harmless. Honoria, in her Lady of the Manor way, was accustomed to giving orders to people like him. "I just want
to sleep. I'm so tired."

The next time Honoria woke up, it was getting light
outside, though it was still pretty dark. She was lying on a
couch, and, yes, the old man must have given her some
clothes because these were dry, and she was covered with
some blankets and quilts. Somewhere close by, she could
hear someone walking around. She could smell coffee.
"You awake?" the old man asked. He was standing in
the doorway, looking at her. "Who are you, anyway?"
Honoria told him that her head still hurt terribly, but she
could remember her name. Her name was Honoria Wells.
She lived in Klover. She'd been going to a restaurant with
a friend, she'd fallen asleep in the car, and then, suddenly,
she'd woken up in some water.

"Your head's all banged up, your face is covered in bruises. You don't look too good, ma'am. I'm gonna take you into the hospital in Hogton; I don't want you to die on me." "What day is it?" Honoria asked. "It's Thursday, round about five in the morning. We're up with the chickens, around here."

Estrella flew to the telephone. It was six o'clock, she'd been awake for an hour, praying in front of the statue of the Virgin of Guadalupe. In her meditative state she heard a voice saying, "Your mistress is alive." All would be well. And then the telephone rang. It was the police.

"Mrs. Wells is alive," the policeman said. "She's in the hospital. She's asking for you. Can you come down?"

"*Sí, sí*," Estrella shouted. "Right away, right away."

There was a policeman in the room, and a doctor, and a nurse, and the doctor was saying that Mrs. Wells might have a concussion, that she shouldn't talk, and the policeman was saying that it was important and Estrella was nodding, yes, yes, *muy importante*, and Estrella reminded her mistress that she had left the house with Harry Clark last night, to go to the restaurant, and that Harry Clark had come back to the house and told Estrella that he and Mrs. Wells had had an argument and that she'd run away, and that he couldn't find her. And then Estrella had called the police.

Officer Abe Reynolds told another part of the story. That after Estrella's call they'd gone over to Mr. Clark's house and gotten him up. He told them he'd pulled off the road, that he and Honoria were arguing about which restaurant to go to, the argument had escalated to a shouting match, and that Honoria, furious, had slammed out of the car right by the Trout Creek waterfall. He told them Honoria had been drinking. Harry said he'd waited a few minutes, then had gone in search of her. Not finding her, he'd assumed she'd thumbed a ride home, and he'd driven to Honoria's house to ask the servants. Then he'd gone home to bed.

The police had then driven to the Trout Creek waterfall. They'd searched the area, looked in the pool below the falls, but hadn't seen a body. They'd assumed, if Mr. Clark's story was correct, that Honoria had indeed thumbed a ride with someone, and was perhaps spending the night at a friend's house. This morning, if no one had heard from her, they were going to get into the pool and search the banks and bring Harry in for questioning.

Honoria told about banging on the door of a house, and an old man letting her sleep in his living room, then driving her to the hospital. "That's old Smitty, he's kind of simple-minded, but he's a good soul," Officer Abe said. "Keeps a few chickens, sells eggs. He sure was worried about you."

"He saved my life," Honoria told them.

Abe Reynolds tried, again, to talk Honoria through her side of the story. She and Mr. Clark were going to a restaurant. They were driving in Mr. Clark's car. Honoria thought she'd fallen asleep, she'd had two big drinks. Oh, yes, it was coming back now. She'd woken up in the car, and Harry had his hand raised, and there was something in his hand covered in white, and he'd smashed her on the side of the head with it . . . and then she'd woken up in some water. No, she and Harry Clark hadn't had an argument, she'd been dozing.

Abe showed Honoria a white handkerchief that they'd found clinging to some brambles, and told her that up on the little hill overlooking the waterfall and the pool they'd found footprints sunk way down, as if someone had been standing there holding something heavy, like a body . . . Did that handkerchief look familiar?

Honoria looked at the white-linen handkerchief that she'd given Harry. Something clicked. "Harry Clark was trying to kill me," she told Estrella and Abe Reynolds and the doctor and the nurse. "I'd told him earlier that I'd included him in my will, then later on I told him I wanted to go away for a few months and think things out. He decided to kill me before I had a chance to change my will back again."

"Just like Mrs. Estrella figured," Abe said. "She told us a bit about Mr. Clark. Mr. Clark has quite a reputation. Not for killing. He usually tries to blackmail 'em. But we haven't been able to catch him. Yet. If you'll sign a statement saying Harry Clark tried to kill you, we can arrest him."

"Bring me a pen and some paper," Honoria said.

Charly sat at his desk in the little office beyond the kitchen and made lists. He made a list of the specials that he would offer in the restaurant this evening (braised lamb shanks; short ribs in red wine; pasta with creamy vegetables) and he made a list to telephone in to Elmo Richards, who would deliver tomorrow. Had Elmo found another Gorgonzola cheese? If not, they would have to substitute, they needed a blue-veined cheese for Walter Maxwell's big cocktail party on Saturday night . . . the lists went on and on.

Benny appeared in the doorway. "We're offering chicken noodle soup and Scotch broth for lunch, right, Charly? And I've just made two egg pies, and now I'm going to cut the potatoes for french fries. Anything else?"

Charly thought for a bit. "The leftover pork, is there enough to offer hot pork sandwiches? We could offer them as a special, with mushroom gravy, which you could make."

The kitchen door banged open, and a voice called, "Hello? Hello?"

Benny looked out. "Why, it's Julius."

"Julius!" Charly exclaimed. "What are you doing here? Why are you not at work in Albany?" Julius took off his jacket. He was dressed in jeans and a tee shirt: his cooking uniform.

"The police called me about Honoria. Have you heard what happened?"

"Mon Dieu," Charly said when Julius had finished his story. He reached for his dropper bottle of Dr. Bach remedies and plopped a few drops onto his tongue. "They think this Mr. Clark tried to kill her?"

"That's what they know. Honoria signed a statement."

"And she is still in the hospital?"

"Well, right now, she is. But I think she's going home this afternoon. They want to keep her, but she won't stay. When has anyone been able to tell my aunt anything?" Julius chuckled. "She's got her lawyer, her masseur, and her nutritionist all lined up, and she's telling them about bad Harry Clark. She's been on the telephone all morning."

"We must send something," Charly fussed. "Let me see, some fruit? A bottle of champagne?"

"No booze," Julius said. "That's the last thing she needs. She's excited enough already; we need something to calm her down. She's treating this like an opening at an art gallery: something to celebrate, a big event. Someone tried to kill her—a first. Hey, Benny, your Scotch broth about heated up? Let me take a container of that. Then, maybe you can send some flowers to her house, she'd love that."

"Excellent," Charly agreed, noting that the flower shop that he used was right next door to The Paint Barrel, Win and Morty's place, and that this would be the perfect excuse to drop in and question Win further about his dead lady. Perhaps he should call Stark, too, and tell him about his conversation with Jean Maille.

Yes, the more he thought about it, Charly must call Stark. There was, even he realized, a limit to his own detecting skills. He must show Stark the pen and the other clues he'd found at the fire; he must tell him his suspicions about Peter Vann.

But not right now. Right now, he had to go to Walter Maxwell's. He'd promised to stop in and present the final list of foods for the big cocktail party on Saturday. Charly smiled as he remembered the lobster and steak dinner last night that Walter's friends had thought so highly of. This cocktail party would be another exemplary culinary event. He wondered if Walter's friends would still be here. They might look like garbagemen, but they clearly knew a thing or two about fine meals.

CHAPTER TWENTY-ONE

A Small
Disagreement

When Walter, Ricky, and Marty drove back to Walter's house after that incredible dinner at La Fermette, Ricky told Walter he and Marty had very serious doubts about doing Charly.

First of all, Ricky loved the guy's food and to pop someone who made such great lobster, not to mention shrimp, steak sauce, creamy potatoes, salad dressing, and flourless chocolate cake, was a crime. The man was world-class.

Second, Charly was obviously well respected, and Ricky felt that the police would make a big effort to find his killer. "It's not like he's some worm that everybody, cops included, are glad he's gone."

"Sleep on it," Walter told them, not showing his annoyance. He'd see them for breakfast. They could make their final decision then.

But the next morning, Richard Zampone and Martin Scungilli were of one mind: To kill Charly would be a big mistake. Doing Charly was a big no.

"Ya know Big Walt," Little Ricky told Walter, "I'm nearly fifty. Bernice and me have a terrific pension plan. We got savings up the kazoo. We don't need the cash, the aggravation."

Marty noted that he had a good pension plan, too. He'd already bought a house in Hallandale, Florida, with two lemon trees in his backyard. No, sorry, but the decision was made. They would not terminate Charly Poisson.

Ricky and Marty had privately decided that Walter was losing it—going soft in the head. This wanting to kill the restaurant guy—that clinched it. Big Walt was senile. Of course, they didn't tell Walter.

Charly drove to Walter's house and parked in front of the farm office. He knocked on the door. No answer. The lights were on, he could hear a vacuum cleaner. He opened the door.

Marian Arnold was vacuuming the floor. "Allo," Charly called. Marian looked up, saw Charly, and turned off the machine.

"Yes? Help you?" There was no recognition in Marian's blank eyes.

"I have appointment with Mr. Maxwell." Charly stared at Marian. There was something unpleasant about this woman. She wasn't at all like the Jehovah's Witnesses, earnest but harmless, who had, in the past, knocked on his door. *She has a look of evil,* Charly thought dramatically. Then an idea popped into his head: *Could Marian Arnold have killed my lady?*

Marian's knocking on his door with that feeble excuse about the Bible, Charly decided, was part of a plan: After all, he had discovered the woman's body. Surely the murderer, knowing this, would be nervous. She'd wanted to feel him out, find out what he knew.

"He's still up at the house," Marian said. "He'll be right down."

"And Mr. Tom, your husband?"

"He's gone into town, doing some errands for Mr. Maxwell." Charly thought, *she wants to get me alone here.* He felt quite nervous. He was convinced, suddenly, that

Marian was the killer of his lady. Nervously, he watched her start packing up her vacuum cleaner.

Charly fingered the little flashlight in his pocket. If worse came to worst, it would not be a bad weapon of defense. Marian didn't seem interested in attacking him right then, so Charly, intending to trap her into an admission of guilt, said very loudly, "I can see that the Bible is a book filled with death and destruction and killing."

Marian frowned. What in goodness was the man talking about? Was he liquored up, like Tom? She shifted her feet uneasily. She didn't like this man.

Charly tried another tack. He said craftily, "What is the name of your church? In case I would like to join?"

Marian said uneasily, "New Awakenings Church. Pastor Pflugg."

"And you knock on people's doors? To get them to read the Bible?"

"The Bible has all the answers. People can find comfort in the Bible. The end of the world's coming soon, and them that reads the Bible will be saved."

"Yes, yes, I see," Charly said. "The end of the world. That is why you must kill the unbelievers. *Smite the infidel.*" Charly shouted this. "Like the woman in my field."

Marian was confused. "What woman in what field?" She was accustomed to Pastor Pflugg's shouting from the pulpit, but he said things that made her feel comfortable. The sinners were always "they," never her. This man made her feel all katty wumpus, as her grandmother used to say.

Luckily, Walter Maxwell came in the door and Marian, after a terrified look at Charly, grabbed her vacuum cleaner and fled. "Marian's not quite right in the head," Walter told Charly. "But she's a good cleaner."

"She looks like an evil woman to me," Charly said. "Has she ever tried to convert you to her Bible? Or is that a ruse."

Walter snorted. "A ruse? No, I'm sure it's not. But no Bible talk in my house or she's out, she knows that. She belongs to some dumb cult."

Charly felt his fear ebb. He wouldn't tell Walter that he suspected Marian of being a killer, not until he got more proof. He produced the contract: "I want to go over the food, just so we are in agreement."

"Of course," Walter agreed. "Let's have that menu again."

Charly cleared his throat. "A round of Gorgonzola, surrounded by slices of pear and onion sticks. The filet mignon, on rounds of French bread, toasted; the miniature crabcake with toothpicks, and a mayonnaise of curry and herbs; small salmon roses, to be eaten on rounds of black pumpernickel, buttered. The garlic shrimp with toothpicks and garlic dip; the steak tartare on rounds of rye bread; miniature quiche; the two tins of Ossetra caviar, surrounded by chopped onion, chopped egg, and snipped chives."

Charly put down his list and continued. "Then as for time: the catering team arrive at four to set up, and I will come too and stay until six or so, when I will go back to my restaurant until seven; then I return to your party."

Walter sat at his desk, staring at Charly. He sensed that Charly had come here to interrogate him about Candy, that Charly knew far more than he was telling. Walter felt confused and angry.

"Wait a minute. I thought you'd be here the entire time." Walter's face had drained of color; his lips were a thin line. Spoiling for a fight.

Charly felt uneasy. He'd seen Walter like this before: that time when customers were sitting in Walter's favorite banquette and Walter had shouted for Charly to move them. Charly had refused, Walter quieted down. *Keep your dignity*, Charly told himself. Walter, like a child, was having a temper tantrum.

"No, Walter. It is all written out in the contract." Charly spoke slowly, clearly. "We do it just like we did it last year, and the year before that. From six to seven, I must be at my restaurant to greet my own guests. I am with you from seven o'clock on . . ."

Walter's face had become a thundercloud. Charly was trying to trick him in some way. "You were here the entire time last year. That's what I pay you for. To be here. Every single solitary fucking minute."

Charly shrugged. Never argue with a customer. But never give in, either. "I am sorry that we are not in agreement . . ."

"In agreement?" Walter shouted. "This party's costing me five big ones, and you're talking about not being in agreement?"

"The party is costly because you rent from Party Rentals, the most expensive firm in Albany, and because you order the most expensive foods on my party list. The caviar alone is over six hundred dollar."

There were a lot of Walters out there, and Charly had dealt with many of them: backing out of contracts, refusing to pay the final installment because "It wasn't what we'd agreed," paying with dud checks, or calling the bank afterward to cancel the check—oh, yes. He sighed. "It is all in the contract. I don't deceive my customer. I have been in business for many years."

"You know what you can do with your contract?" Walter grabbed the papers, ripped them up, and threw the pieces in the air. He turned, shouted, "You don't fuck with me, buster," and stalked out.

Charly sat, stunned. Poor Walter. He seemed to be going through some sort of crisis. Perhaps a nervous breakdown? Perhaps he has lost money in the stock market? Something was going on. A minute later, Tom Arnold walked in. "Oh, Mr. Charly. You waiting for Walter? I just saw him stormin' up to the house. Looked mad as anything."

"We have just had a small disagreement."

Tom sniggered. "Yeah, I'll bet. He's been real weird, lately."

"How, weird?"

"Real jumpy. Loses his temper all the time. Yelled at me cause I couldn't find something; says he's got to do something, leaves, then comes back and says he forgot what he was going to do; forgot an appointment the other day with some buyers—I had to go into town, chase him down."

"*Ah, la la.* Perhaps he have a lot on his mind?"

"And the cops come out the other day, just routine they said, and he really went crazy after that." Tom didn't mention that he'd panicked, too.

Charly drove back to his restaurant. Julius and Benny were preparing lunch. He told them about his disagreement with Walter.

Benny was shocked. "You mean, he's going to back out at the last minute? Just like that? Why, that's crazy. People don't behave like that."

"So you might not have a party?" Julius asked. "After getting all the food in? Guy's nuts. Who's going to call his guests, tell them the party's off?"

"Ah, Julius. It is like this in the restaurant business. People change their minds. Is very difficult. You who want to open an inn, you must be aware of these things. The general public is not reliable."

Julius nodded. "I'm beginning to find that out." Then he grinned. "Is the great detective going to find out what's really happening in Walter's mind? The great psychiatrist, I should say."

"Oh, Julius, you make the joke."

The telephone rang, and Benny picked up. "For you, Charly. A Mister Chenny from Boston."

"Ah, Andre Chenier. I will take it in my office."

". . . and I speak to my waiter at great length," Andre was saying in French, "and he knows nothing about a Houghton family, but he remembered quite a bit about a Mr. Maxwell. Here, I will put him on."

After formal greetings had been exchanged, Charly explained that the name of the man might have been Talbott, not Houghton, but he wasn't sure. Had a Mr. Talbott been involved in a hunting accident?

"Yes, yes," the waiter recalled. "Now that was *Le Grand Scandale*. A Monsieur Talbott used to come to Café du Midi with a man named Maxwell. The Maxwell man was reputed to be part of the underworld, tall, handsome, tip very well, very polite. *Un gangster*, nonetheless. But popular with the waiters. Very polite, gave magnificent dinners, once he tipped the chef a thousand dollars. Everyone love Monsieur Maxwell."

"And Monsieur Talbott," Charly asked. "What was he like?"

"A man of little personality, though the Talbott family was an old and distinguished one. But the man was under the thumb of this Maxwell, that was plain for all to see."

"And the scandal?"

"All that was ever known was that the man Maxwell killed Monsieur Talbott in a hunting accident. There was a trial, and Monsieur Maxwell was acquitted. There were witnesses attesting to the fact that Monsieur Talbott had gotten in the line of fire, that he'd been drinking. It was ruled an accident."

"But what was suspected?" Charly asked.

"What was *suspected* was that Monsieur Talbott had angered the Mob in some way: he was often drunk; he bragged about his connections with the Mafia. The talk was that Monsieur Talbott had been deliberately murdered."

There was funny business afoot, but Charly couldn't figure out what it was. That such an epicure as Walter Maxwell could also be murderer was something that Charly, in his innocence, found hard to believe. And yet, why not? History was filled with epicurean murderers— look at the horrific Astyages in Herodotus' *Persian Wars*, who killed the son of Harpagus, cut him up into bite-sized pieces, roasted him, then fed the child to his own father. The Frenchman Gourier was more subtle: He killed men by feeding them many rich meals, so that they expired from liver failure. Gourier himself, Charly recalled, was finally hoist by his own petard, when he tried to feast an executioner to death and himself died of a surfeit of steak. Yes, Charly thought, it would indeed be possible for Walter Maxwell to kill someone. He must investigate Walter Maxwell's background further. But not at the moment. And as for Jimmy Houghton, well, what was there to say? Poor Jimmy. A tragic childhood.

"Will you stay here for a few days?" Charly asked Julius.

"Yes, I told Honoria I'd stay through the weekend, but that I'd cook here, if it's okay with you. Now, is everything ready? It's almost lunchtime."

Benny came back from the cold room. "Show me where you put that cheese, Charly, in case you go out. You said you put it on the shelf by the door, but I can't find it."

"Of course it is there," Charly said. "Come, I will show you."

CHAPTER TWENTY-TWO

+-+-+-+-+-+-+

Making Visits

+-+-+-+-+-+-+

Charly and Benny stood in the cold room, looking at the shelf where the cheese had been placed. "Is gone," Charly affirmed.

"Maybe someone moved it," Benny said. "Who'd steal a bag marked 'DO NOT EAT—POISON'?"

Charly shrugged. "It will turn up. Maybe Mick take it downstairs, to the big refrigerator. I will look later, after lunch."

But after lunch Charly, in the confusion of worrying about Walter's party, had forgotten about the cheese. Benny went off to his gym, Julius went to the hospital to bring his aunt home, and Charly, finally, was going to sit at his desk and pay bills, make lists, go over the menu. There was a knock on the door.

"Monsieur Poisson?"

"Yes? Ah, it is Monsieur Tigre, who work at the Vanns'. Your family name I do not recall."

"Cavett, Tiger Cavett. I've come to ask if you need anyone in your kitchen, or in your dining room or bar. I'm looking for another job."

"But you just start at the Vanns'."

"It's not working out," Tiger said briefly.

"Ah?"

"No, they want a maid of all work. This morning, when
Mrs. Vann asked me to wash out her silk underwear, I
quit."

"Come into my office," Charly said, chuckling. "Ah,
those Vanns. The *nouveaux riches* never keep servants.
They have no respect."

Once seated with coffee, Tiger expounded. Mr. Vann
downed a shot of schnapps every single morning and
wasn't sober the entire day—Tiger felt like a nurse shep-
herding him around, half-crocked. Mrs. Vann, besides
wanting her underwear washed, wanted Tiger to bring her
tea and toast every morning in bed. "And there's something
else. I gather you found a woman's body buried in your
fields?"

"Yes, that is so."

"Well, the night of their party, I overheard them talking.
They know who she is. Mrs. Vann asked Mr. if he'd killed
her, and Mr. said no, that she must know someone else up
here."

"Ah-ha," Charly said. "Did you hear the woman's
name?"

"No, I didn't. Someone who worked for Mr. Vann. I
don't really mind him, he's a laid-back guy. But Mrs. is not
a nice lady at all. Just a petty snob."

Charly agreed. "Mrs. is a different type. Now, as far as
a job. At present, I do not need anyone. But leave me your
name and telephone number, you never know. Do you have
a résumé?"

Tiger presented a neatly typed page.

Charly was impressed. "You are not afraid of hard
work, I see—dishwasher, sous-chef, barman, waiter,
chauffeur, gardener."

"Start low, aim high, that's my motto." Tiger grinned.

"Well," Charly said, "there is a lady, one of my customer, she is aunt to Julius, my weekend cook. Rich lady, in hospital now, but I hear she just lose her farm manager. Perhaps you could wait for a few days, then call her? I give you her name, Mrs. Wells, also the name of Mr. and Mrs. Crisp and a few others." Charly scribbled away, checking his Rolodex from time to time.

"Let me hear from you," Charly urged, as Tiger took his leave. Charly had no sooner sat down at his desk and pulled out his big checkbook, when the telephone rang.

Patty Perkins was crying. "Oh, Charly, have you heard about Linda Okun's boy, Robby?"

"Yes, that he is in hospital with a broken leg."

"Charly, he's dead."

Charly slumped down in a chair. "*Oh, mon Dieu.*"

"A nurse found him Wednesday evening around five, he was curled up in bed with a pillow over his head. She thought he was asleep. They don't know if it was an accident, or what. Maybe he was strangled, maybe he choked on something, maybe he had a bad reaction to some medication. The funeral's Saturday afternoon. I told Linda I'd send over desserts."

Charly called Linda, completely overcome. For a child to die was surely one of the world's great tragedies. After expressing his condolences, he told Linda he would deliver food. Just like in France, people here gathered after a funeral to talk, eat, offer sympathy. "Some roast beef, some ham, baked beans, enough for a crowd." Linda was still in shock, and Charly didn't question her. He simply repeated that the food was taken care of.

Charly called his butcher and ordered meats for the funeral, then he went to his basement to check his big refrigerator: He'd suddenly remembered about the cheese, but there was no cheese. Freezer, no cheese. He rechecked the cold room next to the kitchen: between a crate of celery and the wall, Charly found a crumpled sheet of paper: DO NOT EAT—POISON, the paper said. It was ripped in half.

Charly remembered that Tommy Glade had found a glass in his sink, yesterday. Could Maurice have come in, as he sometimes did after lunch, had a drink, and taken the cheese? Charly called Maurice. No answer. Charly drove up to Maurice and Barbara's house and pounded on the front door, then went around to the kitchen and pounded on the door, there. Nothing. Charly peered in the garage: Maurice's Mercedes was there, Barbara's sand-colored Cadillac was not. Should he try and force the door? No. "Ah, well, it will not kill him," Charly reasoned. "But it may make him sick, and teach him a lesson."

There was only one place that Charly could go to get information about Robby Okun, and that was Steak Heaven. Charly decided to stop in for an espresso before driving the three miles into Hogton to visit Win Crozier and Morty Cohen at their shop, The Paint Barrel, and ordering flowers for Honoria Wells. He checked his watch. No time to waste.

Rex was not at his restaurant but Bobby Matucci was behind the bar (did he *live* behind the bar?) and he told Charly the latest news from Vince.

"Kid was all doped up, some marks around his neck. Coulda been choked to death. On the other hand, he could have gone into anaphylactic shock, started to choke, grabbed his own throat, trying to breathe, Vince said. Them tranks and painkillers are terrible, I wouldn't take 'em for anything." Bobby shuddered. "Kid probably didn't even know what was happening."

"You right, those painkillers are terrible." Charly said. "One time, a doctor prescribe an antidepressant for me, I take one pill, I sleep for two days."

But Bobby wasn't interested in Charly's medical problems. "The trouble is," he continued in a low voice, "according to the nurse who talked to Vince, place is understaffed, they don't even know when the kid died. One nurse said she checked late in the afternoon, kid was asleep, she thought; then the orderly came round with the supper trays, he thought the kid looked funny, and he notified the nurses. They'll do an autopsy, of course."

"And the hospital, it is cautious, because of lawsuit," Charly concluded.

"Vince got a list of people on the same floor, and guess what?"

"What?"

"All old, senile people except for Walter Maxwell," Bobby said. "Why would Mr. Maxwell kill a kid like that? Doesn't make sense. Of course, maybe one of the old people went crazy, I've heard they sometimes do that."

"Does Maxwell know Robby?" Charly gulped the rest of his espresso.

"Vince is going to ask Robby's folks. Tune in tomorrow, Charly. Oh, hi, Tom, what brings you in here, this time of day?" Tom Arnold had just walked in, and he sat down at the bar in the seat vacated by Charly.

"Just time for a quick one, Bobby," Tom said. "I'm in town getting some stuff for Mr. M. And I need this . . ." Bobby drew a mug of beer and placed it on the bar. "Mr. M's going crazy, and at home, my wife's going crazy, too. All this Bible talk about revenge, and punishing people, I can't stand it."

Something is going to happen, Charly thought, as he left the bar. His nose was tingling: a sure sign of trouble.

At The Paint Barrel, Win and Morty were happy to talk to Charly, since there were no customers. Win apologized: They'd forgotten all about Charly's dead woman. A company had shipped the wrong paint, they'd had to drive to Red Hook on a consultation, they'd had to dust and vacuum the store themselves, since Marian Arnold didn't come last night, hadn't called or anything, though she was usually so reliable.

"We know you want to identify her," Win told Charly, "So we'll really try to think who she might be. I wouldn't count on the police."

"Does the name Candy mean anything to you? I speak with a restaurateur I know in New York and he . . ." Charly decided not to go into the Peter Vann angle. Now that really was grounds for a lawsuit, defamation of character. "He say that he remember a famous model with a birthmark near her eye called Candy, back in the sixties."

"Candy? Bianca? Carmen? Twiggy? Maybe," Morty said. "I was with a big florist, then, we provided flowers for lots of fashion photographers, I knew all the names, way back then. I'll think."

"We could call John Stark," Win suggested. "Maybe we will, when we've thought. But I hate to bother him if we've got nothing concrete."

Charly thanked the two men, then told them he was going next door to order flowers for Honoria Wells, that she was in the hospital.

"Oh, poor lady, I hope it's nothing serious," Win said indifferently. Honoria bought her paint elsewhere, and moved in a different crowd.

"Nothing serious," Charly said, and left the store.

"Now, here's a lovely orchid plant, *Dendrobium aggregatum*," Mr. Hitchcock, the florist, told Charly. "Very easy to take care of. And look at that flower spray. Isn't it luscious?" The florist hefted the plant onto the counter, so Charly could admire. It was only a foot high, but the clay pot was heavy. Charly breathed in. Marvelous. The scented, vivid flowers hung down from the big, fleshy leaves in sprays of yellow blooms.

"It is for Mrs. Honoria Wells, she has been ill," Charly said.

Mr. Hitchcock peered at Charly through his bifocals. "She hasn't been ill, that Harry Clark tried to kill her," he told Charly. "And you know, and I know, that she probably deserved it." Mr. Hitchcock tutted. "At her age."

"She is a good customer of mine," Charly said briefly.

"She is a good customer of mine, too," Mr. Hitchcock said. "So we'll say no more, agreed? Since it's Mrs. Wells, our good customer, I'll put the orchid in a basket and decorate it with Spanish moss, free of charge. And I'll deliver it this afternoon, to her house. She got out of the hospital, already. Doctors wanted to keep her, she kicked up a big fuss."

"How," Charly asked, "do you know all of this?"

"My deliveryman's girlfriend is a nurse; you'd be surprised at all the stuff I know."

CHAPTER TWENTY-THREE

Maurice's Muffler

✛✛✛✛✛✛✛

Business always picked up on Thursdays. Tonight was no exception.

"And guess who's coming to display her wounds?" Julius chuckled.

Charly paused in the making of curry mayonnaise: "Not your aunt. Why, she is just out of hospital."

Julius laughed and nodded, and his halo of curls bounced. "She's bringing the Vanns. Harry's in jail, so she feels safe. She's had guys beat her up, she's had guys try to con her out of her money, but this is the first time someone's actually tried to kill her. She's loving it, all the attention."

"The first thing that she should do," Charly counseled, "is to tear up her will. If Harry were to get out . . . or have a friend kill her . . ."

"Our first stop out of the hospital was Jonathan Murray's office," Julius confided. "She ripped up her newly made will. She may be a flake, but she isn't a fool where money's concerned. Well, most of the time."

"She should take lessons in self-defense," Benny said.

"My aunt lives on another planet, Benny; she's a member of royalty. She should take lessons in reality. Here's a woman who's always had money. Never had to worry about paying her bills. Can you imagine?"

"I can't imagine," Benny said. "It's all I can do to pay off my motorcycle."

"And guess who she wanted to make the beneficiary of her new will?"

"You?" Charly and Benny both said.

"You got it. I said, no thanks. And have her playing games with my head? Being rich is worse than a disease." Julius gave the veal cutlets he was pounding a resounding whack.

"I wish I was rich," Benny said, stirring a mushroom cream sauce.

"So do all young people." Charly sighed. "But there is more to life than being rich. When you become rich, then what? People try to steal from you."

"I'd like to be wise and rich," Benny said. "And a black belt."

"And I'd like to be a nineteen-year-old sous-chef," Julius said, laughing.

It would be an early evening, Charly predicted. The dining room was three-quarters filled, and no more customers were arriving.

At eight o'clock, Charly put on his white jacket and toque and went out into the dining room. He bowed deeply to Honoria, Peter, and Dinah.

Dinah was wearing too many sapphires and diamonds, but Honoria, sensing the drama of simplicity, wore a simple white-cashmere tunic which showed off her tan. She wore little makeup. Her bruised face was still arrestingly handsome, and she'd arranged her pale blond hair into a simple chignon. She looked like the heroine of a Greek tragedy—Jocasta, perhaps, having learned that her husband Oedipus was in reality her son. Her posture was superb. Charly sensed that, having made a fool of herself, Honoria was out to demonstrate that her dignity was still intact.

Regally, Honoria inclined her head toward Charly. "That orchid plant is lovely, Charly dear. Harry used to bring long-stemmed red roses—so dull."

Charly bowed, as if in the presence of royalty. He felt that to mention his dead woman would be inappropriate, but he was anxious to draw Peter out. Peter and Marian Arnold were still his two chief suspects.

"I am delighted you survived the attempt to kill you, madame," Charly said to Honoria. And then, with a sidelong glance at Peter, "It must be quite terrible to kill someone. I cannot imagine such a thing."

"I can't imagine it either," Peter said. "All these shoot-em-ups on TV, they give people the idea that killing's okay. Bang, you're dead. So simple." Peter, surprisingly, seemed sober. He was drinking club soda. "Harry Clark fits the bill. I interviewed him once."

Charly, Dinah, and Honoria all exclaimed, "You did?"

"When?" Dinah said. "I didn't know that."

"You were in Mexico, after you had your eyes done. It was last winter."

"Good heavens," Dinah said. "And you never said a word."

"And during the whole interview," Peter continued, "that guy didn't look me in the eye, once. Shifty. But you should have seen him looking around the house—like an appraiser. Nope, didn't like that guy at all."

Charly had another idea. "You think he killed the lady I found?"

Peter said, "But did he even know her? Harry's not a professional killer. He's just dumb as two planks."

Charly tapped his lips with his index finger. "Win Crozier and Morty Cohen think she look familiar, my dead lady. Did you, Monsieur Vann, think she look familiar in the photograph the police show?"

"She might have," Peter said evasively. "Looked like a woman worked for me long ago. But, you know, you can always find resemblances."

"Can you, indeed?" Charly said. He cleared his throat to continue.

But Peter had lost interest in the conversation. He

mopped up some sauce with a piece of bread. "Damn good,"
he told Charly.

"Both Madame Wells and the lady I find are bashed on
the head," Charly mused. He'd pursue the dead woman's
identity with Peter at another time. "The same *modus
operandi*, if you will permit me."

Honoria said, "Why don't you call Stark and tell him
that, Charly?"

"Stark can figure out," Charly said. "He think that I
meddle."

"Listen to me, Charly," Peter said. "Stay out of the cops'
hair. If you don't, they'll try to pin something on you. Your
dead lady might have been killed by Harry Clark, but
frankly I doubt that. I think it was a drug killing. Especially
considering Hogton's reputation. But it's not your problem."

"Maybe we could get the FBI involved," Honoria said.
"All those delicious-looking tough men."

Peter snorted. "Probably all gays. You know why J. Edgar
Hoover told everyone the Cosa Nostra was a figment of
their imaginations?"

Charly, Honoria, and Dinah shook their heads.

"The gossip was that Hoover, who was gay, had been
photographed in the nude with young men, and the mob
threatened to show the snapshots around if Hoover started
an investigation into the Mafia."

"*Tiens,*" Charly said. "Imagine." He'd heard the same
story, years ago.

Honoria, nettled that the conversation was drawing away
from her, said, "Well, tomorrow I'm going to call John Stark
and tell him I think Harry killed your dead woman. I want
him put away for a long, long time."

Dinah, currying favor, said, "Tell us again, Honny dear,
just what you felt like when you woke up . . ." and Charly
bowed and moved away.

In his big white house on the hill, Maurice Baleine sat at
his kitchen counter, nibbling on that wonderful Gorgonzola,

sipping scotch. Earlier, he'd lain down in the living room. He was feeling strange—so hot he was burning up, yet shivering. He looked at his Patek Philippe: half past three in the morning, but the morning of what day? Time seemed to undulate, fast, slow, fast, slow, like that painting of wavy watches by Dali in the Museum of Modern Art in New York. He was having trouble getting his breath. Shapes seemed to be materializing around him, perhaps spies? Ghosts?

With the paranoia that often accompanies a drinking spree, Maurice felt distinctly edgy. But being a Princeton man, Maurice knew that he could beat the bad guys. *Take a walk in the moonlight,* Maurice thought.

Maurice, dressed in his Burberry and deerstalker, and carrying a flashlight, stumbled from his house and started walking down the driveway.

Now, as opposed to his last walk when time seemed to fly, Maurice's feet appeared stuck in glue. It felt like he'd been walking forever, and he hadn't even reached the end of the drive. Nevertheless, he walked until he came to the fork in the road. He'd walk to Charly's house, then come back. He didn't want to rouse Charly. His legs felt heavy. At last, Charly's little farmhouse loomed up in the mist. Maurice did a double take.

There was an old beat-up car parked in the bushes just beyond Charly's driveway. Was someone visiting Charly? Did Charly have a mistress? Or perhaps a man? Maurice's feelings of superiority over Charly grew. Now, when Charly said (as he so often did), "Now, Maurice, I will talk to you like Dutch *oncle*," and gave him a lecture on drinking, Maurice could counter with, "Now, I speak to *you* like Dutch *oncle*," and give Charly a lecture on getting sexually involved with the locals, so tacky. Really, it was killingly funny. Maurice gave an inebriated chuckle. Suddenly, everything was so funny. He, Maurice, could laugh and laugh.

Very quietly, Maurice crept around the back of Charly's house. There was that little shed, maybe there was a ladder in the shed, he could put the ladder against the house, creep up, look in Charly's bedroom window.

But what was that odd smell? It smelled like a gas station. Now why would the back of Charly's house smell like a gas station? He wouldn't store gasoline in his shed, it was too close to his house.

Maurice sniffed, and sniffed some more—just as with a great whoosh flames erupted at the side of the shed and Maurice collided with a figure, someone running, panting, pushing at him, knocking him down, down, down. Maurice grabbed at the figure, trying to stay upright, but his hands became caught in something woolly and he fell heavily to the ground. The person above him struggled, wriggled out of something, and then was gone, feet pounding. Moments later, a car started.

Maurice, winded, lay on the ground, watching the yellow-red talons of flame reach up to the sky, heard the roar of the flames, so noisy and crackling they seemed to hum. Maurice wondered if he had stumbled into Dante's Inferno. Was this the price you paid for drinking?

The sky was lit up with an orange glare. Maurice wondered if it was the end of the world. The heat made him gasp and the smoke made him gag. He scrambled up as the sparks burst like firecrackers. Maurice stumbled to Charly's back door, and pounded on it, screaming, "Charly, Charly, fire, fire."

Charly, a little figure wrapped in a woolen bathrobe, unlocked the back door and Maurice fell inside. "Dial 9-1-1, your shed, your shed."

"Yes," Charly said breathlessly, "the light woke me up, and the noise." He turned to the telephone and dialed 9-1-1. Maurice was filling cooking pots with water at the sink. He had sobered up considerably.

Charly hurried outside and dived into a blanket of smoke. He was thankful that he hadn't put his hose away for the winter. He turned on the water and began spraying the back of his house, so that the sparks couldn't ignite the dry timber. The old shed was gone, nothing could save it now.

Maurice threw his pots of water at the house's foundation, then ran into the house to refill the pots. In the distance was the wail of the fire engines. Charly kept spraying the back of the house until the firemen arrived. They dragged hoses to the burning shed, as more and more cars pulled up.

"What is that, wrapped around your arm?" Charly asked Maurice. They were standing to the side, as the firemen played their giant hoses on the shed.

"My arm?" Maurice looked down. "Oh, my God, I grabbed at someone running from your shed, and my hand got caught in this thing."

"Who was this person?"

"I couldn't see," Maurice wailed. "He was running so fast, and he knocked me down, but I could hear him panting, huh, huh, huh, almost like a woman, huh-huh-huh, like that." Maurice illustrated.

"Are you sure it was a man? Or was it a boy?"

"I'm not sure of anything," Maurice said. "Someone about my height (Maurice was five-foot-ten) and sturdy, you know, not fat but sturdy."

Harold Tibbetts, the fire chief, materialized out of the smoke. He stood next to Charly. "This's the person you saw?"

"Not exactly saw," Maurice said, "he bumped into me. And I grabbed this thing, must have been his. See?" Maurice held out a knitted muffler.

By then the flames had burned down. The shed was a skeleton of charred timbers, but the house had been saved. The firemen milled around.

"It's the arsonist for sure," Tibbetts said. "Gasoline, rags, he uses the same method, every time. Just thank your stars it wasn't your restaurant."

"Or your house," Rex Cingale said.

"Yes," Charly said, "I do. I thank God. I am safe, my cats are safe."

Stark had arrived, big, somber, scowling. "Mind if we go into your kitchen, Charly? I want to see that muffler Maurice grabbed."

Inside the kitchen, Stark examined the muffler. It was knitted, bright green, acrylic. It had a slight smell, a trace of body odor. Maurice couldn't remember anything else about the person running away. "Except for that huh-huh-huh panting. Not like a man."

"You think it was a kid?" Stark asked. Maurice shrugged.

"What about the car?"

"Just an old car, kind of beat-up, must have been a light color, grey or light brown, I couldn't tell the make. A small car, though, a compact."

It's a wonder he saw anything at all, Stark thought, almost getting drunk from smelling Maurice. The booze was coming out of his pores.

"Where'd you see the car?" Stark asked Maurice.

"It was parked in the bushes, right over there. I was walking down the road, saw the car, thought Charly was entertaining someone . . ."

"At half past three in the morning?" Charly asked.

"Well, I don't know," Maurice said. "You wouldn't be the first."

Charly snorted.

"An old car," Stark said, "light color, kind of beat-up. You didn't notice the plates, did you?" Knowing the answer would be no, and it was.

Rex Cingale cleared his throat, put his hand on Stark's arm.

"Chief?"

"Yeah, Rex?"

"I seen that muffler before."

"Yeah?"

"I seen it tonight. Earlier. In the bar. Tom Arnold was wearing it around his neck. Said he was cold, coming down with the flu."

"Tom's a volunteer fireman," Stark said. "He's at almost every fire."

Rex looked around. "Well, he's not here, tonight."

CHAPTER TWENTY-FOUR

La Synchronicité

It was 7:00 A.M. when the firemen finally left, after drinking all the coffee Charly had in the house. He sat at his kitchen counter, dazed, sipping chamomile tea into which he'd dropped several of Dr. Bach's flower essences. He felt like someone had taken a hammer to his brain. His back ached, too. He must telephone Dr. Regan, his chiropractor. And he must telephone Mrs. Whaley, to order more Bach remedies: olive for exhaustion, elm for feeling overwhelmed. And perhaps chestnut bud, for making the same mistakes over and over. Why couldn't he leave well enough alone? Why must he constantly pry? The arsonist, whoever he was, had obviously taken exception to his investigations: Now look at the result.

Maurice had stumbled home—no doubt to swig down more scotch. Stark had smiled when Charly told him old Doc Ross's story, that Tom Arnold had burned down an old house. "I burned the house down, too, Charly."

"You!"

"Yeah, there was a bunch of us. It was the old Burnell place, empty for years. So, we did just what the arsonist is doing, we got some gasoline, and stuffed newspapers around the foundation and set light to it."

"*Mon Dieu.* You, Chief Stark."

"Just for kicks. That's the way kids are. They never think. And," Stark continued, "it just about scared us half to death. That place went up like a rocket. That's why I'm so afraid of fires, today. Tom's told me he is, too. He might be the arsonist, but I doubt it."

"I see," Charly said. "Then what about the muffler?"

"I don't know," Stark admitted. "We'll go question Tom now. But several firemen admitted to having mufflers like that, and I even think Betty bought a couple. They were on sale, at Wal-Mart. They had thousands."

Charly called his cats, but they were hiding. They weren't going out, today, and who could blame them?

He climbed the stairs to soak away his aches in a steaming bath. Friday was a busy day at La Fermette. Thank goodness Julius was here to help. And tomorrow was Walter Maxwell's party. Perhaps. Yesterday Walter had ripped up the contract. Charly chuckled. Was Walter capable of calling the party off, at this late date? Simply to contact all the people . . . madness. And what would he do—plead illness?

Before going to his restaurant, Charly drove over to the Klover Police Station to file a report on his fire, for the insurance. Vince Matucci, who evidently didn't share Stark's exasperation with Charly, took his statement, his estimate of the shed's worth, a list of its contents (spade, shovel, metal rake, bamboo rake, several other garden implements, about twenty bales of hay, trowels, four or five bags of kitty litter, half a cord of wood) and didn't seem averse to imparting information.

"We went over to Tom Arnold's house, Clem and me," Vince told Charly, "guy's sick, you could tell—red eyes, runny nose, feverish-looking. Says he wore a green muffler to work yesterday, he thinks, stopped in at Rex's, had a few beers, then came home, couldn't even eat supper."

"Ah, then he is really sick," Charly said. To miss a meal was serious.

"Marian gave him a couple aspirins, a hot-water bottle, and put him to bed. He woke up this morning, Marian's not there, her bed's made up. They're old-fashioned, still use twin beds, like a lot of folks."

Charly showed no interest in twin beds. "And the muffler?"

"Waal . . ." Matucci smiled, not a nice smile. "We couldn't find it."

"Ah-ha."

"We looked all over, even in Tom's pickup. He thinks he dropped it at Rex's, maybe in the parking lot."

"Could be," Charly said.

"But what the chief's worried about, is a lawyer would make mincemeat of that evidence. Maurice was so drunk he could hardly stand up. Says he grabbed the muffler but, we don't think it'd hold up in court."

"And the little Robby?"

Officer Vincent Matucci pursed his lips: "Chief wants that kept under wraps, for the time being."

"And my dead lady that I find?"

"We're pursuing various leads."

"Has the autopsy taken place, yet?"

"Doc Bingham's scheduled that for this afternoon."

Everything took so long . . . and Charly was impatient for results.

It was a morning of telephone calls: customers calling to ask about Charly's fire, customers calling for reservations, other calls as well: Charly called Walter Maxwell. No more "Walter." "Monsieur" from now on.

"Monsieur, is the party still on?"

"Yes, of course it's on," Walter said affably. "I just lost my temper for a minute." No apologies, Charly noticed.

Old Doc Ross called. He'd spoken to Hy Bingham, the coroner, who'd conducted Robby's autopsy (Robby was priority number one) and Bingham told Doc that slivers of glass had been found in the child's clothing and in the fold of his neck.

Doc continued. "Their guess is, it's from one of those old-fashioned glass carafes, the hospital still has a few hanging around. Robby's carafe was missing, so was a carafe in room 412—that was where Walter Maxwell stayed. But, you know, they're careless in hospitals, they might have forgotten to put the carafes out. They're under-staffed, might have to close down, I hear. Now they're trying to track down the nurse's aide who did that floor on Wednesday afternoon, she's supposed to note everything down. But she's away on a trip; they can't locate her."

"So now they think the boy was killed?"

"Oh, absolutely," Doc said. "At least, that's what Bingham said. Someone pressed on the carotid arteries on either side of his neck until he stopped breathing. Little bone, right in the little depression below the jaw, called the hyoid bone, it's snapped right in two, a sign of frontal manual strangulation."

"Robby was killed when someone press the arteries in his neck," Charly told Benny. "The police say it is murder."

Benny looked thoughtful. "You know, we learned those choke holds in self-defense. They look easy, but they're not. You need lots of practice. First of all, those arteries are hard to find. You have to know exactly where to press. And what's the other person going to do, just stand there while you cut off the flow of blood? No, Charly, he's going to twist and turn and fight like crazy. So, the person has to have a good knowledge of where to press—a doctor, say, or a cop, or well, I don't know. Someone really knowledgeable."

"It could be a professional killer," Charly said matter-of-factly, as though Van Buren County were bristling with professional killers.

"Sorry to interrupt," Julius said laconically, "your *fascinating* discussion, but lunch is about ready. I think I'll make some fish fumet, then make some more salmon rillettes for tonight. Okay?"

"*Oui.*" Charly went back to his office and called the Baleine residence.

"Well, he seems comatose," Barbara said dubiously. "He seems feverish, says he's burning up; he's just sitting at the kitchen table, staring at nothing."

Charly explained about the cheese, about—he rummaged through the notes on his desk—*Listeria monocytogenes*, with flulike symptoms.

"Oh, yes, there was a big round of blue-veined cheese in the refrigerator," Barbara said. "I wondered what it was doing there."

"You have not eaten any?"

"No, I'm on a new diet, no dairy at all," Barbara said.

"Perhaps you should call a doctor?" Charly said, "Because on top of all of the alcohol he has drunk, it might be a serious situation. A crisis of the liver."

Barbara said that she'd call Hy Bingham's office later on, when she got back from her appointment, if Maurice was no better. "He's pretty indestructible, Charly," Barbara said heartlessly. "But now, I've got a business to run, so I'll talk to you later."

Charly returned to his work: He boned a salmon; he bearded mussels; he opened clams. This was soothing work.

There was a sameness about kitchen prep that Charly found
very calming—and there was excitement, too, of knowing
that you were transforming raw materials into a work of
epicurean art. Raw salmon, for instance, has a wonderful
texture: but cooked *a point*, and drizzled with a reduction
of white wine, vinegar, and cubes of butter, the famous
beurre blanc sauce, the salmon was no longer simply a
fish: It had become an edible masterpiece. Mussels were
good raw, too, though so salty, sometimes, that they
scratched your throat. But fat and fleshy mussels steamed
with white wine, shallots, a suspicion of garlic, chopped
parsley, and a big lump of butter—Charly's stomach gave
a small pleasant rumble at the thought. Add a plateful of
pommes frites, french fries, the way the Belgians ate
mussels, and you were talking about some very serious
food.

So Charly, immersed in soothing epicurean dreams,
jumped when Julius spoke to him.

"What you say, Julius?"

"I said, Charly, that I had a long talk with my aunt last
night. She was telling me about the love of her life, Ralph
D'Annunzio. He'd been a big Mafioso, a Don, but then he
retired, bought a farm in southern Jersey and lived the life
of a country gentleman. He got out of the Mob."

"That is a surprise," Charly said. "He came sometimes
to the restaurant in New York, a good customer. But I did
not know about him being in *La Mafia*, and I did not know
about him and Mrs. Wells. He always came to the
restaurant with other men, never women. He knew a lot
about food. 'The only way to eat American oysters,' he
once told me, 'is with Mignonette Sauce: vinegar,
preferably champagne vinegar, chopped shallots, and
mignonette pepper.' Mignonette pepper is white pepper,
you know." Charly paused, then said; "And do you know,

he did come once with Walter Maxwell. I had forgotten that. Or I never make the connection."

"Did you know that Walter Maxwell was a protégé of Ralph's?"

"*Tiens*," Charly said. "That I did not know."

"Honoria only met Walter once, way back then. But he was with the Mafia, too, she's pretty sure."

So it must be true. First, the waiter's story, now this. "Walter is so distinguished. He does not look like *La Mafia* at all."

Julius shrugged. "Well, neither did Ralph D'Annunzio, I gather. Honoria doesn't like Walter much, she says he's not a gentleman, whatever that means. Harry Clark's a gentleman? She didn't even know Walter lived up here until about five years ago, then she ran into him somewhere."

"*Mon Dieu.* So Walter Maxwell is, or was, *un gangster.*"

"Well, you know my aunt, Charly. I'd take everything she says with a grain of salt."

Charly turned to Benny. "You hear that, Benny? A gangster. And now we find out that Mr. Maxwell and Robby Okun are on the same floor in the hospital. Is that a coincidence? Or, should I say, too much of a coincidence? *La Synchronicité*, as the good Dr. Jung would say."

"An Englishman called Colin Wilson wrote a book about coincidences," Julius said, "Maybe I should try and find it. Or root out my old Jung. It's in his autobiography, *Memories, Dreams, and Reflections.* Jung was fascinated by coincidences, or synchronicity, as he called it."

Benny said, "But why would Mr. Maxwell kill Robby? I don't think he even knew Robby. Unless he just kills for the sake of killing."

"I am taking food over to the Okun family tomorrow morning," Charly said. "The big roast beef in the oven is for them, and the ham, so are the beans baking, the potatoes boiling for real American potato salad, *les macaronis* boiling for *macaronis au gratin* with cheese. Perhaps I can find out a few things. Patty is going to speak to Linda, too."

Julius chuckled. "Operation Charly is under way, I see."

"*Mais absolument.*"

CHAPTER TWENTY-FIVE

Friday Morning with Chief Stark

Meanwhile, at the Klover Police Station, Chief John Stark was having a meeting with some of his men. The first order of business was the arsonist.

"I gather," Stark addressed Abe Reynolds, Vince Matucci, and Clem Hughes, "that you don't think it's Tom Arnold, despite that green thing Charly's partner grabbed."

The three men shook their heads. "Tom's a shiftless little s.o.b., sneaky, but he's too small for this, know what I mean?" Clem said. "It just doesn't fit, him burning barns at all."

"Tom's not a nut," Abe said. "We're hunting a nut."

"My gut feeling is, it isn't Tom," Vince said.

"What about Harry Clark?" Stark asked. "'Course Harry was in jail last night, when Charly's shed burned. But he could have hired someone."

No one liked Harry for the arsonist. "He's crazy," Clem said, "but not crazy-crazy, know what I mean? He's crazy about money. Do anything for money. So if he did burn down those barns, it's because someone paid him to do it. Now, who would want those barns burned down?"

"The answer," Stark said, "lies with the farmers. I'm convinced of that. It isn't a random thing. Something they've done, or something they are, that offends someone.

I've already spoken to them all, but maybe there's something I missed. So this afternoon, I'd like to ask Abe and Vince to visit those five farmers. Talk to their wives, this time. You work out who'll visit whom, I don't care."

"So we cover schooling, religion, politics, kids, how they spend their money, charities they may or may not contribute to . . ." Abe said.

Clem snorted. "Charity begins at home with these folks."

"Clem and I," Stark continued. "We'll deal with Robby Okun's death. Clem's going to the hospital again. Nurse's aide who cleaned Wednesday afternoon, for instance: She had to leave suddenly, there was an illness in her family up in Maine, and the hospital can't locate her. I'm going to talk to Linda and Bob again, and also talk to Marian Arnold, she's Bob's sister."

"She's pretty slow," Abe said.

"That's okay. She also cleans for Maxwell. I can't believe Maxwell would kill the kid in the hospital, but you never know."

"I've already talked to Tom Arnold, he's in charge of hiring the kids in the summer, when Maxwell needs help with the haying," Clem said. "Tom says he looked up Robby's name in the hiring book, no Robby Okun. But Tom acted kind of funny, like he was hiding something. Robby's his wife Marian's brother's child, so I figured maybe Tom knew something bad about Robby and wanted to protect the Okun family. Tom's a sneaky little s.o.b., too sneaky for his own good. Why not just come out and say it?"

"He'd act sneaky if he was buying a candy bar," Abe said. "Just his way."

"Well maybe, maybe not," Clem said. "But I got the names of four other boys hired last summer, and I've only contacted one, so far. Negative. This kid's allergic to hay, so he left after one day. Didn't remember Robby."

Stark said, "We've already visited the high-school principal. Matt Murdock's going to talk to the kids, make a list of the children Robby associated with. Trouble is, Matt says, *everybody* hated that kid. He disrupted classes, blackmailed younger children, if he found them smoking pot he'd demand money or threaten to tell their parents."

"Tell about the sex part," Clem said.

"He sexually molested a couple of younger girls, few months ago, they only told their parents recently. He just fondled them, I gather, nothing serious," Stark said. "But he threatened to harm them if they told anyone."

Clem Hughes took up the thread, "So of course our first thought was, it's one of the fathers, come to the hospital. Both fathers were at work when Robby was killed, and have witnesses. But they may have gotten someone to do it. Kid was a horror show. Everyone says it. Maybe even dealt drugs."

"What do we know about Maxwell?" Abe asked.

"Very little," Stark said. "He's never been in trouble since he's lived here. Originally came from Massachusetts, he told us, he had a farm up there. When he moved here he had a wife, but she died in a car crash, that was before my time."

"Very polite feller," Clem said. "Called me 'Officer' and 'sir.'"

The telephone rang. Stark picked up.

"Yeah? She's gone, huh? No one knows where she is? Oh, boy."

Stark put down the telephone and told his men, "That was Tom Arnold. He's been getting telephone calls all morning, people asking where Marian is. She didn't work yesterday afternoon; she was home when Tom came in last night, but then when he woke up this morning she was gone."

"She's Bob Okun's sister," Abe reminded them, "but I know there was bad feeling. Bob told me Marian used to come round, try to convert them to her religion. Bob finally told her to get out and not come back."

"What about the dead woman Poisson found?" Vince Matucci asked.

"Well," Stark said, "Charly tells me he found out the Vanns do know who the dead woman is; they were overheard talking about her. I'll just swing out there this morning—it's on my way to Linda and Bob's."

"You going to call first, make an appointment?" Clem asked.

"No, I'm not," Stark said. "What's their names again? Pete and Diane?"

"Yeah, Pete, I was just drivin' by," Stark said. Peter Vann had answered the door, dressed in jeans and an old flannel shirt, and invited Stark to "Come on in, have some coffee, sir."

Stark took his thin-looking coffee into Peter's office, following the man. Pine paneling, big walnut desk, leather chairs. Nice office.

"Nice office," Stark said.

"Yeah, thanks. You want some?" Peter gestured, bottle in hand: Going to zip up his coffee with brandy, it looked like. Stark shook his head.

"I dropped in because someone overheard you and Mrs. Vann discussing that dead woman. I gather you knew her."

Peter was not to be hurried: He sipped his coffee. "Mmmm—no, Chief Stark, I didn't say we knew her. I said she looked like someone who had once worked for me."

"Oh. Well, whom did she look like?"

"When your man showed me the picture, I told him I didn't recognize her. And I didn't. But the more I thought about it, the more I thought she looked like an employee of mine."

"Her name?"

"A Mrs. Moran. She was a model, went by the name Candy. Just Candy, no last name. She used to work in my showroom, nearly fifteen years ago."

"Then how come you didn't recognize her, she worked for you?"

"Lotta water over the dam," Peter said, sipping his coffee. "Didn't look like the same woman. Bet she's had a face-lift or two." Peter grinned. "Should have said something, but I didn't. My wife thought she looked familiar, too."

"But you still didn't say . . ."

Peter sat up straight. "Look, Chief. Put yourself in my position. I know what the locals think; they probably think we have wild parties, crazy stuff. Locals never like out of towners. I'd be the first one you'd suspect."

"That's true," Stark admitted.

"So if I did admit to knowing her, you'd think right off the bat that I killed her, right? Am I right?"

"Probably."

"Because," Peter continued, "I didn't know she knew anyone up here and she never knew we lived up here. And, hey, here she is. Turns up dead. Little town hundred and fifty miles from New York City, this woman used to work for me—wouldn't it be simple to pin the murder on me, then no locals are involved, everything's tidy, huh?"

Stark nodded. The guy was right. "What do you know about her?"

Peter listed on his fingers: "Fairly well-known model in fifties and sixties; then she starts looking old, disappears. All the models have short working lives. They begin to look tired, fast. Then Candy shows up again, maybe eight, ten years later, looking for work. That age, early forties, they take what they can get, unless they're smart enough to save their money. Candy had no money-smarts. When I knew her she was always broke."

"Probably made a lot of money, in her day," Stark said.

"A thousand, two thousand a day, back in the sixties,"

Peter said. "That was big bucks, then. As I say, the smart ones salted it away, but not Candy."

Big money then? What about now? "She ever marry? Have children?"

Peter shrugged. "Never talked about herself. Just about how broke she was, how she'd just bought some new cosmetic—a real airhead. Typical model, all wrapped up in herself and her looks."

"And you have no idea what she was doing up here." Stark drained his tasteless coffee, got up to go. Peter rose, too.

"Nope, no idea. She never called me, and as I say, she didn't even know we lived up here. But hey, Chief, it might not even be her."

"You have any idea where she was living, this Candy Moran?"

"Fifteen years ago, she lived right in Manhattan, I'd have her address in my files, but they're in boxes in the barn. I could dig them out, if you'd like. But I do remember she'd take a cab to work every day. I always took the subway, and I figured she couldn't be too poor, riding around in cabs." Peter chuckled. "Even my stockbroker took the subway, and he had more money than the Catholic Church."

Stark realized why he'd been stalling, when he should have been with Bob and Linda Okun. Nobody liked to question bereaved parents. It put him in mind of his own case, five years ago, car-insurance adjusters tackling him after Johnny's death. He'd been so numb, he couldn't even think.

Big Bob Okun came in from his workshop. Curls of wood clung to his overalls, sawdust sprinkled his undershirt. He sat down heavily on a kitchen chair. Linda was at the stove, getting coffee. "Cream and sugar, John, right?"

Stark sipped. Tasted like coffee ice cream, it was so rich. Real heavy cream, strong coffee. My, it was good.

"Robby's priority number one, Linda, Bob, we've got almost everyone working on this one, and we won't stop until Robby's killer is caught."

"Thanks, John." Bob sounded exhausted by grief. Linda sobbed.

She said, "I can't imagine who'd do a thing like . . . must be a monster . . . just a little boy . . . fourteen. Oh, I know he gets into trouble, spray painting the school bus, stuff like that, but he isn't—wasn't—a bad kid."

"Yes, Linda. Now I know you and Bob are probably in shock, can't even think, but let me ask you a few questions, okay? Can I do that?"

Stark continued. "Now, we'd like to know what Robby did last summer, after school was out. What sort of jobs he had."

Linda looked at Bob. "Jobs? Well, I don't know . . ."

Bob said, "Who'd want to kill a kid? Just like them horror movies."

"Where did Robby work last summer, Bob?" Stark spoke slowly, making eye contact. Bob Okun stared back, shook his head. He didn't know.

Stark said, "Did he work for any of the farmers? You know, around haying time, they'll get kids in to help, or get kids in to do stable work."

"That's right," Linda said. "Remember Bob, I found out, over at the diner, that Bradley and Slocum were hiring kids, someone else, too, oh yeah, Maxwell's place needed kids, I told Rob about it."

Stark said, "Yeah? And what happened?"

"Nothing, I expect," Linda sniffed. "We never heard. I never nagged."

"Didn't like to work much, you know kids," Bob said, scowling.

"Did Robby ever mention Maxwell? You know, the rich farmer?"

Linda and Bob shook their heads.

"Did you ever meet Maxwell? Know who he was?"

More head shaking. Then Linda said, "Oh, yeah, he often eats at The Firm, I work there on Sundays, just started. I heard Patty talking, she doesn't like him. But my boss, Mister Poson, he's real friendly with Maxwell."

Bob said, "He's a good man, Poson, I made the shelves in his basement. Real nice feller. It's always, 'Want a piece of apple pie? Want coffee? Sandwich?' I 'spect I put on ten pounds, the two weeks I worked there." Bob smiled sadly, and scratched his belly. "He's going to be at the funeral. Said he was bringing over some food, too. Now that's nice."

"Linda," Stark spoke slowly, "tell me what Patty said about Maxwell."

"Oh, nothing special," Linda said. "He's got lots of money, they deliver food over to him once a week, you know, soups and stuff."

"Why doesn't Patty like him?"

"Oh, I don't know," Linda said. "He's just one of the rich folks."

"Did you visit Robby in hospital?"

"Yeah," Bob said, "We went Tuesday night, then the doctor said don't come until Wednesday night, they were going to operate on his leg, he'd be all groggy. Then they called, Wednesday, around five, said he was dead."

"Do you know anyone, didn't like Robby? You know, did he have any enemies? You know, people mad at him for something?"

Linda looked at Stark, amazed. "Who'd ever be mad at Robby? Sweetest little kid you could meet."

Stark nodded. "What about your sister Marian? She been in touch?"

Bob looked angry for the first time. "My own sister, she didn't even call, can you imagine? Here we lost our only son, and she didn't even call."

"Were she and Robby friendly?"

Linda smiled. "Nuh-unh. They didn't like each other one bit. Robby used to poke fun at her Bible stuff, and she said he was a sinner. And Rob said he knew something about Marian, he'd seen her once in the middle of the night doing something she shouldn't be doing, but he wouldn't tell us what. Said if she didn't mind her p's and q's he was gonna tell the cops."

Stark's ears perked up at this: "What was Robby doing out in the middle of the night?" Was Robby the arsonist? Why not? From what Stark had heard, Robby was crazy about money. If you paid him, he'd do just about anything, other than work.

"Me and Linda, we couldn't control that kid, he was wild. Out all night, sometimes, never slept," Bob said, shaking his head. "Not like Robby's sisters at all, they're so much older. To tell the truth, we were too old for another kid. He just mowed us down. He had friends in Hogton, slept there couple times. We just couldn't get Rob to mind us, no matter what."

"And Marian? You told her not to come back, didn't you, Bob?"

"Yep. We had words. That Bible stuff got too much for me. Always talking about revenge and judging people and punishing the wicked."

"And Matt your brother, Bob? You didn't see eye to eye with him, either, now, did you?"

"Nope," Bob said. "He give Rob a ride on his motorcycle once, told Rob he'd teach him how to drive it. I told Matt not to teach him, I didn't want him riding them crazy things. Matt did, anyway. Rob borrowed his uncle's machine without asking, fell off and broke his leg. If he hadn't got on that machine, he'd be alive now, wouldn't he?"

To comment would be pointless. Instead, Stark asked,

"And Annette and Patricia? They coming home for the funeral?" Annette and Patricia were the Okun's grown daughters.

"They're here now," Linda said. "They're upstairs, sleeping. They drove across from Rochester, together, got in late last night, they're both tired, and so sad about their brother, you wouldn't believe. He was their baby."

CHAPTER TWENTY-SIX

Pieces in the
Puzzle

With great satisfaction Clem Hughes, sitting at his desk at the Klover Police Station, put down the telephone. Too bad neither Stark nor Matucci nor Reynolds were around to share his pleasure. He'd finally managed to talk to all the mothers of the boys who had worked at Walter Maxwell's last summer. They'd remembered Robby and the brouhaha over the stableman's wallet. And Mr. Gentleman Maxwell was in room 412 at the hospital, right around the corner from the Okun kid? Okay . . .

Officer Vince Matucci drove up to the Bradley farmhouse, parked his cruiser, went to the kitchen door and knocked. He enjoyed chatting with women. They were much more observant than most men.

Ruth Bradley opened the door, a filled cake pan in her hands. On the kitchen counter was an empty cake-mix box and an eggshell.

"Here, Officer, come in, let me just put this cake in the oven. I can't remember your name, but you look familiar."

"It's Officer Vincent Matucci, ma'am. With the Klover Police."

Ruth Bradley frowned. "I could say a thing or two, but

I won't. About that barn burner. And now he's burning
sheds. One so far, I read in the paper. What next? Our cars?
Our homes?"

"Two sheds, ma'am. He burned another one this
morning."

"Dear Lord. Well, have some coffee, Officer, tell me
why you're here."

Mrs. Bradley poured two mugs of her weak coffee,
added plenty of milk and sugar, and handed one mug to
Vince. "It's someone with a grudge against us. I know that
as well as I know my own name."

"Yes, ma'am," Vince said. "What's the grudge?"

"Well," Ruth Bradley said, "we're fairly successful, as
small farms go. And so are the others whose barns burned:
Jim and Mary Halloran, Helen and Abner Wilcox, Luke
and Amy Chilten, Pierce and Lucille Sadowsky. We all had
help from our folks. See, I've been thinking. Why us? Why
not the rich weekenders? Or the poor farmers who can't
meet their payments?"

Vince sipped at his coffee, said nothing. Just nodded,
from time to time.

"Officer—Matucci, is it? Now that's a foreign name,
I'd say."

"Born and raised in Klover, ma'am. Of Italian descent."

"Oh, Eyetalian, of course. So that's my theory, Officer."

"I agree, ma'am. Now who do you know, might have a
grudge?"

"Well, the farmers who've gone broke, last five, six
years, for starters. I've made a list, I'll give it to you before
you go, all farms within a twenty-mile area, like the
Cooleys, the Blodgetts, I feel sorry for them. And I've also
made a list," Ruth Bradley continued, "of folks I consider,
well, peculiar. Like that man, killed his own son when they
were deer hunting, everyone said it was an accident, but

I've heard it said they never got along. Excuse me, I want to look at my cake."

"Yes, but . . ." Matucci tried, and failed, to get a word in.

"Like that old Mrs. Peabody, goes around in rags, drives that broken-down old pickup, and Mary Halloran tells me she's got a pile of money in the bank; and that feeble-minded feller looks after the Bible Church on Route 33, mows their lawn and shovels their snow, I think he lives in the basement. And what about Marian Arnold? I went to school with her. Now, would you believe, a couple of months ago she comes knocking on my door."

Vince knew better than to interrupt. Ruth Bradley was in full flow. This was her chance to shine. Probably didn't talk much around her husband. She stayed home and figured things out.

"Marian Arnold, huh?" Vince said. "You think she's crazy, too?"

"Not crazy, Officer, but peculiar. I wouldn't let her into the kitchen, so she stood there on the stoop tellin' me I was a sinner and I had to read the Bible to be saved and I should beg God's forgiveness for bein' a bad person."

"Why, that's terrible," Vince said. "I'd be mad as anything."

"Well, I was. And then, do you know, some man from her church, they're a queer lot, run by a man named Pflugg, none of the other churches will have anything to do with him, anyway a man calls up the police and says the farmers had it coming to them, that they were godless folk, John Stark told my husband. Now, did you ever?"

Matucci said well, he never did. Shocking, that's what it was.

"Oh, there's another group, too, farmers who bought up a lot of land along Route 8G, they want it zoned commercial, and they'll get it, too." Ruth Bradley looked knowing. "I hear money changed hands, and someone, I'm not mentioning names, just bought himself a fancy car. Wants 8G turned into strip-mall country."

Ruth Bradley—now who did she remind Vince of? The common scold, who, in colonial days, was ducked in the pond when her gossip and vicious talk got out of hand. Practically everything Mrs. Bradley had said was actionable. If there was a local Ku Klux Klan, which there wasn't, Ruth Bradley would be the Grand Marshal or Vizier or whatever he called himself. Maybe talking to the wives wasn't such a hot idea, after all.

"Oops," Ruth Bradley said, "my cake." And she hurried over to the stove. Vince rose to go.

"Van Buren's an agricultural county," Ruth Bradley told him. "But Walton, he's on the town board, he wants to turn it into some cheesy shopping area, filled with Wal-Marts and McDonald's and such. I'll bet you anything he's behind the barn burnings, wants to discourage us, wants us to sell out to the developers."

"Yes'm," Vince said, edging out the door.

"We've got some beautiful farms here, dairy farms, fruit farms, vegetable farms, some horse farms, and that man up the road raises Black Angus bulls. Beautiful place, he has. And the town board wants it all to die: they're probably getting bribes from some contractors. A whole new element has come into the area."

"Yes, ma'am, we've noticed that. Crime's way up."

"All those drugs in Hogton. You ever wonder why the kingpins never get caught? All you read about is little piddly amounts, a hundred dollars here, sixty dollars there, they never catch the millionaire drug pushers, now isn't that curious?"

"Yes, ma'am," Matucci said, talking over his shoulder as he fled to his cruiser. "I've often wondered why that is."

• • •

Back in his office, John Stark dialed Manhattan information and learned that there were no Candy Morans, two Catherine Morans and eight C. Morans listed. He jotted down all of the numbers and started dialing.

Both Catherine Morans picked up, both elderly ladies. There were two no answers and two answering machines, telling the caller to leave his number. The seventh answering machine said, "This is Candy. If you're calling on business, you might try the gallery, at 821-2619. If you're calling for gossip, darling, leave your number and I'll call soon's I can. Bye."

Stark dialed 1-212-821-2619.

"Hapworth Gallery." A plummy man's voice.

Stark identified himself, gave the reason for his call. The voice, which belonged to Forrest Hapworth, became less plummy.

"Candy Moran works here, but hasn't been in all week, Chief Stark, and that isn't like her not to call. Doesn't answer the phone. I went round to her apartment and the super let me into her place, but there's no sign of her and nothing in her appointment book. I was going to call the police."

Stark asked if Candy knew anyone upstate.

"Not that I know of. She represented the gallery at an art symposium in Albany on Sunday. I called, she was there. But she left there around five, to get the Amtrak back to the city. Yes, a middle-aged woman, good-looking, beauty mark just below her left eye."

Yes, Mr. Hapworth did have a fax and yes, he'd call Stark as soon as he received the photo.

Everything happened very quickly: Stark faxed the photo, Hapworth immediately called back to say yes, that was Candy. She'd never mentioned Klover, New York. Never mentioned husbands, lovers, though she had friends all over the globe. A worldly woman. An asset to the gallery. They were devastated, simply devastated, to hear that she was dead, and so on.

"Was she a partner in your gallery, Mr. Hapworth?"

"Oh, do call me Forrest, Chief Stark. We'd invited her to join us, and I had the feeling she was going to accept, as soon as she got some money."

Hapworth gave Stark Candy's address, but claimed he knew next to nothing about her personal life. "I think she'd been married several times, but she never spoke about it. Clients were impressed with her. She used to be a model, you know."

Ah, well. Now Stark would have to deal with the New York City police, something he hated to do: They were even busier than he was, and just as understaffed. It would take months. And they weren't very pleasant to upstate cops, treated them like hayseeds. Which the upstate cops probably were. Well, at least now Doc Bingham could fill in the death certificate.

Even though Stark was annoyed with Charly, he found himself dialing the number of La Fermette. In spite of all of Charly's prying and snooping, Stark liked the little guy. He was a compassionate man, and he was good to his help. Stark told Charly the dead woman's name.

"Tiens," Charly said. "Imagine that. I speak to a restaurateur in New York, he remember Mr. Vann bringing a model named Candy for dinner, but he does not recall the woman's last name."

"You weren't going to report this to the police?"

"But, of course, Chief Stark. However, I want to wait until I get more information, something useful, that can help you. I do not want you to think that I pry."

CHAPTER TWENTY-SEVEN

Danger at
La Fermette

Walter Maxwell was in a bad way. He couldn't sleep at night without Seconal, then he'd drag around all morning, drinking coffee. His hands shook, and he'd developed an annoying tic, his left eye squeezing shut involuntarily, his mouth forming a grimace. "I look just like Candy did," he thought as he peered in the mirror. He wondered if he'd had a small stroke.

He had lost his appetite, developed diarrhea, and vomited several times—nothing but yellow bile. Everything was closing in on him, making him want to scream. He found it difficult to breathe. His heart pounded.

Charly Poisson was the cause of all this. He had to disappear. But how to do it? Walter didn't want to touch Charly, himself. No more killing: He'd spend the winter someplace warm, have a rest. But that Charly—damn little snoop, knew about Candy, somehow. What to do about Charly?

The best way would be to lure Charly to Hogton, get someone to shoot him in an alley and let him be found by the police in the drug-infested part of town. Hogton, three miles from Klover, had a big drug trade. A hit of crack, called a crill, sold for $15–$20 on the street. In New York City, the same amount went for $3–$5. Young drug dealers in Tommy Hilfiger jackets came up on Amtrak, stayed a couple of weeks, made a little money from the tourists, then went back to the city, and other drug dealers took their place. A never-ending cycle. But luring Charly into Hogton, at night? Impossible. Walter sighed, lay down on his big leather sofa, and slept.

Lunch was over at La Fermette. Thirty-five people, everyone wanting to hear about Charly's fire, discuss the arsonist, speculate on who it might be, and talk about Robby Okun's death. Charly's dead woman was forgotten. Too much else was going on. Theories started up like brushfire, then were swept along: The barn burner was a paid hoodlum hired by the commercial interests who wanted to build a strip mall on 8G, but were prevented from doing so by the folks who wanted to keep Van Buren County agricultural.

Charly shrugged. He didn't believe it. He thought the answer lay much closer to home. But where? And who? Someone mentally unbalanced, who probably never came to Charly's restaurant. Like Tom Arnold. Or even Marian. But why they would want to burn the farmers' barns, Charly couldn't imagine. The jangling of the telephone interrupted his speculations.

"Ah, my dear Barbara. And how is our patient? Still the hangover?"

"Charly," Barbara sobbed. "It's bad, really bad. I'm calling from the hospital, I've just talked to Hy Bingham. Maurice's liver is failing."

"Oh, *mon Dieu*. Is it the drink? Or the cheese, that listeria?"

"Both, probably," Barbara said. "The alcohol, with the listeria on top . . . well, I don't think Maurice can pull out of it. I think he's going to die."

"I come right away," Charly gasped.

• • •

"Well, his liver's definitely enlarged," Hy Bingham told Charly. They were sitting in Hy's office at the hospital. "Vomiting, claylike stool, dark urine, yellow skin, bleeding gums, abdominal ascites—that's fluid collecting in the stomach—and given Maurice's history of alcohol abuse, plus eating the tainted cheese, makes it certain that we're talking about liver failure."

"Serious," Charly murmured, shaking his head. To the French, a *crise de foie*, liver failure, was the classic gourmand's (and/or drinker's) death.

"Oh, we'll run the tests, have to for the insurance, don't want to get sued," Dr. Bingham continued. "But," he shrugged, "looks pretty obvious."

"And his chances for pulling through?" Charly asked.

"You know, that's up to him. He's got a strong heart, he might make it. He's really not in too bad a shape—for a drunk. Sorry, Barbara, but let's not pussyfoot around. We're cleaning out his system with a glucose drip now."

"Can we see him?" Charly asked.

"Sure, why not? He's in a private room right next to the emergency room, nurses will be checking on him every few minutes. He's pretty out of it, but he might recognize you."

"Barbara," Maurice said. "Charly." His voice was raspy, skin yellow-grey. "My throat—all that smoke—and that woman knocked me down."

Charly leaned forward. "Why do you say a woman, Maurice?"

"Been thinking. Jus' before I grabbed that scarf, I put my hands on her chest—could feel breasts. Didn't think of it at the time. Not thinking. Out of it. And she ran like a woman, it was a woman, all right. Knocked me out? That's why I'm here? I remember being at the fire, then I woke up here."

"You went home after the fire," Charly reminded Maurice.

"I did?"

"You came in the back door, said you felt sick," Barbara said. "I left you sitting at the kitchen table. When I came back an hour later, you'd collapsed in the kitchen. Passed out on the floor. I called the ambulance."

"Gotta go home," Maurice said. "Drive into New York. Squash date with Piggy, then lunch."

Charly looked at Barbara.

"He was playing squash with his old classmate Piggy Carmichael tomorrow, Saturday. I'd better call Piggy," Barbara explained. And to Maurice, "You're not very well, Maurice. I'll call and postpone, okay? Hy Bingham says you'll be in the hospital a few more days."

"Few more days," Maurice repeated. He closed his eyes.

"And you are sure it was a woman who ran into you," Charly said.

"*Absolument, mon cher Charly,*" Maurice said. "*Cherchez la femme.*"

Charly was sitting in old Doc Ross's dusty living room, sipping tea so strong it looked like coffee in the cup. He shuddered. Such strong, acid tea would give him indigestion. He would have to take a Nux Vomica pill.

"Says it's a woman, huh?" Charly had just told old Doc about Maurice's insisting that it was a woman who had knocked him down.

"What do you know about Marian Arnold, Doc? Or Mrs. Dinah Vann?" Charly had always been suspicious of Dinah, he didn't know why.

Doc Ross thought for a bit. "Marian was an Okun before she married Tom. Her parents were drunks; her brother's Bob Okun, the carpenter. She was slow in school. There was some trouble, as I recall, some girls, classmates, laughed at her, teased her or something, she beat one of 'em up pretty badly. She's a strong woman, you know. Always was big for her age."

"So," Charly said thoughtfully, "she could have a grudge against those girls. Who were they, do you know?"

"Well, Charly," Doc continued, "I think probably some of the well-to-do farmers' daughters. They were a snobby bunch, always thought they were better than everyone else. But that was a long time ago."

Charly thought of the schoolboy slights from his childhood. Children remembered things like that. He did. And so would Marian Arnold.

Doc said, "Ever since then she's been cleaning folks' homes, and I gather she does pretty well. People like her. I wouldn't like to have her around, she's a gloomy soul, but I hear she's a good cleaner."

"And the Bible business?" Charly asked.

"All I can tell you," Doc said, "is that the New Awakenings Church has a reputation for being a cult. That Pflugg fellow isn't liked. Meant to be a rabble-rouser. He gathers together all the misfits. I don't know anything else about them, I steer clear of troublemakers. Why? Are you suspicious of Marian? Or of that cult? They're strange folks, all right."

Charly got up. "Oh, Doc, I am suspicious of everyone. This morning, I was convinced that Marian Arnold was the murderer of my dead lady. Now, I do not think so. Now, Maurice tells me a woman bumped into him at my fire. What woman, I ask myself? Could it be this Marian Arnold?"

"The Okun clan has a bad reputation," Doc said, "and much of it is deserved. Marian's always seemed pretty harmless to me, but I don't know her well. She was a cleaner at the hospital back when Alma was dying, and she did a good job, there."

"And Mrs. Dinah Vann?" Charly asked.

Doc shook his head. "Never met the Vanns. Man who mows my lawn says Mr. tried to stiff him on a job, once."

Charly got up from his seat. "Well, Doc, I think I must go, now. We have quite a few reservations for tonight. Lobster; beautiful salmon; Moules Marinière, lots of good thing to eat. You want to come, be my guest?"

"Not tonight, Charly, but thanks. I had a big lunch," Doc said. "One big meal a day is my limit. Sure you won't have more of my good, strong tea?"

"It is truly delicious," Charly lied, "but one cup is my limit."

Charly drove back to the restaurant and parked in the big lot by the kitchen. There was a lot to do tonight, and he was late. Thank goodness Julius was here to help Benny, though Benny was becoming more and more capable. "He is a born chef," Charly mused, proud of his young assistant.

He walked to the kitchen door, making lists in his head . . . and heard something whistle past his ear. At first he ducked, thinking it was a wasp. It all happened in a split second: There was a thud in the wooden clapboard, and a hole appeared as, at the same time, he heard a noise like a truck backfiring, a short, sharp crack. But maybe it wasn't a truck backfiring. Fear flashed in his head. Was that a shot? Was someone shooting at him? He wrenched open the kitchen door and dived in.

"What was that?" Benny and Julius both said, looking up at Charly, who was hanging on to the counter, breathing hard.

"I think someone shot at me," Charly said, gulping air.

"I know someone shot at you," Julius said, dialing the police.

"It looks like a bullet from a rifle, and rifles aren't allowed in Van Buren County anymore, too populated," Stark said about fifteen minutes later. "I've got two men tracking that field beyond the restaurant parking lot. There's a little hill up there. If the shooter stood on it, he'd have a clear view of the back of the restaurant, get you right in his sights, then, bam."

"Lucky he's a bad shot," Benny said. He was nervously chewing on a clove of garlic, a habit he'd picked up from Charly.

"We'll have someone out here tonight, in case he tries again," Stark said. He'd dug the bullet out of the clapboard and held it in his hand, a small, misshapen object. "Looks like a .22 long. I used to have an old Marlin rifle, called a Little Buckaroo, single shot, came with a little scope. Used to fire bullets like this one. It's not really my choice if I wanted to kill a man."

"So, Chief, you're saying the shooter isn't a professional," Julius said.

"Oh my, no, I think he's an amateur. But they're the worst kind."

"How so?" Charly asked. He was chopping garlic, occasionally popping a small bit in his mouth. He still felt dazed.

"They take terrible chances. They can't gauge distance. And, as you can see, they miss. God knows what else they hit while they're banging away. Charly, I think we've got some old bulletproof vests down at the barracks. I'd be grateful if you'd wear one, tonight."

"Anything you say, Chief. You the boss."

After Stark left, Charly poured some olive oil into a small Dutch oven, the ones made for individual service. He added a small handful of chopped garlic, let it sizzle for a bit. Then he dumped in a measure of mussels, sprinkled parsley on top, sloshed in some white wine, dropped in a big spoonful of butter, and put the lid on. He shook the pot, to distribute the contents. In a minute, he lifted the lid. The mussels were open. He carried the pot over to the big pine table, set it on an asbestos mat.

"You have no idea how hungry this has made me," he said to Julius and Benny, who were staring at him. "If I am going to die, at least let me have a last favorite meal."

MOULES MARINIÈRE
Yield: 2 servings

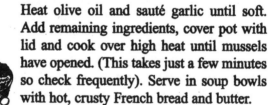

¼ cup olive oil
4 cloves of garlic, finely chopped
2 pounds mussels, cleaned
  and bearded
½ cup chopped flat-leaf parsley
1 cup white wine
2 Tablespoons butter

Heat olive oil and sauté garlic until soft. Add remaining ingredients, cover pot with lid and cook over high heat until mussels have opened. (This takes just a few minutes so check frequently). Serve in soup bowls with hot, crusty French bread and butter.

CHAPTER TWENTY-EIGHT

✛✛✛✛✛✛✛

Oyster Stew and Secrets

✛✛✛✛✛✛✛

Jimmy Houghton returned home after work to an un-cleaned house. He lived alone, and was fastidiously tidy, so there was no mess, but he enjoyed seeing his small house sparkle the way it did after Marian Arnold had been there. She used marble polish on the coffee table's top, lemon oil on the furniture, and sprayed the rooms with a woodsy air-spray that Honoria Wells, one of his clients, had given him, so that when Jimmy opened his front door the house smelled like a perfumed forest. But not tonight. The house remained exactly as he'd left it that morning, a bit dusty, a bit tired-smelling.

Jimmy stepped over to his answering machine—there were no messages. He looked up Marian's telephone number and dialed it—after five rings he hung up. He opened the drawer of his Shaker chest of drawers in the dining room and removed the things that he had hidden so that Marian couldn't accidentally break them, and replaced them in their accustomed spots in the living room.

Stepping back to his telephone, he called Walter Maxwell, who was home, and asked if Marian Arnold had been in today to clean. No, and neither had she called.

Walter was annoyed. Then Jimmy called Win Crozier and Morty Cohen at their shop; they stayed until six on Fridays. No, Marian hadn't been in to clean their shop last night, nor had she called. Most distressing. Where the hell was the woman?

However, it was suppertime. First things first, and Jimmy was looking forward to his meal. Jimmy Houghton, né Talbott, was a traditionalist when it came to food. Fridays he always ate fish, usually one of the dishes his mother's Irish cook had taught him. He'd picked up a pint of shucked, pasteurized oyster from the supermarket on the way home and now set about making oyster stew. He poured the oysters and their liquor into a stainless-steel saucepan, turned on the heat, and let the oysters cook for a few minutes. Over this he poured a carton of heavy cream, plopped in a chunk of butter, salt, freshly ground white pepper, and the tip of a knife's worth of red pepper. Then he poured the mixture into the bowl he always used for oyster stew: a seventeenth-century Kakiemon bowl with a molded rim, which had been in his father's family for generations.

Win Crozier, who knew something about old china, had told him the bowl was worth a lot of money, which was nice to know, but didn't stop Jimmy from using it. If you have beautiful stuff, Jimmy believed, why stash it away in a cupboard? Life is short. His dad's life had been very short, he had died at forty-three, when Jimmy was ten. And who knew how long Jimmy had left? He had set himself a task, thirty years ago, to avenge his father's murder, and once that task was completed . . . well, he just didn't know.

He had waited patiently. "I'll know when it's the right time," he told himself. And now, the time was approaching, he could sense it as surely as an animal senses the approach of winter, or the nearness of an enemy. His period of waiting was about to come to an end.

As he sipped his creamy stew and nibbled on oyster crackers, Jimmy recalled eating this same meal on Friday nights in Boston. His parents, who loved Mary Scully's oyster stew, would eat a small bowlful with Jimmy and his sister Christina (nicknamed Sissy) and Nanny Briggs in the breakfast room, before going out to a dinner party. His dad would be sipping a clear drink in a heavy glass tumbler, and would josh his children.

"I spoke to those oysters just this afternoon," he'd tell them, "and they said they were going to be eaten by a very nice family who lives on Beacon Hill. They were very excited about that."

"We live on Beacon Hill," Sissy said importantly.

"Are we the nice family?" Little Jimmy would ask.

"We're the nice family," his father would admit. "And the oysters promised me that, once they were in your stomachs, they'd report back to me, when Mommy and I get in tonight, whether or not you behaved yourselves with Nanny Briggs."

"These children always behave themselves," Nanny Briggs would say, staunchly sticking up for her charges, who were the best-behaved children in Boston she'd declare, even after Sissy bit the dog or Jimmy hid the checkers and then forgot where he'd put them. Nanny Briggs would make shepherd's pie or bubble and squeak on cook's night out.

"I always talk to the oysters," his dad would say, solemnly. "They tell me things you'd never dream of."

"They just told me you're not going to have any more martinis tonight," Jimmy's mother cautioned.

"No more martoonies, no more martoonies," Jimmy's

dad would sing, tossing his head and making saucer eyes, while the children laughed. He was a gin comedian, after a few martinis the funniest man in the world. To his children. Jimmy's mother wasn't so amused.

Now, finishing his bowl of oyster stew, Jimmy sighed. It was amazing (well, it was sad) how much of their fun had depended on the lubricating effects of liquor. His father was only jolly after a glass or two. That's why Jimmy never drank. Not one drop, ever.

"Told a friend about you," old Shep Richardson said, had to be ten years ago. "Told him you made a lot of money for me. Guy's name is Maxwell. Has a farm, raises Black Angus. You think you might have enough time to take him on? Guy's got a few bucks. His money manager died."

"Maxwell," Jimmy had said, feeling his stomach drop. Oh, come on, it couldn't be. Maxwell's a pretty common name. "Where does he live?"

"Going from Hogton, East on 23 to Wimble Corners, then turn left, just after Orchard Road. Big place. Guy's got some bucks, I tell you."

He was shaking when he and Shep pulled up to the big house at Black Bull Farm. Coincidence? Or chance? Or perhaps justice waiting to happen? He recognized Walter immediately when Shep introduced them, in spite of his thinness, his white hair, but of course Maxwell didn't remember him, Jimmy had been ten years old at the time. Nor did the name Houghton ring a bell, since he'd been Jimmy Talbott, then.

Sure, Jimmy told Walter, he could help him with his investments. His father's killer. No escape for you now, Walt. But Jimmy wasn't in a rush. Ever cautious, he was waiting for the proper time to avenge his father. He wasn't sure what he would do, but he'd know when the moment presented itself. And the moment was approaching. Something was happening in Walter's life—he was nervous, jumpy, suddenly wanted all that money. Walter was going down, and down was when you kicked a man like Walter. Kicked him so hard he'd never get up again. Jimmy made a mental note to check his pistol, make sure it was oiled and loaded: a lightweight Colt automatic that he kept in his bedside table.

Jimmy washed his Kakiemon bowl very carefully, dried it and replaced it in the linen drawer, and he washed the remainder of his dishes and put them away. Then he went into the garden room, so called because it was filled with plants, lay down on his wicker chaise lounge, and opened his book. He was reading Elmore Leonard's *Stick* (for the third time) and imagined himself to be the tough but quixotic Ernest Stickley, while his adversary, Walter Maxwell, was none other than the psychotic Chucky Gorman, who would set up his grandmother if the price was right.

It was past five o'clock, shutting down time, and Walter Maxwell was clearing up the papers on his desk, down at the farm office. Tom Arnold had his coat on, ready to go, thinking to himself, *Now or never.* It was the moment. He took a deep breath and walked the few steps to Walter's chair.

"Walter? You remember my dad? All the things he done for you? I think I could keep quiet about what went on in Massachusetts, all that stuff my dad told me about, if I got a little something extra in my paycheck."

There, he'd said it. Biggest bluff in his entire life. He had no idea what had gone down in Massachusetts, except that his old man had testified in court—well, lied in court, committed porjy, some word like that his dad had told him—about something that Walter Maxwell had done.

What Tom wasn't prepared for was Walter's response. He thought Walter would fly into a rage, or at least say, "Nothing doing." It had taken Tom the better part of six months to work up the courage to say what he'd just said. And then, bang, spur of the moment, almost without thinking, he'd said it.

What Walter did was throw back his head and laugh and laugh. "So now you're trying to blackmail me, too," Walter had gasped, as if it was the funniest thing in the world. "Okay, twenty-five dollars a week more, how's that? You think you can live with that?" Walter went right on laughing.

Tom had been hoping for thirty, but knew when to quit: while he was ahead.

Walter couldn't stop laughing. "Oh, Sweet Jesus, now there's a list," he'd said: Cross off Candy. Cross off that little bastard from the stables, pure luck, that one, (The daily paper had the kid's obituary. It simply said the kid had died in the hospital.) Who was left? Charly and now Tom.

Tom was so easy, he could do that one himself. Knock him out near the tractor shed, use a monkey wrench, sometime when the two of them were alone, then get on the tractor and run over him. Tell the cops Tom was repairing the machine, God only knew what had happened, he'd heard a scream, gone outside, the tractor was still running. Yes, simple. Walter felt better than he had in days. And on the strength of this good feeling, he decided to go over to La Fermette, have some shrimp in the barroom.

• • •

Tom Arnold, knowing that there'd be nothing in his refrigerator at home, with his wife disappeared (a not very great tragedy, in Tom's eyes, only he wondered where she'd gone to) leaned his elbows on the bar at Steak Heaven and sipped his mug of Genny, listening to the shouting, bragging, and laughing that was the usual bar scene at Steak Heaven.

"Here you go," Bobby Matucci the bartender said, sliding over a Macho Burger De Luxe platter, two burgers on toasted onion buns, with a mound of potato salad, another mound of coleslaw, and a mountain of fries.

"Thanks, Bob, I can sure use this. My boss? Maxwell? He's drivin' me nuts. Go here, go there, call the oil-burner repair place, I go, 'Yeah, Walt, you told me to do that yesterday, they're comin' tomorrow.' So he goes, 'Yeah? I never told you tomorrow, tomorrow's no good, it's gotta be now, today.'"

"Yeah? Pain in the ass," Bobby sympathized. He didn't mind Tom. Little, puny feller married to that weirdo, but he was a steady customer, all right. Give the guy five bucks, he'd spend three at Steak Heaven. Paid on the nose. Not a drunk, either. Never had more than four beers—well, five, six on occasion, never the hard stuff. He'd probably die in here.

"So I gotta call 'em back, then I call the vet, same thing happens, vet's gotta be there in an hour or don't bother, he'll find another vet, I think the guy's what's it called, senile, maybe Alzheimer's. Gotten so bossy."

"No lead in his pencil," Bobby said authoritatively. "Old guys, they try to get it up and they can't, so they go all macho on you, tryin' to prove theirselves, prove they're still tough guys. You should hear them yelling during the Monday night football games. Like their lives depended on it. Uh-oh, I says to myself, there's another one, gone soft."

"Yeah? Well, I was the tough guy 'bout an hour ago. Told Maxwell I wanted a raise and, know what?"

"No, what?"

"He gave it to me. Just like that." And Tom snapped his fingers.

"Son of a bitch," Bobby said admiringly. "Way to go, big Tom."

CHAPTER TWENTY-NINE

✛✛✛✛✛✛✛

A Visit to
Pastor Pflugg

✛✛✛✛✛✛✛

John Stark sat in his office, talking to some of his men.
Vince Matucci had just reported on his visits with the
farmers whose barns had burned: The general feeling with
the Hallorans, Bradleys, Wilcoxes, Chiltens, and Sad-
owskys was that they were being targeted because they
were considered successful in the farming community.
Jealousy, pure and simple.

Vince said, "Listen to this, Chief: they all had help from
their families; all five of the men married women who
came from good farm families; they all went to the local
high schools; I swear to God there's something there. All
the farmers got suspects, we gotta check them all out."

An officer stuck his head in. "Chief? Sorry to bother
you, but I think you'd better come outside."

Stark and the cop confronted the young man at the
desk. His jeans and shirt were beyond dirty: threadbare
clothing that smelled of the barnyard. Looked about sev-
enteen, eighteen, like that, as thin as a broom. His face was
grey and streaked with dirt. Thinning, lifeless hair. He
looked up at Stark, and told him, "I shot my wife; she's
sittin' in the pickup outside."

The emaciated child-woman was wedged into the passenger seat of the battered pickup. Her face was grey, eyes

closed, teeth clenched. Her hair was stained red; it looked like a bullet had grazed her scalp. Stark stared. She was breathing in short, labored gasps. "Call the ambulance," he yelled to one of the cops. "She's still alive."

After the ambulance had left, Stark walked heavily to the holding cell where the youngster waited, sitting calmly on the bunk.

"Okay, son, why'd you do it? And why not take her to Emergency?"

"Thought she were dead. Jesus told me to. She were a wicked woman."

"Jesus told you, huh?"

"Yessir, Jesus told me. Punish the wicked."

The glimmer of an idea surfaced in Stark's brain, but he couldn't quite catch hold of it. "You belong to some church, son?"

"New Awakenings Church. Run by Pastor Pflugg."

Stark told the officer in charge to handle the matter. Every year or two there were incidents like this one, where some personage "instructed" someone to take justice into his own hands. The idea in Stark's brain surfaced, and he hurried after his officer and the young executioner.

"Say, son, did Jesus ever tell you to burn down some barns?"

"No, sir. Not me, he didn't."

"But Jesus told someone to do it, didn't he?"

"Yessum, sir, he might have."

"Who'd he tell?"

"I don't know."

"Would Pastor Pflugg know?"

"I don't know."

Pastor Pflugg was short and fat, looked like Humpty Dumpty in the Tenniel illustrations for *Alice in Wonderland*. He certainly didn't look like a guru, the leader of a cult. He and Stark sat in Pastor Pflugg's white, bare office. Stark passed over a Polaroid, slightly sticky. The minister took the snapshot and studied it. "Eddie Felton, in my congregation. That's him."

The minister sat at his desk in an expensive leather swivel chair, the kind Stark would have liked but the budget wouldn't allow. Pflugg's wire-rimmed spectacles glinted. He wore a shiny brown suit, soiled white shirt, and a narrow nylon necktie, black decorated with jags of lightning in gold. He sighed. "A sad case, Chief Stark. I was trying to straighten him out, his body was polluted by drugs. I'm saddened. He has a very spiritual side."

"Oh, really?"

"The Lord spoke to him at our meetings. Told him to give up the drugs, for instance, and he did that."

"Did the Lord ever tell any of your parishioners to set fire to farmers' barns? To punish them for something?"

Pastor Pflugg pursed his lips. "Not to my knowledge." He looked at the wall, wouldn't look Stark in the eye.

"Halloran, Bradley, Sadowsky, Wilcox, Chilten—those names mean anything to you, sir?"

The little fat man pursed his lips some more. "No."

"They're the farmers whose barns were burned down. You called the station, spoke to one of my men. Said you'd pray for the farmers but they were wicked people, maybe the Lord was teaching them a lesson."

"I didn't *say* wicked people. I don't know them. Only what I hear."

Stark shifted in his hard wooden chair. "What do you hear?"

"I hear they put mammon before God. I hear they are consumed by greed. I hear they are cruel people who make fun of those less fortunate."

"How many people are there in your congregation, Pastor?"

"We're small, Chief Stark. Only twelve, something like that."

"I've heard that Marian Arnold is a member of your church. Could you tell me the names of some of the others?"

The little fat man looked up at Stark. "Not unless you have a court order. You will persecute us, as those before you have done."

"Where were you before you came here, Pastor?"

The little fat man looked at Stark. He shook his head. "I think our meeting has ended, Chief Stark."

John Stark strode into the police station. He spoke to Clem Hughes and Vince Matucci, who were at their desks. "I think we've got a lead on the barn burner. Get a court order, and bring in Pastor Herman Pflugg, New Awakenings Church, Mott Road. He's knows something, but he's not talking. I think we're justified in getting a search warrant, too, go through his papers. You won't have any trouble with Judge Ottinger. His niece is Ruth Bradley. Then question that kid, Felton, who shot his wife. He'll give us some names. Pflugg says there are only a dozen or so in his group. The Arnold woman, this kid, we've got to get the names of the other ten."

Hughes and Matucci stood up. "See, Chief?" Matucci said. "The farmers were right. Someone with a grudge."

"As soon as you get some names, Vince, go back to the farmers, run the names by them. I'll contact the National Crime Information Center in Washington."

Vince said, "The Bradley woman already told me Marian Arnold came to her door, tried to talk Bible talk to her. She kicked her out. A high-school classmate of hers. Marian's a member of that church."

"Marian Arnold," Stark said. "She's kind of a half-wit, as I recall. An Okun, Bob Okun's sister." Stark smiled. "For the first time in six months, I feel good about this thing. We're nearly there."

CHAPTER THIRTY

✦✦✦✦✦✦✦

Walter Has
a Few Ideas

✦✦✦✦✦✦✦

Charly smiled as he peeped out at the sizable crowd in La Fermette's dining room. Customers were eating lobster (a Friday special) boiled or broiled: bouillabaisse; several shrimp specialties including the famous Shrimps Charly; Moules Marinière; poached salmon with Hollandaise. For some reason the Friday crowd was always loud and full of fun.

Although he still felt shaky, the showman in Charly rose to the occasion, the occasion being to provide epicurean fare for his customers. Caught up in the festive atmosphere, Charly almost forgot the attempt on his life. He broiled clams topped with his special butter, (Pernod, chopped shallots, and a touch of garlic), stirred the creamy seafood sauce for pasta, plated the buttery pan-sautéed salmon filets. What madman would want to shoot him? It wasn't as if he had a long list of enemies—as far as he knew, he had none. Well, he amended, he obviously had one, the shooter. What secrets had he uncovered? There was the barn burner, the dead woman, and the mysterious death of Linda Okun's son, in the hospital. Were they tied together? It would make things very tidy if this were so. Unfortunately, life wasn't very tidy. So the incidents probably weren't connected.

Julius and Benny had sheets of brown paper covering the kitchen windows, and Charly was wearing a bullet-proof vest. It was hot and uncomfortable.

"Walter Maxwell just arrived in the barroom," announced Elton the waiter. "He never eats this early. Says he just wants a snack."

"Tiens," Charly murmured, as he plated a thick slab of broiled halibut. "I am surprise. He was here Wednesday, and he usually come on Sunday."

"Well, he's here now, and he just wants an order of Shrimps Charly and an order of celeri remoulade, that's all."

Charly always had celeri remoulade on hand: matchsticks of celeriac, blanched, then dressed with a mustard, olive oil, wine-vinegar dressing. Celeri remoulade was a French bistro favorite, and all of New York's French restaurants had offered it in the sixties. Now, for some reason, it was out of fashion, but Charly had certain customers who would have kicked up a big fuss had it been removed from the menu. Walter was one of them. "I will go and greet him," Charly decided, remembering the altercation over the cocktail party. "Maybe offer him dinner on the house." Walter was no longer a loved customer, but he was still a good customer.

"Monsieur," Charly bowed, "allow me to offer you your dinner on the house, in anticipation of a wonderful party tomorrow night. And perhaps a split of champagne? Or sparkling cider?"

Walter smiled insincerely. "That's very kind of you, Charly. Some sparkling cider would be nice. I'm off on an adventure, after I eat: I'm meeting someone in Hogton, a man who says he can let me have a dozen sides of Scottish smoked salmon for about $10 apiece. Would you be interested in coming with me?"

Charly didn't like Walter's smile, nor his ingratiating manner—this wasn't Walter the arrogant, his usual stance.

And surely Walter knew that Charly only bought his foods from reliable sources. No, something was wrong here. So he offered an insincere smile back, and said, "Thank you very much, but I am not interested. It sound, you will forgive me the pun, fishy. Either stolen or not of good quality."

"Well, maybe it is," Walter said, "But I want to check it out, anyway."

"If it is for your party, be very careful. Much of this food, sold at cheap prices, is merchandise that has been condemned by the FDA because it has a too-high bacterial count and is meant to be destroyed."

"Hmmm," Walter said. "Maybe you're right."

"And," Charly continued, "to meet someone at night? In Hogton? Where the drug dealers are? Not wise, Monsieur."

Walter sighed. "So, you wouldn't want to go, check this guy out?"

"With certainty, no. But I thank you for the offer."

Charly returned to his kitchen, shaking his head and muttering. Something was definitely not right. Walter's behavior was decidedly odd. He confided in old Mick, Julius, and Benny.

"He was lying to you, for sure, but I don't know why," old Mick said.

"Did it ever occur to you," Julius speculated, "that Maxwell could be getting someone to burn all those barns, in hopes that the farmers would get disgusted with farming and sell out? To him?"

"They're rich farmers, so that won't wash," said old Mick. "And where would they go? They've been here all their lives."

"Don't go with Walter, Charly," Benny cautioned. "Or else, I'll go with you. Whatever he's up to, it's no good."

"Oh, I have no intention of going." Charly sprinkled parsley on an order of Sole Bonne Femme. "I wonder, that is all."

"Don't forget what my aunt told me," Julius said, "about Walter's being in with the Mob."

"No, I do not forget." Charly smoothed his mustache. "Monsieur Maxwell, he is up to something. Benny is right. This I feel in my bones."

Walter thanked his waiter and began eating his meal. It was tastefully arranged, a mound of celeriac in the center of the plate, surrounded by Charly's famous shrimp. He took a bite of shrimp, chewed. It didn't taste like it usually did. Not enough garlic, the tomato sauce was too runny, and Charly—or someone—had forgotten the final fillip of hot red pepper. He tasted his celeri remoulade: the freshly ground pepper had been omitted. Very bland.

When Elton stopped to inquire if everything was all right, Walter mentioned the badly cooked shrimp and the inadequately seasoned celeriac.

Elton chuckled. "Well, I'm not surprised. He's in a state. Someone took a shot at him this afternoon. We had the cops here and everything."

"What?" Walter upset his water glass.

Elton grabbed a napkin and mopped up, telling Walter what he'd heard.

"Someone tried to kill Charly?"

Elton said it looked that way.

"Good God," Walter said. Then he started to laugh, a high-pitched whinny that caused people at other tables to look over. "Excuse me," Walter said to Elton, "but it's too ludicrous. A rival restaurant owner, perhaps?"

"Perhaps, sir," Elton said cautiously.

"Who would want to kill Charly?" Walter spluttered, still laughing. *Except me*, he added to himself. Maybe the entire matter would be taken out of his hands. Walter asked Elton to tell Charly to stop by his table, when he had a moment. He wanted to hear the story straight from the horse's mouth.

• • •

"Is true, Monsieur," Charly nodded solemnly. He'd just told Walter about the shot and the visit from the police. "The bullet was from a deer rifle, Chief Stark thinks."

Walter mused. "And he only shot once, and missed. It doesn't sound like a professional, does it? In fact, the whole thing sounds strange—as if someone wanted to warn you, not kill you. Oh, by the way, Charly, I'm going to need a cleaning lady; Marian Arnold seems to have disappeared. Can you think of anyone, or should I just ask Party Rentals to send someone down?"

Charly didn't want to involve himself in any more problems with Walter, so he said, "At this last minute, I can think of no one. Party Rentals can send someone down. Their help is bonded, and they will do a good job."

"You haven't seen Marian Arnold, have you? She's vanished. Her husband Tom doesn't know where she is, either. She was always a strange one, but she's a good cleaner."

Charly wondered if he should take Walter into his confidence. Why not? "You know that my shed was burned down the other night, Monsieur. And now my partner Maurice tells me that the person running away was a woman. Do you think this person could be Marian Arnold?"

"Could be," Walter said. "You know, I always thought she'd crack up, one day. She's a strange woman. Tom told me she's been obsessed with the Bible since she joined that cult a year ago. That she talks nonstop about vengeance. Maybe that cult's behind everything—all the barn burnings, shooting at you, the death of that child in the hospital . . ."

"And the dead woman I find in my field?"

"Oh, that's right, I forgot about her," Walter said.

"But," Charly persisted, "why should Marian Arnold kill the child in the hospital?"

"He's her nephew," Walter said. "She hates her brother Bob Okun. I think she's jealous because he has children and she doesn't. I generally don't listen to servants' talk, but she's always muttering about them. She told me once the little boy was the devil's spawn. Made fun of her, I suppose. Told me once it was just a question of time, that God would strike him dead."

"*Tiens,*" Charly muttered. "And then he die. Very convenient, yes?"

"Everyone has enemies," Walter continued. "And it's easy enough to spread the word that they're evil, that Jehovah has them earmarked for destruction. Then when the person dies, well, it was preordained by God. Kind of like pointing the bone in primitive religions: You point the bone at someone, and he dies."

"Yes, I have heard of this," Charly reflected.

"Sometimes the person dies of fear," Walter continued. "And sometimes, I think he's given a little nudge. But everyone believes that he was killed by the evil spirit behind the bone, the curse."

"But Mrs. Marian, she is not a thinker."

"No," Walter agreed. "She's very slow. But she follows orders. If that guru at her church told her to do something, she'd do it."

An idea was taking shape in Walter's mind. Marian had disappeared. Marian wasn't too bright. The townspeople thought of Marian as a strange person. What if Marian should die? And what if, before she died, she confessed to Walter (without any witnesses, of course) that she'd killed Candy? And the kid in the hospital? and then Marian would try to kill Walter and he'd have to shoot her in self-defense. After she had confessed to two murders. Yes, it would work perfectly. And, Walter thought, he had a few ideas about where Marian might be hiding . . .

CHAPTER THIRTY-ONE

+-+-+-+-+-+-+

Pulling the Plug
on Pflugg

+-+-+-+-+-+-+

John Stark, walking into his office at six o'clock on Friday evening, had a smile on his face. Everything was coming together. He'd just gotten the information, via the state police and the NCIC on Pastor Pflugg, who had conveniently left his fingerprints on the Polaroid snapshot Stark had showed him. Pflugg had quite a little reputation in Ohio, Kentucky, Pennsylvania, and in the Syracuse area of New York State. He was wanted on several counts of larceny and grand larceny, and suspicion of many more. Stark called Syracuse, and got even more information.

"It couldn't be simpler," Stark told Matucci and Hughes. "Pflugg induces about a dozen simpleminded people to join his church, never too many, all people who are paranoid and easily led."

"Plenty of them around," Hughes said.

"All looking for a leader," Vince Matucci agreed.

"And," Stark continued, "he also gets to know the scumbags in the community, he probably has referrals from other locations: the crooked lawyers, the doctors who are looking for fast bucks. Then he pulls a scam or two, for a fee, of course: back injuries requiring thousands of dollars for treatment that the doctors claim from insurance companies; factories or houses or barns to burn down so the owners can collect; blackmail. The pastor gets a cut on everything. He's behind the barn burnings here, for sure. I suspect he'll go around to those farmers in a few months, try to intimidate them into giving him money for extra 'insurance' so there won't be any more barn burnings. But he's messing with the wrong crowd, here."

"It's a wonder he hasn't gotten caught before now," Clem said.

Stark continued, "The secret of his success is that he never works these scams on a large scale. He makes himself five, ten grand, then he moves on. That's a lot of money for a man like Pflugg, who's probably never had two nickels to rub together. Also, he never cheats poor, honest people who might report him. Always people who might find it embarrassing to report it to the authorities. Like blackmailing a doctor who has a couple of hundred grand in his safe, so he never has to declare it to the IRS. Pflugg never stays in a place more than a year. Guy's not stupid. Maybe psychotic, though."

"Looks like that Ruth Bradley, the farmer's wife, was right." Vince said.

"Where there's smoke, there's fire," Stark agreed. "Maybe he's in with some mob, maybe not. Maybe he's a loner. My guess is, he's a loner. We're all Mafia-crazy from watching all those Mob movies."

"You sound like my Uncle Rex," Vince said. "He hates anything to do with the Mob, feels it's a slur on Italian-Americans everywhere. He also thinks we see gangsters when it's the little guy next door, just getting even."

Stark said, "I called the cops over in Syracuse. A Pastor Jones ran around trying to sell insurance to farmers three, four years ago. Those who wouldn't buy, their barns burned down. Sound familiar? Is Pastor Jones Pastor Pflugg? Jones left suddenly, was never seen again in the area."

"Pastor Pflugg's bad news, whatever he's done. None of the other churches in the area will have anything to do with him. They're all talking against him. But, I'll tell you this: The rumor mill is always working overtime." Stark looked at his watch. "But I'm not. Not tonight."

"Nothing we can do tonight," Vince and Clem agreed.

"So I'm out of here," Stark concluded. "Gonna go home, tie on the feedbag then go to bed. The hospital still hasn't found that nurse's aide, the cleaner, the one on the corridor where Robby Okun died. Tomorrow's the funeral; I'm going."

"I am too," Vince said.

"I'll be there," Clem said.

"Then tomorrow night's that guy Maxwell's big cocktail party. He called, asked if we could send a man over, he's afraid the barn burner might hit again when he's got all those rich people there. I said sure, he could help direct traffic, keep an eye on things. I think he's got a point."

"You think Maxwell's up to something, Chief?" Clem asked. "You never know with them rich folks."

"I know he got his investment advisor, Jimmy Houghton, to sell nearly a million dollars' worth of stock," Stark said. "Jimmy called and told me. I was amazed. I said, 'Why tell me?' and Jimmy said, 'Oh, I just thought you'd like to know.' Houghton sounded real strange, too. I can't put my finger on it, just . . . strange. There's something going on, but I don't know what. So go get your beauty sleep, men, tomorrow's going to be a long day and an even longer night."

After Chief Stark left the office, Vince asked Clem how friendly was the Chief with Jimmy Houghton.

Clem shrugged. "It's not Houghton, it's his office manager, Evelyn."

"Who's Evelyn?"

"Evelyn Holmes is the office manager at Houghton and Houghton, Jimmy's firm. They tell rich folks how to invest their money."

"But why Evelyn?"

"Evelyn Holmes was one of John's teachers in high school. He loves the old lady. And she's also his wife's aunt."

"Jeez," Vince said. "Small world, ain't it?"

In the dining room of La Fermette Win Crozier and Morty Cohen were enjoying a supper of bouillabaisse, salad, garlic bread, and a bottle of Châteauneuf-du-Pape.

"This wine is heaven, Charly," Win said. "I always order Châteauneuf-du-Pape with your bouillabaisse, and I'm never disappointed."

"Yes," Charly agreed, "it takes a big wine to marry with all the garlic in the sauce rouille, and the saffron in the soup."

"Oh, I remembered the name of that model," Morty said. "Candy Moran. And I even remembered what happened to her. She left town, was going to marry a gentleman farmer somewhere in New England, guy raised horses or bulls or something, just like Walter Maxwell."

Charly told Win and Morty that the woman was, indeed, Candy Moran.

"Where was Walter going?" Morty changed the subject. "He was tearing out of your parking lot when we pulled in. Didn't even notice us."

Charly smiled. "He is meeting with someone in Hogton, I believe."

"No," Morty shook his head, "he wasn't going toward Hogton. When he left the lot he turned left, toward his house."

"Ah," Charly said, "then I am mistaken."

"We'll be at Walter's party tomorrow night," Win said, "and I'm dying to know what you're serving."

"Only delicious food," Charly said. "Don't you want to be surprised?"

"Oh, thanks for the tip on a house cleaner, Charly," Morty said. "We called Tiger Cavett, we interviewed him last night. He took the keys to the store home with him, and this morning, when we came in, it was cleaner than it's ever been. We're firing Marian, as soon as she appears from wherever she's been. Tiger's the man for us."

"Do not fire her too soon," Charly counseled, "since I believe Monsieur Tigre is looking for a full-time job. Mrs. Wells has lost her farm manager."

"I can't see a sensitive man like Tiger working for Honoria Wells," Win said petulantly. "He'd be much better off with us, and some like-minded souls. Maybe I can find him a few more cleaning jobs."

"Oh, but Honoria Wells would adore Tiger," Morty said quickly. Win had shown preferences before for small, blond men. "And she'd pay him a fortune. Yes, working for Honoria would be great for Tiger."

Charly smiled. "Well, we shall see. And now, may I offer you a slice of Patty's almond cake and a glass of kirsch, on the house?"

"Heaven," Win said, and Morty nodded. "Though I'm cross with you, Charly, not telling what you're serving at Walter's."

"I tell you this, *mon ami*, there is to be a two-kilo tin of Ossetra caviar, and another thing you love, my steak tartare."

"We won't eat all day in anticipation," Win said.

Honoria Wells, exhausted, asked Estrella if she could have a bowl of chicken noodle soup and some toast in bed, after her bath, in lieu of dinner. She was exhausted because

CHARLY'S ALMOND CAKE

Note: A restaurateur named Karen Hubert gave Charly the recipe for her celebrated chocolate cake before she died. Charly adapted the recipe, substituting almond paste for chocolate.

4 ounces butter, melted (1 stick)
½ cup sugar
1 Tablespoon almond essence
6 ounces almond paste (about ¾ cup)
5 eggs, separated, whites beaten stiffly
　　and reserved
1 cup flour
½ cup pignola nuts
Glaze: 1 cup confectioners' sugar
　　stirred with 2 Tablespoons rum and
　　1 Tablespoon water.

 Combine first six ingredients excluding egg whites, one at a time, beating well after each addition. Fold in beaten egg whites after addition of flour. Pour into greased and floured 10" springform pan and sprinkle top with pignola nuts. Bake in a preheated 350° oven, in water bath, 50–60 minutes. Cool, then pierce top of cake with tines of fork and drizzle over the glaze. Refrigerate.

she had been talking to her friends all afternoon—in New York, London, San Francisco, Santa Fe, Bermuda and São Paolo, telling them about her adventure, edited, naturally, to put herself in a good light: Her farm manager, a young man whom she'd asked out to dinner "as a friendly gesture" had tried to murder her.

It wasn't every day, or even every year, that someone tried to murder you, and Honoria hadn't had so much attention since she'd locked a would-be thief in her wine cellar three years ago and the police had found him amidst opened bottles of the 1959 Château Latours that she was saving for a grand occasion. (A resourceful chap, he'd had a corkscrew on his Swiss Army knife, and apologized for opening seven bottles, but five, he'd reported, had turned to vinegar, and one would have to be decanted, it was so filled with sediment.) Now, finally, having exhausted the names in her address book, Honoria lay in her bath and planned what she would wear to Walter's party tomorrow night. There was a knock on the bathroom door, and Estrella called "Señora Vell, there is the *policia* at the door, he tell me that he must see you at once, that someone is trying to kill you, he will explain."

"Dear God," Honoria said. "Show him into the library and give him a drink. I'll be right down."

The handsome young officer—Hackett was his name, Will Hackett—smiled at Honoria and explained.

"Because Harry Clark escaped from jail, ma'am. A guard came to his cell, and he knocked the man out, put on his uniform, and just walked out. He'd been talking to the officer earlier and found out he had a new black Ford, so when Harry knocked him out he took his car keys and just drove off. Naturally, the police think that Harry might drive by and try to kill you."

"My word," Honoria said. She couldn't believe Harry

would try to attack her again, he wouldn't be that stupid. Would he? But how lovely of Chief Stark to provide this toothsome morsel to guard her. Honoria smiled warmly at Officer Hackett.

CHAPTER THIRTY-TWO

+-+-+-+-+-+-+

Shots in the Dark

+-+-+-+-+-+-+

My, Officer Hackett, you certainly do lead an exciting life."

Honoria, curled in a chair in her pale grey living room (tastefully accented in charcoal and fuchsia and white) was giving the young cop what she considered sexy looks: eyes lowered, then raised seductively while batting eyelashes heavy with mascara.

Hackett thought some of that gunk she had on her lashes had gotten stuck in her eye, all that blinking she was doing. He felt uncomfortable, itchy. And her perfume made him want to sneeze.

These rich folks gave him a pain, they were so closed in on themselves. Nobody mattered but them. Living room was the size of the police parking lot: looked like a fancy doctor's office in the movies. Hard to believe one person actually lived here. Everything matched, pink and dark grey and white, even the pink-and-white flowers matched. Hackett couldn't believe Harry had been actually banging this old broad, dressed in a pink knitted one-piece thing, trying to look like a movie star, tits sticking out.

"I'll patrol outside tonight, ma'am, hope to catch Harry. Chief Stark's sure he'll show up here. He's a vengeful son of a gun, probably not smart enough to figure out this's the first place cops'll look. But he told his cellmate he was going to stop by and see you—loves to brag, that guy."

"You, alone? Won't that be dangerous? I thought there were always two of you." Honoria sipped at her ginger ale, batted her eyelashes. Hackett shifted in his chair, he felt weird, sitting here in this movie set. What was it, with this old lady—was she trying to put the make on him? Why was she wriggling around like she had an ant up her butt?

"Not enough manpower," Hackett told her. "Chief Stark needs at least four more men, the drug traffic in Hogton's spilling over into the rest of the county. Right now, we've got that boy killed in the hospital, Harry Clark walks out of jail, there's a religious-cult feller causing trouble . . ."

Honoria switched from seductive to alert. "Religious fellow? Little short, fat man, looks like Humpty Dumpty? Head of some sort of cult?"

Will Hackett leaned forward. "Why, you know him? Name's Pflugg."

"Well, Officer, this awful little man, reverend somebody, came to the door a few weeks ago. Estrella, my maid, told him to go away and he wouldn't. I spoke to him, he said he wanted to invite me and my staff to a service at his church, if you can believe that."

"Did he tell you why?"

Honoria widened her eyes, the picture of innocence. "Why, Officer Hackett, he said the most amazing thing. He said he was rounding up the sinners in this county, wanted to help them. Can you imagine?"

Will Hackett nodded, then realized this wasn't the proper response. He firmly shook his head. "No, ma'am."

"When I said I wasn't interested, he said I'd be sorry. He sort of sneered, like a little fat kid. 'You'll be sorry, real sorry.' Then he left."

"And you never heard any more?"

"Not another word. I asked Harry Clark if he'd heard of him, and Harry said he was the leader of a cult, and also, that he had a bad reputation as a blackmailer. Now really, Officer Hackett, how could he blackmail me?"

Just then Estrella appeared in the doorway. "Telephone for la *policía*."

Officer Hackett picked up the extension outside the living room. He said, "Yeah? You're not kidding?" Then laughed. "I don't believe it. He couldn't be that stupid, Vince."

"Well, that's what Harry did," Vince told Hackett. "Walked right into Steak Heaven, stood at the bar, had a shot of rye with a Genny chaser, told Bobby he was out on bail. I'd already mentioned to Bobby that the judge wouldn't grant bail for this guy, so Bobby calls the station, five minutes later our Harry's cuffed and going back to jail. Chief says come on back, they can use you here. Old Honoria got you inta the sack, yet?"

"Not yet." Officer Will Hackett told Honoria what had happened and left, after promising to stop in again and give her a progress report. "Will do, ma'am," Hackett lied. He didn't like the look in Honoria's eye. *About as old as my granny*, he thought. Honoria and her cosmetic surgeon would have been disappointed to hear this.

Walter Maxwell was convinced that Marian Arnold was hiding on his property. She'd worked here for twenty years, knew his routine, knew the outbuildings, cleaned his office, the bunkhouse, she'd told him once she felt more at home here than at her own house. And he knew just where she'd go: she'd always loved the guest cottage down by the swimming pool, loved to air it out in the spring and had told Walter that someday, she wanted a little place just like that: tiny bedroom, tiny living room, bathroom, and kitchenette. It hadn't been used in a couple of years, Walter guessed, since the few friends who had stayed over now stayed in the big house. Little Ricky said the pool house gave him the willies. All you could hear down there at night were owls hooting.

Walter left the car running, hurried into the house, and grabbed the keys to the guesthouse that were hanging on the panel by the back door. Marian could have had a second set of keys made. He drove down to the pool area, got his flashlight from the glove compartment, and hurried to the guesthouse, which was behind a clump of lilacs. From the outside, it looked uninhabited, totally dark. Walter fitted the key in the lock, and after a bit of twisting—it needed oiling, he must remember to have the gardener oil all the outside locks—the door swung open. Cobwebs framed the entrance, and Walter felt them brushing against his face as he swept in.

It was clear that no one had been here for a long time. The yellow walls and the sisal-rugged floors gave off a pungent odor of mildew, and the sheet-covered rattan furniture stood sentinel like short, squat ghosts. Walter played his flashlight around the kitchenette and the bathroom, and (remembering the movie *Psycho*) pulled the shower curtain out of the bathtub: *nada*. The bedroom smelled just as musty and mildewy as the rest, and mice had been carrying away the cotton batting in the antique quilt that lay folded at the foot of the queen-size bed. The silence was palpable. You couldn't hear the traffic, you couldn't hear anything. Walter felt his heart thudding against his ribs. Little Ricky was right: It was a creepy place. The people he'd bought the house from had told him the pool house had been built in the early twenties by a New York City millionaire who, after losing everything in the 1929 Wall Street crash, had shot himself in the pool-house living room. If Walter believed in ghosts, which he didn't, he'd say the place was haunted. But Marian loved the pool house.

Well, that was a disappointment. Walter would have put money on Marian's being here. As long as he was searching, he checked the tractor shed by the farm office, the office itself, and then went down to the barn, checked the stalls, and opened the door to the bunkhouse where some of the stablemen slept: the valuable Black Angus cattle were guarded like jewels.

"Oh, hello, Denny, I should have knocked. You haven't seen Marian Arnold, have you?" Denny was sprawled on a bunk, reading *Playboy*. Walter wrinkled his nose: the room reeked of old sweat, cow dung, marijuana, and, more faintly, of aftershave and vomit.

"Hi, Mr. M. Marian Arnold? Here? Why should she be here?"

"Just checking. She never showed up yesterday or today, and Tom's worried." *Tom's probably delighted*, Walter thought, but didn't say.

Back in his house office, Walter wondered what he'd forgotten in relation to Candy Moran. Something was nagging at the back of his brain, something he'd told himself to do, and he hadn't done it. Oh, of course. The manila envelope and Candy's toilet kit, up in the small guest bedroom, he'd hidden them. He'd taken the bottom drawer out, dropped the articles in so that they rested on the floor, then put the drawer back. He was going to get them right now, put them in a black plastic garbage bag, take them down to the pond in the rear pasture, weight them with a stone, and drop them in. No one would think to drag that old pond.

Walter went to the pantry and got a garbage bag, then

he mounted the steps to the second floor. In the small guest bedroom he pulled out the bottom drawer of the old pine chest of drawers and felt around: *Where the hell are they?* Then he bent way down and peered into the space. The manila envelope and Candy's toilet case had disappeared.

Julius Prendergast had been sleeping at his aunt Honoria's house since she'd gotten back from the hospital, and when he got in at eleven from the restaurant he expected to find the house dark. But there was a light in Honoria's small study, "my chintz room" she called it, since the walls and chairs and sofa were covered in salmon-colored flowered chintz. The television inside the study murmured softly, but the remainder of the house was still. Julius stopped outside the chintz room and called softly, "Hello?"

There was no answer, so he opened the door and peeped in. A breeze stirred curtains flanking what looked like a bullet-smashed window. Honoria was lying on the thick brown carpet, on her side, arms flung out. By her right shoulder, the one on the floor, blood soaked into the carpet. It looked like molasses in the dim light. Julius felt Honoria's neck: there was a faint pulse. He took three giant steps over to the telephone and dialed 9-1-1. He told the operator there had been a shooting, and it was an emergency; his aunt was still alive but a lot of blood had been lost. Then he went back to Honoria. Her hands were icy cold, and her face had the grey tinge of shock. He grabbed the fur throw from the sofa and covered her up. He took up her hand and held it to his cheek. "Everything's going to be all right," he told her.

The dining room of La Fermette smelled tired, the way it always smelled after a busy evening: too much smoke, too much food, especially fish, too much old perfume from

he customers. Charly loved the smell: It meant money in
he bank. Tommy Glade was tidying up the bar and
:lunking bottles together; one of the waiters was clearing
he tables of their cloths and stacking the chairs on top—
he cleaners came in every morning at six to vacuum and
lust, open all the windows to air the place out, change the
vater in the flower vases, and spray the dining room and
he barroom with the French airspray that Barbara Baleine
lad decreed was the proper restaurant aroma.

The staff had their coats on, ready to go home. Charly
vent back to the kitchen, where Benny was mopping the
loor. Benny had his overnight bag with him: He was going
o spend the night at Charly's house (yes, he insisted, he'd
old his mom) where he hoped to prevent the shooter from
innihilating the most famous French chef in Van Buren
County.

Although Charly pretended that all of this shooting
neant nothing to him, Benny could tell, from Charly's
lervous throat clearings, his constant glancing at the
)aper-covered windows, his shrugging inside the tight
)olice-issue vest, that Charly was, in fact, frightened.
Charly checked the cold room, the refrigerator, and made
ure the stove burners were all off.

"I have a better chance of dying from food poisoning,"
Charly told Benny as they trudged back to Charly's house.
'I was reading article just the other day in the newspaper,
:mployees do not wash their hand after using toilet, then
hey touch food: forty million Americans get sick from
estaurant food each year and eighty thousand die from
'ood poisoning caused by dirty hands."

"Hey," Benny said, "you know what most restaurants
)ay their kitchen help? How they treat those poor guys?
.ike scum."

Charly pretended innocence, teasing Benny: "In those
rade magazine that come for free, I read that restaurant

employees are all so happy, and well paid, is such a wonderful industry . . ."

"You don't read the trade publications," Benny reminded Charly.

"I always keep one or two in employees' toilet. And I know my employees wash their hands, because the soap go so quickly."

Benny snorted. "Not many employee restrooms have special olive-oil soap from France. Everyone loves that soap. It smells wonderful, *and* the aloe gel keeps your hands from drying out."

"If my employees are well fed and well paid, nice soap to wash their hands after they make *pipi*, they give good service. Waiters sell more food. The kitchen crew works well. You know how much it cost to train a new person? Look, the cat."

And indeed, two of Charly's cats were rubbing themselves against Benny's legs. The four-cat crew materialized and rushed into the kitchen when Charly opened the door. They waited expectantly for their snack.

"See?" Charly said, "No one has tried to shoot us." He got the plastic container marked CHATS from the refrigerator, spooned some meat into four bowls, and set them down on the floor.

Benny said, "We're not home free yet, Charly. Could you please get me some blankets or sheets? I want to cover the windows in the kitchen, your bedroom, my bedroom. Those flimsy curtains in your bedroom let in the light. We shouldn't be standing here in the light, you're right in front of the window. I'll need long thumbtacks, or little carpet nails and a hammer. Then we'll go to bed."

The telephone rang. "Allo? Yes, John, good of you to call. I still have on your vest. Benny is spending the night. We have just gotten home, and nobody is here. Everything

look safe. Benny will cover all the windows. WHAT? Oh,
mon Dieu! Is there anything I can do? She is out of danger?
She will live? Julius is with her?"

Charly had just hung up, and was turning to tell Benny
the news about Honoria, when the window above the sink
exploded and there was a loud noise. Charly screamed as
Benny grabbed his ankles and dived with him to the floor.
All four cats, ears back, abandoned their food and raced
upstairs.

CHAPTER THIRTY-THREE

❖❖❖❖❖❖❖

A Most Busy Day

❖❖❖❖❖❖❖

The police hadn't left until after midnight. Benny nailed plywood over Charly's shattered kitchen window and covered the other windows with dark blankets and towels. Charly's bedside clock said 1:04 when he finally crawled into bed. Benny was asleep in the small guest room.

"I shall not sleep a wink," Charly assured himself as the cats, calm now, arranged themselves on the bed and in baskets. The next time he opened his eyes it was 5:32, and Charly stared at the dark blue towels tacked up against his windows. Cautiously he got up and lifted a towel: a misty grey day. If he didn't hurry, he'd be late getting to the restaurant. He listened: silence. He decided not to wake Benny until seven, and he and the cats went downstairs.

"Honoria can't remember a thing," Julius told Charly, Benny, old Mick, and Max Helder and Fred Deering, the two catering helpers. They were standing around the restaurant kitchen, eight o'clock, sipping coffee. Charly and Benny had finished recounting their shooting adventure, and now the conversation had moved on to Honoria's similar experience.

"The cop left," Julius told them, "and she went into her study to get her purse. She remembered hearing some kind of explosion, then she woke up in the emergency room having a blood transfusion. The bullet went into her shoulder and out again, missed everything vital. She's a lucky lady."

Charly said it was lucky that the shooter was such a bad shot. But who could it be? And was it the same shooter who made an attempt on Charly's life?

"Cops are pretty sure in Honoria's case it's that Reverend Pflugg, little fat guy who's head of that cult," Julius said.

"How do you know?" Charly asked.

"Vince Matucci told his brother Bobby; Bobby told one of the ambulance attendants who's a regular at the bar; the attendant told his girlfriend who's an emergency-room nurse, and the nurse told me." Julius grinned. "It's called the county hot line. But who shot at you, Charly, could there be two shooters loose? And did you ever know this cult person?"

"I have never even met him, and he has never come to the restaurant as far as I know," Charly mused. "But now, we must get moving," he reminded them. "This is a most busy day. Patty is baking the cheese straws, the individual quiche, and she is making the blini and the crêpes at home, then she will take them directly to Maxwell's tonight. Benny and Julius, can you get lunch ready? Then start on dinner: I have a list of the dinner specials on my desk. Max and Fred, I have made you a list, it is in my office. Now, can you all help me load the van? I must get the food over to the Okun family. But first, I must call Barbara, to ask about Maurice."

Charly hurried into his office and dialed the Baleines'

number. Barbara, who was hurrying to an appointment in Albany, said that Maurice appeared to be improving, and that Dr. Bingham was talking about sending him to a sanatorium in Saratoga, a drying-out spot, to spend several months.

Charly told Barbara that this was an excellent idea. And, too, it would postpone the splitting up of the partnership. Even though Charly disliked Maurice, he was the son of his old partner, and to buy him out would be closing a door which had been open for many decades. Charly had a dread of closing doors, making irrevocable decisions.

"Ah, the most terrible tragedy, the death of a child," Charly said. He was sitting in Bob and Linda Okun's old-fashioned kitchen, drinking coffee. Bob's bulk was wedged onto a small wooden chair. Linda stood at the sink, dressed in baggy jeans and a sweatshirt.

"He never meant no harm," Bob said, "Just high spirits and prankishness. We all did stuff like that. He was just a little kid."

Charly, Bob, and Linda had emptied the van, Charly had been thanked, the food put on the screened porch, where it would keep cool. Bob and Linda were still in shock. Charly figured it wouldn't hit them for several more days. He remembered his own feelings when his wife and son died: It hadn't happened, it was a bad dream, he couldn't process the information, they weren't really dead. The reality of the situation was a long time in coming, when Charly finally realized that his family was gone forever.

"I am sure that he was a good son to you," Charly said.

"Oh, he was," Linda acknowledged. "Just last month, he gave me twenty-five dollars, said he knew we were going through a bad patch."

"A good son," Charly repeated, and wondered where the boy had found the money. He sipped the good, strong coffee. "And his aunt, Marian Arnold, has she expressed her condolences?"

Bob shook his head so hard his jowls wobbled. "Now, that's something I'll never understand. Never forget, either. My sister Marian and I had words in the past, 'cause of that religion of hers, but we're family. Family. And she hasn't called, hasn't come round. I just can't understand it. Police can't find her, anyplace. Seems like she's just vanished."

Linda smiled. "Maybe Robby's right about Marian. He always said she was crazy. He didn't like her. Nossir. Didn't like her a-tall. He said, now, wait, let me think just what he said, because it surprised me, it really did, coming from him. 'She's mental,' he told me. 'I seen her late at night, doin' funny things, things she oughtn't be doing.' Robby knew right from wrong, he surely did. And he didn't approve of Marian."

"What funny things?" Charly asked. "Did the child stay out very late?"

Bob chuckled. "Couldn't get that child to stay in, just couldn't do it. We were powerless over that boy. Couple times, he'd come in at breakfast time. 'Where you been, child?' I'd say. And he'd just shrug his shoulders, funny little way he had, and say, 'Oh, just around. Seein' things.'"

Charly merely nodded, but he was appalled at parents who couldn't discipline their children. It would never happen in France, he vowed.

Linda said, "Then he used another word about Marian I'd never heard. Pio-maniac. Said she was a pio-maniac. 'That nutty pio-maniac,' he'd call her. Then, he said, couple of times, 'I'll make her pay.'"

"Pio-maniac," Charly murmured. "I have never heard the word. And what did he mean, 'I'll make her pay'?

Would he demand money from his aunt for his silence about something he saw?"

Bob shrugged. "Little kid like that? 'Course not. Least, I don't think so. Basically, Robby was a good boy. Just filled with devilment. Kid stuff."

"There's no such word, Charly," Julius said, back at the restaurant kitchen. "Pio-maniac, no such word. Bet the child meant pyromaniac, which means a mania for setting things on fire. Like, a sickness. They say firemen are sometimes pyromaniacs."

"Like an arsonist," Charly said.

"An arsonist is someone who sets things, usually buildings, on fire," Julius explained, "but arson is a deliberate act. And usually done for money, to get insurance from a burnt building. A pyromaniac sets fire to things because it's a sickness, he can't help himself. Like a kleptomaniac steals because he can't help himself. A pyromaniac has a compulsion to watch things burn. Maybe this Robby saw his aunt setting fire to one of the barns, and he decided to blackmail her. 'I'll make her pay.' Wouldn't that fit?"

Charly arrived early for Robby Okun's funeral. He sat in his van near the church and thought about what Julius and Bob and Linda had said.

If Marian Arnold was setting fire to the barns, it would stand to reason that Robby, who often stayed out all night, could have seen her. And, Robby being Robby, he wouldn't alert the police. He'd want to get some money out of it. And so he would threaten Marian. And Marian would have no compunction about eliminating the person standing between herself and God's word. God's word, to Marian, was vengeance.

Someone tapped on the van's front window and Charly

jumped. It was Rex Cingale, from Steak Heaven. "Oh, Rex, is it time to go in?"

"If you want a seat," Rex said, "you'd better come now. Looks like the whole town's turning out. Everyone feels real sorry for Bob and Linda."

Rex waited while Charly climbed out of his van and locked it. Together, they strolled toward the little white-clapboard church. "Is nice church," Charly said to make conversation. "Is plain, simple. It is what, Methodist?"

"Methodist, Baptist, who knows?" Rex said. "It's not St. Mary's, that's all I know. After you, Charly." They reached the church.

The church vestibule smelled of perfume, flowers, mothballs, and more faintly of alcohol. Clumps of men stood together, talking. Presumably the wives had gone on into the church. Charly and Rex joined Win Crozier, Morty Cohen, and Peter Vann.

"Bob made the shelves in our cellar and our garage," Peter said. "I felt I should be here. Dinah couldn't come."

Of course not, Charly thought. *Why should Dinah bother with such an unfashionable crowd?* Charly's estimation of Peter went up. Peter was swaying slightly, and Charly could smell alcohol every time Peter breathed out, but . . . he was here. That was the important thing.

"Bob's done work for us, too," Win said. "He's a good man."

Rex cleared his throat. "This funeral's costing them a fuckin' packet. I'm going to slip Bob a few bills."

Charly, Peter, and Win agreed that this was a good idea.

The little church was packed, with people standing in the back. Charly nodded to old Doc Ross, Hy Bingham with his wife, to Patty Perkins who was sitting with Benny, to John and Betty Stark and their daughters, to Vince Matucci, Clem Hughes, and a few other policemen. Jimmy

Houghton and Evelyn Holmes were there, too, sitting right behind Charly.

"The Okun clan is taking up four pews," Evelyn whispered to Charly.

"Does Linda have any people here?" Charly whispered back.

"A few," Evelyn whispered. "Her people are from around Syracuse. See her brother? The man in the grey suit, with the woman in the black coat. Bob and Linda's daughters have been working at the brother's grocery store up near Syracuse, learning the business. Uh-oh, here comes the minister.

The minister, an elderly man whom Charly had never seen before, stood to the side of the plain wooden casket decorated with a simple spray of chrysanthemums and announced a hymn. The congregation rose to its feet. After several hymns the minister spoke about Robby, a sunny child filled with good deeds and a respect for the Lord, the pride of his parents, with a funloving nature and an innocent disposition, snatched up in the springtime of his life but now, blessedly, with God where he was enjoying eternal life. Charly, discreetly clearing his throat, frowned at these flagrant lies. He turned around and met the eye of Matthew Murdock, the school principal. He was frowning, too. Bob and Linda were weeping quietly.

Charly was one of the first people out of the church, after the Okun family. He didn't want to appear rude, but there was much work to be done. He shook Bob's and Linda's hands, and started toward his van. In front of him a tall and ungainly woman wrapped in a blue raincoat strode down the sidewalk. She might have come from the church, but Charly hadn't seen her there. She looked familiar. Marian Arnold? It looked, from the back, like Marian. Her head was covered in a flowered kerchief, bent down as if in deep thought. She was walking very quickly. Before Charly could catch up to the woman, she turned the corner and disappeared.

I must call Stark and tell him, Charly thought.

CHAPTER THIRTY-FOUR

Charly Snoops

Charly got in his van and sped off, looking for Marian. At the corner, Charly looked both ways, but she, or whoever it was, had disappeared. He drove back to the restaurant. He'd love to take the afternoon off and hunt for the woman, but he had a business to run. Leave the detecting to the police, he admonished himself, knowing that he wouldn't.

The kitchen of La Fermette was busy. Julius and Max Helder were preparing for Saturday night dinner—several roasts tonight, pork, lamb, veal. Some chickens, partially roasted, were sitting in the cold room waiting to be finished off, per order, with the appropriate sauces (Chasseur; A La Crème d'Estragon; Herbes de Provence;) or simply roasted to sizzling with the crispest skin imaginable on a bed of steamed puréed watercress, butter, and cream. There were beef and lamb steaks, stuffed pork chops, racks of lamb already coated with mustard, parsley, and garlic, and a basin of shrimp. Fred Deering was finishing the miniature salmon roses for Walter's party, and the steak tartare was resting on a bed of crushed ice in the refrigerator. Benny had arrived minutes before Charly, and he set about peeling and carving potatoes for the potato balls that would accompany the racks of lamb.

When Benny had first started working for Charly he had questioned the potato balls: "It's so time-consuming, and what's the difference whether or not you eat a quartered potato or a potato ball. It tastes just the same."

"This is style, not food," Charly said. "Would you pay thirty dollars for a few chops and a mound of boiled potatoes? No. But a crusty rack of lamb, plus tiny, hand-wrought potato balls, making the entire platter look like a work of art—ah, that is a different story, is it not?"

"Probably," Benny said.

"Or take some nice herbs and toasted bread crumbs, pan dripping, mustard, salt, and pepper, and stuff a big pork chop with this, and serve it with sweet-and-sour red cabbage and pommes Duchesse, mashed potato bound together with egg yolk and flour, then piped around the plate and browned under the salamander? So beautiful you want to take a photograph?"

"Yeah," Benny had said. "I see what people pay for."

"The difference between *la grande cuisine* and good plain cooking is not the ingredients but the method of preparation, the garnishes, the decorations on the plate. Why would you take lessons on how to make a spin kick to knock down your opponent, when you can punch him in the stomach with your fist, without taking any lessons at all?"

"I understand, Charly. One is an art, the other's not."

"And that is why we serve the potato ball, which take much time to prepare, with the rack of lamb, and that it is why we can charge thirty dollar. Because the plate is not just food; it is a work of epicurean art."

"But," Benny persisted, "it tastes just the same, doesn't it?"

"Maybe, maybe not," Charly said. "Your mind can influence your palate. Put on a blindfold, and they will taste just the same. But keep your eyes open and eat the same food from a beautifully garnished platter or a plain bowl, and to many people the beautiful platter will taste better. That, my dear Benny, is why you wear the handsome white uniform in Tae Quon Do. To turn simple self-defense into an art which is awesome to behold. Would it not be the same if you wore your jeans and a sweatshirt?"

"We're ready to load," Fred said. "Patty's meeting us at Walter's."

"Then I will get my list, and we will load in order of the list, as usual."

Charly had foregone his afternoon nap to go to Robby's funeral, but he didn't feel tired at all. He was quivering with excitement. In addition to the normal party jitters, Charly felt that something momentous was about to happen.

At the Klover Police Station John Stark met with his men.

"I have a feeling that after his party, Maxwell's going to disappear," Stark told them. "I checked with the bank. They didn't want to tell me, but finally they did. That million dollars is no longer in his account. He had it transferred to a bank in the Caribbean."

"You think he did the kid?" Vince Matucci asked.

"Either he did, or Marian Arnold did. I called the school, got her records. She quit in the eighth grade, which isn't legal, so they kept tabs on her but they couldn't force her to go to classes and none of the teachers wanted her there. She beat up one of the girls in her class pretty badly."

"Yeah," Vince said. "Mary Halloran, Jim's wife. He's the first one whose barn burned, incidentally."

Stark continued: "Marian told the police that Jesus had told her to do it. Even then, she was a Jesus freak. She was hospitalized up at Albany Psychiatric. Possibly schizophrenic. Released after three months. That was 1966, she was twelve. Released to the custody of her parents."

"Which was a joke," Clem Hughes said, "both alcoholics, living on welfare. They're both dead, now. You get anything on Maxwell?"

"Yeah," Stark said. "The Massachusetts State Police found records indicating that he was involved in a shooting back in 1965, but he was cleared at a jury trial. It was a hunting accident, he shot a guy named William Talbott, but the other hunters testified that Talbott was drunk and wasn't where he should have been."

"Think of all the hunting accidents we have around here," Clem said. "I often wonder how many of 'em's really accidents."

"You know who else testified?" Stark continued, "Maxwell's farm manager, acting as hunting guide. His name was Thomas Arnold. He was Tom Arnold's father. I called Tom, he and his family moved down from Massachusetts when Tom was a youngster, his father continued to work as Maxwell's farm manager until he died in 1989, then Maxwell offered the job to young Tom. Tom says he can't remember any shooting."

"Talbott have any family?" Vince asked.

"Yeah, wife and two kids. State police said they moved to Albany, right after the accident, her family came from there. They don't know what happened to them after that. Don't even know her family's name. It was never written down, or lost. The Talbott family, his people, high-society folks, simply closed ranks, wouldn't talk to anyone, acted like it never happened. William Talbott had evidently gotten in with the Boston Mob."

"But don't forget," Clem said, "this all happened thirty years ago. Lotta the players are long gone."

"That's only yesterday, if it happened in your family." Vince smiled. "My parents, my aunts, and uncles, sit around after Sunday dinner talking about things that happened in the family thirty, forty years ago, it's as if they happened yesterday. My great-uncle Angelo, sixty years ago, punched a kid in the mouth, the kid ends up marryin' my great-aunt Cora, they're still arguin' about who was right, wrong. Everyone's in their eighties now."

Stark said, "Well, I still think after his party Maxwell might do a disappearing act. Rich guy like that, probably has a condo in the Bahamas. I want to bring him in for questioning. I'd like a couple of men to keep an eye on things. I told Walter we'd keep an eye out for the arsonist. I have a feeling as soon as the last guest is gone, the help gone home, Walter's going to pack a little suitcase. So, if Clem and Vince could go over, around half past seven, I'll clear it with the party people. I got the name from Charly Poisson. They'll have men there parking cars. I want them to know you'll be patrolling the grounds. I'll stop by around eight-thirty."

"Valet parking," Vince said. "Just like one of those fancy clubs up in Albany. Man, that's the way to give a party."

Maxwell's a businessman," Stark reminded them. "He deals with a lot of rich folks. He wants to impress 'em, so when they buy a bull from him, they'll know it's quality merchandise. That's all this party is, a business thing. And Van Buren County's poor, we could use more Maxwells."

"Not if he's in with the Mob," Vince reminded John. "Like I heard."

"Yeah, Vince, but maybe he's not. And, who knows, couple of the guests might say, 'Hey, this country's beautiful, maybe we should move here, set up business.' That's why I want you to tread real easy."

"Real estate feller told me, other day, sixteen thousand houses in this county up for sale," Clem said. "We're in a bad way, here. Hey, what if Maxwell sees us?"

"Tell him it's routine," Stark said. "You'd gotten a tip about the arsonist, wanted to check out the woods behind his house."

"I think we should grab the guy right toward the end of the party; even before the last guest leaves, we move in."

"Un-unh," Stark said. "I don't want another Scanlon business. Why embarrass the guy?"

Everyone wanted to forget the Scanlon business. It had been a major embarrassment for the county, even though it had happened in another town, with another police crew. Mr. Tobias Scanlon, a distinguished antique dealer, had, in his shop, a sterling-silver tea service that matched the description of a tea service stolen from an estate in nearby Connecticut.

The police had arrived at Scanlon's shop while he was entertaining at a little cocktail party in the garden behind the shop. They'd bumbled in, grabbed Scanlon, made insulting remarks, acted like the Gestapo, and carried Scanlon and his tea service away. Later, Scanlon had produced impeccable provenance for the tea set, as well as a very tough lawyer. And the real thieves were arrested several days later, trying to peddle an almost-identical set in a nearby town. Scanlon had sued the police department (and won), and Van Buren County again made national news of a less than positive kind.

"Yeah, I remember that," Clem said. "Aw, what the hell. We'll be careful. I heard the weather forecast, gonna rain, tonight."

"So wear a raincoat," Stark told him. "You're too big to melt."

• • •

In Walter Maxwell's kitchen (furnished with a stainless-steel Traulsen refrigerator, Garland stove, hanging copper pots, butcher-block island) Patty Perkins was chatting with Ben Bradley, the Party Rentals supervisor, when Charly arrived.

"Charly, you should hear this," Patty told him. "Go on, Ben, tell Charly what you told me."

"Chief of police called me," Ben told them, "said there would be men patrolling the area tonight, around the time the guests were leaving. Something about an arsonist? The chief wanted me to alert my men that there'd be a couple of cops roaming around outside."

Charly said, "Does Mr. Maxwell know this?"

Ben, the supervisor, shrugged. "I don't know, and I wouldn't bother to tell him. He's not in a good mood. He called earlier, asked us to get a cleaning crew in, his cleaner didn't show, and he says our crew chipped one of his glass animals, big thing, looks like a whale. Maxwell says it's worth eight thousand dollars. 'Course we're insured, but now he's got to dig up proof of purchase, and our cleaners say it was already chipped when they got here. They made a note of it. I see a big song and dance, ahead. I tell ya, guy's pissed. So are we. I trust our guys. If they say it was chipped before, then I believe them. When they damage something, they're honest about it."

"He usually comes into the kitchen, wants to taste everything," Charly told them, "but if he is not happy, perhaps it is better he should stay away."

Walter appeared in the pantry beyond the kitchen. "Charly? That you in there? How's everything going?"

"Everything is fine, monsieur. We have just arrived, and we are unpacking the food. Max Helder and Fred Deering, you know Mr. Maxwell."

"Yes, hello," Walter said, nodding at Max and Fred. "I'll

be in my office. Guests are due in, what, forty-five minutes?"

"We are in good time, monsieur. No need to concern yourself. If you would like to sample the food, as is your custom, it will be ready in thirty minutes. We are serving the caviar in its own tin, in a silver bowl filled with crushed ice." Charly displayed the bowl. "Is it not handsome?"

Walter stood, hand on hip, studying the silver bowl. "Passable, Charly. It looks like hotel service. We used it last year, I remember thinking it wasn't quite right. I've got a nicer one, antique pewter, I wonder where it's gone to, I remember putting it away . . ."

"The cellar, monsieur? The storeroom? The attic?"

"Not the storeroom. Marian cleaned it out a few months ago. Possibly the cellar, though I doubt it, or maybe the attic," Walter said. "I haven't been up to the attic in years." Walter stood stock-still, and a curious expression came over his face. "The attic," Walter shouted. "Of course, the attic. Why didn't I think of the attic?" He turned and ran out of the room.

"He's getting pretty excited about a serving bowl," Fred said.

"I think it is more than that," Charly said thoughtfully. Did he have time to follow Walter to the attic? But just then Max came up to speak to him, where was the sauté pan for the crabmeat balls, and Patty wanted to know if it was too soon to put the fruit and cheese out, and one of the party caterers wanted to know if food was to be placed on the two pine side tables, because if so, they should have a tablecloth, and in the busyness of the moment, Charly forgot all about Walter and the attic.

At five-forty-five Patty said to Charly, "Walter never came back with that serving bowl, should I put the ice in the silver bowl?"

"Yes, we can always change it back, later."

The guests began arriving, but still Walter had not returned. Patty went out to play the role of hostess, telling people that Walter was momentarily delayed. When he did appear, breathless and a bit disheveled, a few minutes later, he didn't mention the serving bowl and took over welcoming his guests. He was suave and charming, as usual.

"Something funny's going on with Mr. Maxwell," Patty told Charly in the kitchen. "He never mentioned the serving bowl, and he looked—well, I don't know, like he'd been in a tussle, his clothes were all funny."

"Funny?" Charly asked. He hadn't seen Walter.

"Well, you know, kind of disarranged. His necktie was twisted, and he had a smudge of dirt on his cheek, and his shirt looked dusty, and the pocket of his jacket was torn. I guess he was ripping open old cartons, trying to find that bowl. Funny he didn't mention the bowl."

Charly was already aware that this party had a strange feel to it. Walter, for instance, hadn't come out to the kitchen to sample the appetizers, as he always did; this business about the police patrolling the woods with the story about the arsonist—something didn't turn around, *ça ne tournait pas rond.*

He sat down at the kitchen table, suddenly exhausted. Would this day never end? At six-thirty he had to return to the restaurant to make sure all was going smoothly . . . then he had to come back here, to Walter's, and stay until the end . . . he took his handkerchief out of his pocket to mop his forehead, but his pen, caught in the handkerchief, flipped out, and rolled under the refrigerator.

Oh, merde, Charly thought. With difficulty— his back was a bit stiff, as were his knees—he stooped down and felt underneath the refrigerator for his pen. He couldn't feel anything. He took up a long knife from Walter's knife drawer and waved it under the refrigerator, hoping to flick the pen out. The knife connected with something and clicked, Charly gave a quick sweep, and his gold-plated Cross pen sailed out along with something else, a small piece of—of what? glass? ivory?

Charly picked up his pen and placed it safely in his pocket. Then he picked up the bit of whatever it was and examined it. Not content, he took his magnifying glass from his other pocket, and scrutinized the small white object. It looked like enamel from a tooth. He looked again, and looked again, turning the piece this way and that. It appeared to be the bottom half of a front tooth, not white but more ivory colored, cleanly broken off.

Charly put the object in his pocket and sat down at the kitchen table again, visualizing the fragment. A tooth, a tooth—why would a tooth be under Walter's refrigerator? Walter didn't appear to have broken a tooth, not a front tooth, and this was definitely a front tooth, quite flat on one side. And neither had Marian, when he'd seen her the other day in Walter's office.

And then Charly remembered the corpse he had found in the woods on Monday, six days ago. The corpse of, he now knew, a woman named Candy Moran who worked at an art gallery in New York and who had, as far as anyone knew, no earthly reason for being in Van Buren County.

Charly could see the corpse in its shallow grave, see the woman's face, the mouth grimacing, the broken front tooth, the broken front tooth . . . the tooth of Candy Moran, Candy, C—A—N was inscribed on the smudged pen that he'd found in the fire behind Walter's garage . . . "Oh, *mon Dieu*," Charly muttered.

CHAPTER THIRTY-FIVE

✛✛✛✛✛✛✛

Charly Continues
to Snoop

✛✛✛✛✛✛✛

Vince Matucci and Clem Hughes had parked the cruiser over by Walter Maxwell's burnt shed. The rain, which had begun in a gentle way as they drove, now became more insistent. Felt like the temperature was dropping, too. Vince shivered and said, "Brrrr." He wished he'd worn a sweater under his rain gear. This was going to be a long night.

They didn't want to alarm Maxwell's guests, some of whom, they figured, might be disturbed at the sight of a police vehicle. Unlike their boss John Stark, both Matucci and Hughes were united in their disapproval of Walter Maxwell and his wealthy guests. The officers shared the countryman's view that most rich people were dishonest. Nice guys finish last. And poor. How many backstabbings did that first million entail?

"Buncha crooks, the way I figure it," Clem said. "All standin' around sippin' champagne, showin' off to each other how important they are. All gussied up in their fine feathers."

Vince said, "I went up to Maxwell's earlier this week, you shoulda seen his kitchen—bigger 'n my uncle Rex's, at the restaurant. He seemed normal enough, though. Offered me coffee, passed the time of day."

"Hmpf," Clem said. "Look out on your side, into the bushes. Can you get out without scratching the door?"

"No," Vince said. "Back up, then nose in more to the left. See? Some branches are all broke, there. Oh, boy, it's really started to rain, now."

"Hey," Clem said. "You see what I see?" Just in front of the cruiser's nose, wedged deep into the bushes, was the back of another vehicle. It was an old white car. Clem and Vince pulled up the hoods of their rain ponchos and stepped out of the cruiser.

"Engine's cool," Abe said, feeling the hood. "Coulda been here for months. Old battered white car—wasn't Marian Arnold's car old and white?"

Clem had returned to the cruiser and was relaying the license plate number to the station. Within minutes, the message was returned: It was Marian Arnold's license plate. Clem told the dispatcher to alert the chief. Meanwhile Vince was snooping around the car, flashlight out, checking the tires, the trim, the dents and scratches, all of which appeared to have been made a long time ago. The car doors were locked.

"Oh, boy, think we'll find a body in the trunk?" Vince asked Clem.

"It's a hatchback."

"Oh, yeah, 'course. Well, nobody's in the car, far as I can see." Vince peered in the car windows. "Big stack a pamphlets on the backseat. See? 'If It Ain't King James It Ain't Bible'. Oh, boy, Father Evangelista would sure have something to say about that. Catholics use the Douay version."

"You get your prints all over, Chief's gonna be pissed," Clem told him.

Vince drew back from the car. "Lookit that bumper sticker: NRA ALL THE WAY. My uncle Rex belongs to the NRA, National Restaurant Association."

"It's also the National Rifle Association," Clem said. "As you should know, bein' a cop. That tells us something about Marian, don't it?"

"Tells us she likes guns, like everyone else in this county."

"Yep, I'd guess old Marian's a shooter. Her dad, poor as he was, had an arsenal. Big deer hunter. Big drunk, too. Bet he taught her to shoot." Clem sniffed. "Cold as a bitch, ain't it? My wife made me put on my long johns."

"Maybe Marian's gonna lean in the window over at Maxwell's, take a shot at some of those fancy horse doovers," Vince told Clem. "Charly told my uncle Rex, Rex told Bobby, Bobby told me—raw ground filly mignon, caviar, that's fish eggs from sturgeon, little crab cakes, little roses made outta smoked salmon—impressed the shit out of Rex. Not me."

"You won't catch me eating raw hamburger," Clem said. "Or fish eggs or crabmeat, neither. Glad I'm poor, if that's what the rich eat."

By this time it was past eight o'clock and Vince and Clem had made their way up to the front of Black Bull Farm, dripping all the way, brushing against wet branches. Their whispers were muffled in the misty dusk. Cars were parked along the driveway and to the left of the house in a field. Two young men were standing near the front walk, dressed in rain ponchos. Seeing the two police officers, they walked over.

"No one's left, yet," one of them said, "but we checked with the kitchen. Party's beginning to wind down. They figure another half hour, guests'll start leaving. You want to stand on the porch? Rain's soaking through this rag."

"Maybe later," Clem said. "We'll walk around for a bit." The officers strolled around to the back of the house, then down to the garage, where they found Stark sheltering from the rain in a doorway. The three-car garage was built on a stone foundation, with a 1920's cottage framework above.

Vince had heard that the Shelbys, an old Van Buren County farm family, had sold out to some New Yorkers about seventy years ago, and they'd turned the farm into an estate, with a swimming pool, guest cottage, fancy garage, and other outbuildings. Then the Depression had come along and they'd lost everything. Something about a suicide. The place had stayed empty for a good ten years before Maxwell bought it in the late seventies, for about a fifth of its real value. Supposed to be haunted, or jinxed, or something.

"I got the message about Marian's car; good work," Stark said. "We'll do a quick search after the guests leave, be real polite to Maxwell, but let him know we're serious. I'll bet Marian's hiding somewhere in the house. Maybe the cellar, or the attic. It's a big place. Bet there's a lot of little rooms Maxwell never goes into. Charly Poisson called this afternoon, said he thought he saw Marian leaving the funeral. But when he went to look for her, she'd disappeared. But with her car here, she must be nearby."

"Maybe Maxwell killed her," Clem said, darkly.

The party had, indeed, wound down. In fact, the party was over. The guests had left, Walter standing at the door shaking the hands of the men and kissing the cheeks of the women for over half an hour. Charly, in passing, had nodded to the few guests he knew: Win and Morty, Jimmy Houghton, Dinah and Peter Vann, the Warburtons. Honoria Wells would have been here, Charly knew, but she was in the hospital. Poor Honoria, she loved parties. Then, guests gone, Walter had disappeared.

Charly, standing in the kitchen in his chef's whites, popped a cold crabmeat bouchée in his mouth and chewed. "It is perfect," he complimented Fred, who was pouring the oil from the portable fryer into the small tin drum they used for that very purpose. "Crispy on the outside, soft and tasty within. Too bad they are so costly to make."

"You ever try that fake crab, Charly?" Fred asked.

"Not good," Charly replied. "Too much salt and chemical. You want to make for your friends, use tuna fish. We serve that at a graduation-from-high-school party last summer. Very nice. Benny think of the name, Tuna Pepper-Pops. We put in tiny, tiny little bit jalapeño pepper, the children think it is very daring to eat something so spicy. Uh-oh, I hear . . ."

What Charly had heard was the sound of breaking glass, and he hurried into the corridor. A waiter had dropped a glass toward the back of the front hall, and Charly bent down to help the young man retrieve the pieces.

"It's my own fault," the waiter told Charly. "I wanted to get all of the glasses at this end, and I tilted my tray when I put it down. You think there's any glasses in that room over there? I think it's Mr. Maxwell's office—he told us to keep the door shut, but it's open, now." He gestured with his head.

"Just a minute, I will see," Charly said, and darted into Walter's office. He stopped suddenly, seeing Walter sitting at his desk with the middle drawer open. He had something in his hands which he replaced in the drawer when Charly burst in.

"Oh, forgive me," Charly said, "I did not see you, monsieur. I am so sorry to interrupt. We are looking for empty glasses."

Walter looked at Charly. "This room is off-limits, Charly. No guests were in here, I shut the door." Walter slid the drawer shut, and stood up, waiting for Charly to leave. "I've got some telephone calls I have to make," Walter explained, "then I'll come out to see you off. I'll make out your check now, Charly, and see you in the kitchen in about fifteen minutes."

Apologizing profusely, Charly backed out. Walter had been loading a pistol. If Charly had known anything about pistols, which he did not, he would have recognized a 9mm Parabellum Beretta semiautomatic pistol with a fifteen-round magazine. What Charly did notice was that the pistol looked extremely deadly. He was sorry, now, that he hadn't searched Walter's house, looking for Marian. But how could he, with a big, important party to supervise? He had a reputation to maintain.

CHAPTER THIRTY-SIX

Seek and Ye Shall Find

Instead of returning to the kitchen, Charly hurried down the hall to the back corridor leading to the servants' wing. Here was a back staircase, so that in the days when nearly everyone had help, the servants could come downstairs early in the morning without disturbing the rest of the house.

Only once in his life had Charly been upstairs in Walter's house. Walter had been sick in bed with the flu, and Charly had delivered some food. Walter had told him to come up the front stairs, turn left at the landing, and walk down the corridor to the master bedroom at the end. Charly, who often confused right with left, had turned right, instead of left, and opened the door at the end of the corridor to find steps leading up to the attic. That was where he was now headed. Walter had seemed inordinately excited about the attic, just before the cocktail party. And Charly, goaded by his own curiosity, simply had to find out why. He knew it couldn't be a mere pewter serving bowl.

Charly tiptoed up the attic steps, holding tightly to the banister, for the steps were steep. Charly hadn't been in many old attics, but he knew, from his own big restaurant farmhouse, that attics in these old houses were divided into storage areas and extra rooms for servants. When people had gone visiting a century ago they often brought their help, nursemaids for babies, ladies' maids, perhaps even valets for the men. Visits could last for weeks.

He played his flashlight on the steps, noting that the dust on both sides had been wiped off the middle, no doubt by recent footprints. At the top of the steps, Charly played his flashlight around. It was a clean space, filled with cobwebs but tidy, with boxes and trunks arranged around walls that had been Sheetrocked but never painted. At the far end of the attic were three doors leading to, Charly assumed, servants' rooms.

He tiptoed across the space and tried the first door. The door swung open to reveal a metal bed frame with sagging mattress, a window curtained in torn white cotton, a bureau, and, under the bed, a chamber pot. Although the room was empty, this part of the attic had an odor—an unpleasant odor combined of sweat, excrement, and other things that Charly could not, at the moment, define.

Charly backed out and moved to the second door. He turned the door knob, but the door was locked. Looking down, Charly saw that the key was in the keyhole. He turned the key and walked in.

The room was identical to the first room, except that here there was an oblong woven reed baby basket, the kind that Native Americans made, under the window, and in it was what looked like a mound of herbs and something old and shriveled, like a piece of dried cod. An elegant toilet case lay on the floor by the bed. And on the bed lay a body covered in quilts. Charly came over to the bed and peered at the head sticking out. Marian Arnold.

Marian lay under a pile of old quilts. There was a piece of rag tied around her mouth. She looked half-dead—eyes sunk in, grey coloring, her breath coming in little, shallow spurts. She rolled her eyes up to the ceiling, then down to the bed. Did she even notice that Charly had entered the room? She gave no sign. He found a light in the ceiling, and pulled the cord, flooding the room with the feeble light of a sixty-watt bulb, turning off his flashlight as he did so.

Charly flung the quilts aside. Marian's hands and feet were bound with clothesline cord, a gag made from an old towel covered her mouth. She looked at Charly, now, and seemed to recognize him. She banged her heels against the metal bed frame, and shook her head from side to side.

Charly pulled the gag from Marian's face and, removing his pocketknife, began slicing at the cords. Marian's mouth worked. She ran her tongue over her teeth and tried to speak, but only a croak came out. Charly looked around the room but found neither water nor a glass.

"How long have you been tied up?" he whispered.

Marian croaked, "Lotta hours. Came this aft'noon after funeral. Mr. Walter come up, found me when it got dark, tied me up."

"You have been staying here? Hiding?"

"This's my room. My room. Always come up here to rest."

"Always?"

"Years 'n' years. Used to spend night, when Ma and Pa were so liquored up. They used to beat us, me 'n Bob. And worse."

"Did Walter know?"

"I don't know. Maybe he knew. Mrs. Walter told me I could stay here. She was scared of Mr. Walter. He killed her. She knew he would. He did something to the brakes on her car. I saw 'im. Thought he was fixin' something; I didn't say nothing. But afterward I knew."

Marian wet her lips with her tongue. Charly had finally sliced through the cords, and he massaged Marian's ankles as she rubbed at her wrists. She smelled strongly of urine and feces and Charly wrinkled his nose but didn't say anything. Charly was intent on watching for an attack from Marian, whom he both pitied and feared. Was she a murderer? An arsonist? And more to the point, should he question her? Probably not, she was in shock. He nodded to the basket in the corner of the room. "What is in the basket?"

"My baby."

"What happened?"

"Baby born, in this room. Too small to live. Little bitty thing. I tried to take care of him, but he died."

"Walter Maxwell was the father?"

Marian shook her head. "My dad. I think."

"So what did you do?"

"Baby didn't move. Just lay like my dolly. I got some tansy, like Indians do, wrapped baby up in tansy. Baby dried up. I visit with him every day."

Charly moved over to the window and picked up the little woven grass basket. It was as light as a bunch of feathers. He sniffed at the desiccated little mummy cradled among the dried herbs. It gave off, faintly, the odor of long-dried fish at the seashore, washed up beyond the tide line and left to dry in the sun—a faintly saline smell, not unpleasant. He took some of the dried herbs and crumbled them in his fingers, then sniffed: It was, indeed, dried tansy. In France, women supposedly drank tansy tea to abort.

"How could no one know that you were expecting a baby?"

Marian shook her head. "No one knew. I was fat, is all. I prayed to the Lord to do the right thing. He told me it had to die. He told me it was best."

Charly decided to chance a few questions: "And the Lord told you to kill that little boy in the hospital."

"No, I never did."

"The Lord told you to burn my shed."

Marian nodded. "You was argant in the face of the Lord. You spoke in blasphemy against the Lord."

"What does argant mean?"

"Don't know. Pastor Pflugg told me. Argance must be punished."

"And the six farmers, you burned down their barns . . ."

"Pastor prayed with me, told me to do the right thing. They was argant, too. Argant in the face of the Lord. Pastor was goin' to visit them, pray with them, tell them the Lord was punishin' them." Marian took a deep breath and recited, singsong: "'And the fearful, the unbelieving, the 'bominable, the murderers, the idolators, all liars, shall have their part in the lake which burneth with fire and brimstone, which is the second death.' And after I burned down seven barns there would come unto me seven angels, and I would become purified."

"That is the Book of Revelation," Charly said, thinking, *She cannot be too stupid, if she can memorize parts of the Bible.*

"The magic book," Marian clarified. "I learned it for Pastor Pflugg."

"And so," Charly said, "they were Godless souls, the farmers."

"Prideful, Godless souls."

The prosperous farmers, who were so proud of their well-kept farms. And the women, who had poked fun at the poor, dull, lumpy girl. So it was jealousy, after all. Jealousy and a madness for vengeance. Charly looked at Marian. He tried to see inside her, to imagine the tortured soul that lay in this lumpy, ugly body. The wounds had festered like wet hay, baled too soon. Then they had burst into flame, a combustion not so spontaneous as progressive, one hurt building on the next, and the next, and the next.

Charly heaved a great sigh. The police would come, Marian would go back to Albany Psychiatric, or to some prison hospital for the criminally insane. While the man who had used her, that Pflugg character, would pack his bags, hop in his car, and journey onward to find more Marians to use.

"And Honoria Wells? You shot her? And tried to shoot me?"

"Godless souls," Marian mumbled. "You, too. Godless."

Of course, Charly thought. *The Godless must be punished.* Charly shook his head and wished devoutly that he was elsewhere. He felt that his legs couldn't hold him any longer. And yet to sit on the bed would put him closer to Marian, to the revolting smells. Marian made his stomach lurch, just the person she was, never mind the smells.

"Well, well," said a voice behind Charly, "I didn't expect to find you here, Chef." Walter Maxwell was standing in the doorway. With a very ugly-looking pistol in his right hand.

CHAPTER THIRTY-SEVEN

✛✛✛✛✛✛✛

Last Meals

✛✛✛✛✛✛✛

Charly sighed. "*Mais oui*, monsieur, I am always around, like the flies in a summer kitchen. I am always buzzing around. This poor lady tell me that you have tied her up and threaten her with death."

"Poor Marian," Walter said, and sighed, keeping his pistol aimed at Charly. "She's gone completely round the bend, you know. She killed that little boy in the hospital, and she set all those fires, besides. She also killed that woman you found in your field, Charly. Didn't you, Marian?" Walter spoke softly, almost caressingly, but kept his eyes on Charly. "Poor Marian. Too bad she won't be alive to testify."

"Didn't kill Robby, no woman in no field," Marian mumbled.

Walter continued, as if Marian hadn't spoken. "Poor Marian, she's not normal, you know. Typical schizophrenic. Voices tell her to do things. Voices, for instance, told her to burn down those barns."

"The barns, yes, I believe she did that," Charly said sternly. "But the people, no, that I do not believe. It is not in her nature."

"Perhaps," Walter said. "That preacher got her all fired

up, excuse the pun, so she believed the farmers' wives were wicked because they used to poke fun at her, so their barns had to burn to teach them a lesson. The woman and the boy, too, for reasons we'll never know."

"Are you certain that Marian kill the Moran woman?" Charly asked. ("Sometimes I think you have a death wish," Julius would later tell Charly, when he recounted his story.) "I think *you* kill the Moran woman, and try to put the blame on this poor creature, who is, I agree, not normal. I find a broken front tooth under your refrigerator, Walter, and the woman that I find, this Candy, she have a broken front tooth."

"Oh, Charly." Walter sighed. "I hate to do you. Little Ricky's right, you're too good a chef to die. But you have to be a detective right to the bitter end, don't you? Playing at Sherlock Holmes. But, yes, if you insist, I did kill Candy Moran. I'm sorry, Charly. I have to hit you and Marian. You're the last people I'll ever kill, though. I hate all of this butchering." Walter held the pistol in firing position, with both hands, legs apart, slightly bent. "It's not the gentleman's way." He lowered the gun. Wanted to talk some more.

"You never learn, do you?" Walter continued. "Always nosing around. But before I kill you, give me the recipe for your Shrimps Charly. I've tried to make them, but I never get the recipe quite right. Either the sauce is too runny or the shrimp cook too long and are rubbery."

"You want my famous recipe? Before you kill me?" Charly's voice rose to a squeak. "Oh, Walter, Walter, you have the *culot*, the testicle of the whale. I say to you, take some shrimp and stuff them up your *derrière*. I will never give my recipe to my murderer. It is too *grossier*."

Charly heard a creak on the stairs, and thought, *Keep him talking, someone is coming.* Walter had heard nothing. Charly looked at the pistol, which appeared to be aimed at his stomach. He imagined the bullet traveling across the room, hitting his navel, grey and pink intestines spilling out like the innards of slaughtered pigs. It was not a happy thought. *I would make a very good andouille,* Charly thought, andouille being made from intestines. Andouille, actually, would make a very good last meal. Grilled, and served with a mountain of deep fried, shoestring potatoes, some good Dijon mustard, a *bock* of Alsatian beer, or a robust Belgian beer that he enjoyed, Stella Artois. Charly's mind floated in a reverie of last meals. Sweetbreads Financière, Tripes à la Mode de Caen, steamed clams, artichokes, Belgian endive, deep-fried clam bellies, pigs' knuckles *au vin blanc.*

"You would not shoot me, Walter." Charly simply couldn't believe that he was about to die. Something would happen to save him, like the cavalry arriving at the last minute. Faintly, he heard more creaks. Someone was definitely approaching. "Imagine life in Van Buren County without my good pâtés, my soups, no more Shrimps Charly, no more salmon roses, no more Sauce Marchand de Vin on your steak. You would eat, where? At the restaurant of my friend Rex Cingale? You would eat, what? The frozen green bean? The soup from the can? Good grilled steak, but would you eat steak every night? Not healthy, at your age."

Perhaps, like Scheherazade spinning her stories for the old sultan so that she wouldn't be put to death, Charly would keep Walter interested with talk of food. "A light Poule au Pot with leek and organic carrot, that is nourishing for a man of your age; or a bowl of oysters on cracked ice, with mignonette pepper and red-wine vinegar; or a mound of fat asparagus, to be dipped in a Sauce Poivrade made with finely chopped shallot . . ."

"I won't be in Van Buren County, Charly," Walter said

softly. "My bags are packed. Tonight I'm driving to Kennedy airport, and from there I'm flying to the Bahamas. I'm going to shoot you and then Marian is going to shoot herself, I'll put her hand on the pistol and she'll hold it in her mouth, 'eating your gun' the cops call it, my gun, which she'll have found in my office."

Walter chuckled. "You find Marian, she shoots you, then shoots herself. What could be simpler? I've been working down in my office on a letter, written by Marian, confessing to Robby's and Candy's murders. I have it in my pocket, it's nicely done. I thought I heard a noise, and I imagined that somehow Marian had gotten loose. So I hurried up. I never expected to find you here."

"Why did you kill Candy, monsieur?"

"She was my ex-wife and she wanted to blackmail me over that shooting in Boston thirty years ago."

"A man named Billy Talbott," Charly said.

"A man named Billy Talbott," Walter agreed, not asking how Charly knew. "Which was ironic, because I'd been instructed to kill Talbott. He was a loose cannon. He was involved with the Boston Family, but they realized he was a disaster, always shooting his mouth off, and he was a drunk to boot.

"But I was going to do an execution-style shooting, no witnesses. A little twenty-two behind his right ear. The actual shooting was an accident. I shot at a pheasant, and Billy, who should have been behind us, stood up in front, right in the line of fire. Talk about irony. So when Candy wanted to blackmail me, I lost my temper. It was a stupid thing to do, killing her like that."

Keep him talking Charly thought to himself. "Yes, most stupid, Walter. Because it uncover the entire bowl of worms. And did you know," Charly purred, putting on his best customer-relations voice, "that this William Talbott you killed was the father of our investment advisor, yours and mine, Jimmy Houghton? I bet you didn't know that, Walter."

Charly, out of the corner of his eye, saw a figure approaching the doorway. In the gloom of the attic the figure was not identifiable, but Charly assumed it was the police.

"What?" Walter screamed. He really was surprised. "Jimmy Houghton? My investment advisor? Jimmy Houghton is Billy Talbott's son? Are you serious?" Walter, for a fraction of a second, lowered his gun and Charly dived for his knees: made a sudden, flying tackle, the way he'd seen it done on television by players of *le Foot*, butted his head into Walter's stomach, and wrapped his arms around Walter's knees.

Walter collapsed on top of Charly and his gun went off, a deadly little *Pffft*. His finger had pressed the trigger as he fell. Another pistol fired from the doorway, a sudden, quick *splat*, and Charly's head, which was still buried in Walter's stomach, throbbed with the loud gunshots. Walter slid off Charly as the bullet bored into his head, and Charly, wiping Walter's blood off his face with his handkerchief, smelled the acrid odor of cordite and the sweet, sickly smell of blood.

Marian, her face distorted, had collapsed on the bed, with blood pouring out of her chest from Walter's stray bullet. Turning around, Charly saw Jimmy Houghton standing in the doorway. "Jimmy!" Charly cried. "It is really you. *Quel miracle*. You are my guardian angel. You have saved my life. Never again will I say you are the pest."

Jimmy looked at Charly curiously, then strode over to Walter, put his pistol behind Walter's left ear, and fired again, even though Walter had, Charly felt sure, been killed with the first shot.

"I've been waiting thirty years for this," Jimmy said calmly. He could be discussing the merits of a certain stock fund. "Waiting for thirty years to get the bastard who killed my father and ruined my family." He closed his eyes, the pistol clattered out of his hands, and he slid down the door-frame to collapse in a heap on the floor.

Charly heard a noise like a thundering herd, and Stark, Reynolds, Hughes, Matucci, and several other cops erupt-ed into the little attic room.

"I do not understand," Charly said to Jimmy sometime later (they were sitting in a room at the Klover Police Station), "what your father, a cultured man from Boston society, see in Walter Maxwell."

"Charly," Jimmy chided, "you adored Walter. My father saw in Walter exactly what you saw. A glamorous, exciting, wicked man. Boston society was a lot of stiff-necked little Wasps, dreary dances and balls, games of tennis and croquet and golf. Walter was dangerous. He was handsome, rich, suave, and it was whispered around that he'd killed people, that he was a member of the Mob. He was forbidden fruit, high-profile glamor. Walt the Stone Killer the Mob called him. Even the damn Mob thought he was glamorous."

"He never visited France, the home of glamor," Charly said disapprovingly.

"No, he probably hadn't. But Walter would take my dad down to New York, they'd visit the Stork Club and the Co-pacabana, they'd go out with chorus girls, it was all pretty heady stuff for a young man who usually spent his Sat-urday nights at the country club eating overdone scrod and gossiping about boring people like himself. Walter was Houdini to my dad."

"Walter was nothing but *un gangster*."

"As romantic as a crown prince. Everything in dad's life was upright, moral, rigid, ethical. New England Puritan. And then along came Walter. Dad forgot that Mom and

Christina and I existed. It was Walter, Walter, Walter all the time. He started wearing jeans and V-neck cashmere sweaters over bare skin, and soft Italian loafers without socks—just like Walter. He bought a sports car, an old Bentley convertible. He started serving wine with dinner, and had the cook make French food."

Stark cleared his throat. "Excuse me for interrupting, but I'd like you to sign these papers, Jimmy. They're what you dictated to Vince. And don't travel out of the country for the next few months, and let us know if you're going out of state. It's just a formality. We know you shot in self-defense."

"When will you know about Marian Arnold?" Charly asked.

"Well, she was still alive when they got her to the hospital," Stark told them, "but it doesn't look good. The bullet appeared to be lodged in her lungs. They're probably operating right now."

"What will happen to her?"

"Oh, poor Marian, she'll go away forever," Stark said. "My guess is that she'll never stand trial."

"And the wicked Pastor Pflugg? It was he who incited Marian to burn the barns."

"Gone, Charly. Some officers went round, about eight o'clock, while I went to Walter's. He'd already cleared out. But we'll pick him up, I'm sure, sooner or later. Types like him always get caught in the end."

"Tomorrow—no, today, it is past midnight, Chief Stark, today, I would be honored if you and your men would come to dinner at my restaurant. I will call you later on, you can tell me how many. Jimmy, of course, will be the guest of honor. Now, with your permission, we will go home and sleep."

As they walked out into the misty, rainy night, Jimmy turned to Charly, who was just stepping into his van, and asked casually, "What did you mean, Charly, never again would you call me a pest?"

Charly, suavely and smoothly, said, "I must have been hallucinating and thought you were Walter. He, of course, was the pest, everything always had to be just so for Walter."

"Of course, Charly," Jimmy said just as smoothly.

CHAPTER THIRTY-EIGHT

✦✦✦✦✦✦✦

Sunday Dinner at La Fermette

✦✦✦✦✦✦✦

It was Sunday afternoon, four o'clock, and Charly and his guests were sitting at a long table at the rear of La Fermette's dining room. Benny and Julius were being helped in the kitchen by Max Helder and Fred Deering, since Charly was too exhausted after last night's excesses to pay much attention to *la grande cuisine.*

Jimmy Houghton sat at the head of the table, and John Stark sat at the foot. In between were Charly, Abe Reynolds, Clem Hughes, Vince Matucci, Evelyn Hughes, and Patty Perkins. Doc Bingham had been invited, but he was on duty at the hospital. Honoria would have been a guest, since she had been the recipient of Marian's bullet, but she was still in the hospital, as was Maurice Baleine, Charly's almost invisible co-owner, who was recuperating from his liver ailments. Marian Arnold had died that morning.

"Thirty years," Jimmy said, "I've been waiting to expose Walter. I was ten years old when my dad was shot. Pass the shrimp, please, Clem."

"Tough for a kid, losing his dad," Stark said, helping himself to sausage in pastry and thinking, *Tough for a dad to lose a son, too.*

"My world fell apart," Jimmy said. "My mom moved us to Albany, and took back her maiden name, and we adopted it, too. Then we moved down here; she didn't want to face Boston society after what she'd been through."

"You and your sister must have been in a state," Stark said. "Whatever happened to your sister?"

"She and my mom moved to Florida. My mom's dead, now. Sissy's still there, works in an antique shop. We don't keep up, much."

"But you stay here," Charly reminded Jimmy. "You found yourself."

"Yes, my uncle took me under his wing, took me into the firm. I like to work with money. It's so cold, it can't hurt you, unless you get hooked on it. And then, by chance, years later, I got Walter as a client. I invested his money for him and he made many more millions. Recently, he'd started selling off stock. I was pretty sure he was stashing the money in some tax haven. I knew he had a condo in the Caribbean."

Charly said, "He was a very rich man, and with the riches, he had acquired power. He felt very powerful, and his world revolved around protecting that power. More *celeri remoulade*, Vince?"

"Maybe so, Charly," Jimmy said. "I knew I'd get Walter eventually, I just didn't know when." Jimmy buttered a piece of bread. "And all the time, I was waiting for Walter to do something so that he could be caught. I knew he would, eventually. I'd always assumed he kept up with his Mob friends."

"We knew a branch of the Mob was operating across the river," Stark said, "and we knew it was just a matter of time until they moved over to this side. We never thought of Walter."

Clem asked. "Any more of that sliced meat loaf left? What did you call it, partay?"

For once in his life, Charly didn't feel like giving a customer a lesson in French pronunciation. He was so tired, he could do little but eat bread, drink wine, and think his private thoughts. *Walter, Walter, what a fool I was,* he thought again for the millionth time.

"My uncle Rex told me all about the Mob," Vince told them. "He's very sensitive, anyone who's Italian is. Italians hate the Mob. It's turned Italians into a joke, in this country. If you have an Italian name, everyone thinks you're the Mafia. Pass the sausage, please, Clem."

"How did you know where we were, Jimmy?" Charly asked. "And where did you hide yourself in Walter's house?"

"Easy. I got my coat out of the coat closet when the party was over, said good-bye and thank you to Walter, then I pretended I'd lost something out of my pocket and, when no one was looking, I simply walked back to the coat closet and disappeared inside. It's a big closet, I just hid behind Walter's coats. I heard Walter hurrying upstairs, and I followed him."

"I try to keep him talking," Charly said. "He say he want my shrimp recipe, I tell him I never give it to him . . ."

"This the shrimp?" Clem asked.

"Yes."

"Good, but not that good," Clem snorted. Charly shrugged.

"It's wonderful," Evelyn said loyally. "Are you giving out the recipe?"

"Shrimp Charly is dangerous to make at home because the oil must be heated until it is smoking," Charly said. "I gave the recipe to a customer once and he not only burned himself, but his kitchen caught fire. Now, I do not give the recipe."

"Very wise," Evelyn said. "Now, as I was going to say, no one knew this, though there was no reason why they shouldn't, but I was Jimmy's mother's second cousin, and after they'd stayed in Albany a few months, with Jimmy's mom's parents, I invited them to come down here to Van Buren County and share my big house. I taught school, taught John, as a matter of fact, and later Jimmy. Of course I knew the whole story."

"Well," Stark said, "for some reason, we thought you'd all be in the cellar, so that's where we started to look. We were out in front, saw Walter run into the hall, then saw Jimmy run after him. But we couldn't see the front stairs, and we couldn't see the cellar door. We guessed you'd be in the cellar, but when you weren't, we ran upstairs."

Waiters now appeared with platters of roast chicken, stuffed pork chops, roast beef, potatoes au gratin, green beans with parsley and garlic, roasted peppers and eggplant and onions, herb-stuffed tomatoes, Yorkshire pudding. All of the good, hearty fare that Charly knew his guests enjoyed.

"When did you know that Walter killed Candy?" Charly asked Jimmy.

"As soon as Officer Reynolds showed me the photograph."

"How did you know?" Charly persisted.

Jimmy smiled. "I was in New York City a few months ago. I stopped in an art gallery. And there was a woman at the desk who looked familiar. I started talking to her, and asked if she'd ever lived in Boston. She was Maxwell's former wife, Candy Moran, a greedy, conniving woman. We had a long talk."

"And what did you say to Mrs. Moran?" Charly asked.

"I asked her if she'd kept up with Walter. She said she didn't know where he lived. I told her he was fabulously wealthy, living the good life in Van Buren County. I gave her Walter's address and telephone number."

SHRIMPS CHARLY
Serves 2

This is a tricky dish for the home cook as the smoke is fierce. That's why it's so popular at La Fermette—no one wants to smoke up his house. Do not attempt this recipe unless you have a powerful fan and a wire-mesh grease protector. A fire extinguisher is useful, too, especially if you panic easily, for if hot oil spills on the burner it will ignite.

SEASONING MIX:

2 teaspoons salt
2 Tablespoons sugar
2 Tablespoons best Hungarian
    hot paprika

12 large shrimp, peeled and
   deveined, patted dry
4 ounces butter, melted (1 stick)
1 cup peanut oil (this oil has a
   high smoking point.)
8 cloves garlic, finely chopped and
   sautéed gently until soft in olive oil
½ cup flat leaf parsley, chopped

1 cup homemade tomato sauce made
   with garlic, onions and as much hot
   pepper as you can stand. Reduce this
   to a thick paste.

Combine ingredients for seasoning mix.
Dip shrimp in melted butter and roll in seasoning mix, coating well. Heat oil in heavy-
bottomed skillet to smoking and, using
tongs, place shrimp in smoking oil. Immediately cover with grease protector. Cook

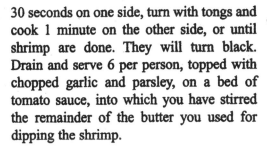

30 seconds on one side, turn with tongs and cook 1 minute on the other side, or until shrimp are done. They will turn black. Drain and serve 6 per person, topped with chopped garlic and parsley, on a bed of tomato sauce, into which you have stirred the remainder of the butter you used for dipping the shrimp.

ABOUT THE AUTHOR

Cecile Lamalle spent her working life in the food-service industry as restaurant cook, food editor, writer and recipe developer for mainstream U.S. companies. She lives in upstate New York.